Praise for the
A Sprinkling of

ELIZABETH ...

"Rolls starts off with a mystery and unravels it g...
The sexual tension is strong between the hero and
heroine, and it seems that every time they begin to get
close, another bit of the mystery is revealed, and they
are kept apart. This technique keeps the reader engaged
from beginning to end."
—*RT Book Reviews* on *A Compromised Lady*

"Rolls has written an entertaining, delightful romp full of
engaging characters, outrageous misunderstandings and
inspiring trysts. Readers are in for a real treat."
—*RT Book Reviews* on *The Chivalrous Rake*

BRONWYN SCOTT

"Scott delivers a story reminiscent of Virginia Henley's
works with its naughty, bawdy overtones. Sexy, smart and
delightfully sinful, this steamy tale features characters
who know themselves well and will take extraordinary
risks to succeed despite the odds. This is
a wonderfully satisfying read."
—*RT Book Reviews* on *A Lady Risks All*

"Sexy, seductive, satisfying. Book two in Scott's
Rakes Beyond Redemption trilogy is another keeper,
with strong characters and a well-written story."
—*RT Book Reviews* on *How to Ruin a Reputation*

MARGARET McPHEE

"This Gentlemen of Disrepute tale is mysterious and
alluring, with unexpected twists that will both startle the
reader and draw them into the mystery and suspense.
McPhee's talent for creating intense, tension-filled,
passionate love stories, tinged with the darkness of
modern urban suspense, will captivate the reader."
—*RT Book Reviews* on *Dicing with the Dangerous Lord*

"Ex-lovers, secret babies, lies, betrayals and blackmail
make McPhee's new romance a winner. This latest is
fast paced, suspenseful and wildly romantic."
—*RT Book Reviews* on *Unmasking the Duke's Mistress*

Award-winning author **ELIZABETH ROLLS** lives in the Adelaide Hills of South Australia in an old stone farmhouse surrounded by apple, pear and cherry orchards, with her husband, two sons, three dogs and two cats. She also has four alpacas and three incredibly fat sheep, all gainfully employed as environmentally sustainable lawnmowers. The kids are convinced that writing is a perfectly normal profession, and she's working on her husband. Elizabeth has what most people would consider far too many books, and her tea and coffee habit is legendary. She enjoys reading, walking, cooking and her husband's gardening. Elizabeth loves to hear from readers, and invites you to contact her via email at books@elizabethrolls.com.

BRONWYN SCOTT is a communications instructor at Pierce College in the United States, and is the proud mother of three wonderful children—one boy and two girls. When she's not teaching or writing she enjoys playing the piano, traveling—especially to Florence, Italy—and studying history and foreign languages. Readers can stay in touch on Bronwyn's website, www.bronwynnscott.com, or at her blog, www.bronwynswriting.blogspot.com—she loves to hear from readers.

MARGARET McPHEE loves to use her imagination—an essential requirement for a trained scientist. However, when she realized that her imagination was inspired more by the historical romances she loves to read rather than by her experiments, she decided to put the ideas down on paper. She has since left her scientific life behind, retaining only the romance—her husband, whom she met in a laboratory. In summer, Margaret enjoys cycling along the coastline overlooking the Firth of Clyde in Scotland, where she lives. In winter, tea, cakes and a good book suffice.

A Sprinkling of Christmas Magic

Elizabeth Rolls
Bronwyn Scott
Margaret McPhee

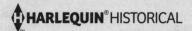
HARLEQUIN®HISTORICAL

ISBN-13: 978-0-373-29759-7

A SPRINKLING OF CHRISTMAS MAGIC

Copyright © 2013 by Harlequin Books S.A.

The publisher acknowledges the copyright holders
of the individual works as follows:

Recycling programs
for this product may
not exist in your area.

CHRISTMAS CINDERELLA
Copyright © 2013 by Elizabeth Rolls

FINDING FOREVER AT CHRISTMAS
Copyright © 2013 by Nikki Poppen

THE CAPTAIN'S CHRISTMAS ANGEL
Copyright © 2013 by Margaret McPhee

This edition published by arrangement with Harlequin Books S.A.

For questions and comments about the quality of this book,
please contact us at CustomerService@Harlequin.com.

® and TM are trademarks of Harlequin Enterprises Limited or its
corporate affiliates. Trademarks indicated with ® are registered in the
United States Patent and Trademark Office, the Canadian Trade Marks
Office and in other countries.

HARLEQUIN®
www.Harlequin.com

Printed in U.S.A.

CONTENTS

Christmas Cinderella

Elizabeth Rolls

Dear Reader,

Most of us love Christmas. It's a time of year when we get together with our families to celebrate and look back over the past year—and wonder where it went! We spend time making gifts or buying them, preparing food that we eat only once a year, and eating far too much of it. But most of all it's being with our families that makes it special.

So I have always wondered how Cinderella coped with Christmas before she went to that ball. Because Christmas must be the loneliest time of all if you've lost your family. It's hard to watch others celebrating together and yet be alone. My heroine, Polly, believes herself alone and has a hard time realizing that sometimes you get to choose your family and where you belong. Those who have read my earlier Christmas story, *A Soldier's Tale,* may recognize the unshockable Reverend Alex Martindale. I hope you all enjoy this story and have a wonderful and blessed Christmas with your own families.

Best wishes,

Elizabeth Rolls

DEDICATION

For Trish Morey, Anne Oliver and Claire Baxter—
you're my touchstone.

Chapter One

The Reverend Alex Martindale looked down at the innocent babe in his practised arms and braced for the inevitable storm. Red-faced, eyes scrunched up against the holy water dripping into them, the Honourable Philip Martindale, heir to considerable estates and, far more importantly, apple of his parents' doting eyes, roared his displeasure.

Having baptised every infant in the parish for the past two years, Alex was used to the noise. Nevertheless he shot a look over the aristocratic squaller to its father, Viscount Alderley. 'Takes after you, Dominic—temper and all.'

The Viscount grinned. 'Not me, cousin.' He glanced at his wife. 'Must be Pippa.'

Alex snorted and continued blessing his little cousin, the child who—thank God from whom all blessings flow—had displaced him as Dominic's heir. There was a tug at his surplice and he glanced down.

His goddaughter, the Honourable Philip's elder sister, looked up at him solemnly. 'You got water in his eyes, Uncle Alets,' she explained. 'Mama or Nurse better give him his next bath.'

'Ah. Was that it?' he said, preserving a clerical straight face. 'Thank you, Emma.'

* * *

The christening party in the Great Hall at Alderley was a rowdy and cheerful affair. It was conspicuous for the absence of the guest of honour and his sister, both of whom had retired early to the nursery in the company of their nurse.

Alex toasted the heir to Alderley with as much, if not more, enthusiasm as the next man. He gazed around the Hall, noting that the party, attended by many of Dominic's tenants, was winding down. A far less boisterous gathering of the local gentry, including himself, had been entertained in the drawing room, but Alex suspected that Dominic and Pippa, having seen the last of those guests off in their carriages, were just as happy mingling with the tenantry.

He made his way across to them. Dominic laid a friendly hand on Farmer Willet's broad shoulder and shook his hand in farewell, saying, 'I'll find out about that bull', and turned to Alex with a grin.

'Staying to supper?'

Tempting, but— 'No, thank you. Mrs Judd would kill me.' His housekeeper was the sort of benevolent tyrant it was unwise to offend. Staying out to supper without notice would ensure his breakfast eggs were boiled, not poached, for a week.

Dominic snorted. 'Why the devil didn't you just tell her you'd be supping here? You must have known one of us would ask you.'

He had, of course. Dominic was his cousin and closest friend, but he preferred not to take his welcome for granted.

Pippa smiled at him, her oddly penetrating gaze suggesting that she knew precisely how he felt, and understood. 'Tomorrow, then?' she suggested. 'We do need to talk about this village school you're starting.'

He returned her smile. 'Tomorrow. And perhaps you'll return the favour next week.'

'That will be lovely,' said Pippa cheerfully.

'Do you want the carriage, Alex?' asked Dominic.

'Thank you, but no. I'll enjoy the walk.'

* * *

He did enjoy the solitary walk. Twilight had closed in and a rising moon glimmered on the frost crunching under his boots. Another year was nearly gone, four weeks until Christmas; tomorrow would be Advent Sunday and he should have been thinking about his sermon, but instead gave himself up to the crisp, cold moonlight that spilled over the fields he was crossing. The familiar path ran clear before him, an ancient right of way. Sometimes he wondered about all the people who had used this path before him, the ancestors of men and women he now served as their rector. Romans, Saxons, Vikings, Normans: all of them coming as invaders, but being tamed by this land until they all belonged to it under God, as much as it belonged to them.

Not for the first time he thanked God that he had been called to serve Him in such a place. A place he had known and loved all his life. The place that had been his home since his father's early death. His uncle, Dominic's father, had taken him in, along with his mother, and educated him as a younger son, making little distinction between his own sons and an orphaned nephew. Except that he had understood that his bookish nephew would do far better being schooled by Mr Rutherford, the rector, and had not sent him off to Eton with his cousins.

He had been very, very lucky. Blessed. And his widowed mother had been able to live out her days in safety and peace. He knew of other women, bereft of family and fortune, who had not been so lucky.

He will lead me to lie down in green pastures…

Counting his blessings was one thing, but if he lay down in this particular pasture right now he'd catch his death of cold and Mrs Judd would be more than annoyed at the waste of his good supper, so he hurried on.

He didn't enjoy his solitary meal nearly as much as the walk. It wasn't Mrs Judd's excellent cooking, but the fact that there was no one to share it with him. He had shared the rectory with his predecessor and mentor Matthias Rutherford for several years before the old man's death earlier that year.

Rutherford had resigned the living a year earlier, but stayed on in the rectory, increasingly frail, but alert. It had been like losing his father again. Worse, in a way, because this time he had known exactly what he was losing. He had known Rutherford far better than his own father. And now Christmas was coming, the first without the old fellow. Grief was no stranger; he had buried his mother and his elder cousin, Dominic's brother Richard. It was part of his calling to comfort the bereaved. Sometimes he thought it might be nice for the comforter to be comforted…

He caught himself up at once, rising from his chair and deliberately sloughing off the melancholy that had crept over him. Grief was one thing, self-pity quite another. One of the more insidious sins. And he *had* comforters: Dominic, Pippa, even little Emma and Philip. He chuckled, remembering Emma's critique of his handling of Philip.

Still, it would be something to have a companion. Someone to share the rectory with him. Someone with whom to talk on quiet evenings. Someone to share his now solitary post-dinner brandy and assist with the parish.

Now that he thought about it, the more he realised what an idiot he'd been not to think of it earlier. His gaze fell on the chess table, its armies frozen for the past ten months. It was obvious: he needed a curate, one who played a decent game of chess and could take up the post of village schoolmaster.

In the opinion of Miss Hippolyta Woodrowe, Cinderella was a complete ninnyhammer. Of course, Cinderella had been extremely lucky. But in Miss Woodrowe's opinion it was a great deal better not to rely on luck. Let alone relying on Prince Charming to gallop up waving a glass slipper to save a damsel from destitution.

Having foolishly cast her cousin Tom in that role two

years ago, Polly Woodrowe had learned her lesson. Prince Definitely-not-so-Charming preferred to forget your very existence, let alone your claim on his affections, once your fortune was gone.

She snorted. Easier to believe in the fairy transforming pumpkin, rat, mice and lizards into an equipage suitable for a princess, than that Prince Charming would still have loved Cinderella when he found her in rags.

'Toss her down the Palace steps more likely,' she muttered, as she walked along the village street. Of course, it seemed that Cinderella had been sweet-natured almost to a fault, because not only did she never become bad-tempered at her lot, but she actually forgave her beastly stepsisters in the end.

Clearly Cinderella had possessed a much nicer character than Polly Woodrowe could lay claim to. Cinderella had waited patiently, suffering in stoic silence, waiting for her prince. Polly felt like kicking someone. Several someones.

In the two years since her remaining trustee had explained that her fortune was gone, gambled away by his fellow trustee's son, Polly had learnt to depend upon herself. She shivered a little and lengthened her step. Only the other day her younger cousin, Susan, had complained that, 'Hippolyta walks much too fast. Ladies shouldn't stride so, should they, Mama?' Well, a lady who wanted to keep warm in a cloak of inferior quality, and reach her destination before her toes froze quite off, walked as swiftly as she could. Especially if she wanted the officially sanctioned errand to the village shop to cover her real goal.

And there it was—the rectory gate. Her stomach churned at what she was about to do. Perhaps Mr Martindale would not be home. He might be out visiting parishioners, or…or burying someone. Her steps slowed. He was bound to be out. She could return another time. Or not at all. He would think her forward. *Pushy.* Her aunt thought she was pushy now. When she had still been wealthy her father's merchant status hadn't mattered. Now apparently she gave herself airs, her father's connection with trade abhorrent to her cousins...

She hesitated. Since when had she cared what a mere country rector might think of her? But she had always liked Alex Martindale. A much older schoolboy, he'd been kind to the little girl visiting her cousins. Sometimes she'd watched him going to and fro from his lessons at the rectory, dazzled when he'd given her a kindly greeting. The same friendly greeting he'd given to the village children, a smile in the grey eyes—the Alex Martindale she remembered was not one to look down on those less fortunate than himself.

People changed, though. Or perhaps as you got older you simply learned more about them. A great deal of it unpleasant. She knew a pang of regret for the innocent young girl who'd had a definite *tendre* for a handsome boy. Brought up to know her duty, she had obediently turned her eyes to her Cousin Tom, who she was assured by her aunt had a great fondness for her.

She snorted and kicked at a clod of mud. Alex Martindale had probably changed anyway. Everyone grew up. And her idea was a foolish one, especially since it would be bound to get back to her aunt and cause even more trouble.

Polly had half-turned away from the rectory gate when she realised what she was doing: giving in before she'd tried, bowing meekly to her fate instead of doing something about it as she had decided yesterday while her cousins were in church. Her aunt had decreed her bonnet and cloak far too shabby to attend church with the family—although apparently not too shabby to walk in to the village on an errand today—and there *had* been a pile of mending. So if Mr Martindale thought her an ungrateful, grasping, *ill bred*—that comment of Aunt Eliot's had really stung—pushy baggage who gave herself airs, then so be it. That pile of mending had been the final straw in a week of slights and snubs.

Gritting her teeth, she stiffened her wilting spine and set her hand to the gate. He would either listen to her, or not.

Think ill of her, or not. A lady with only herself to depend on could not afford scruples about being thought forward. And if she had not her own good opinion, then that of others counted for nothing.

'Miss Woodrowe to see you, Rector.'

Alex looked up from the letter he was writing to the bishop, outlining his plans for the school and his intention to employ a curate. 'Miss Woodrowe?' For a moment he was puzzled. Then it came to him. Miss Hippolyta Woodrowe, of course. Niece to Sir Nathan Eliot, that was it. The *wealthy* Miss Woodrowe. Heiress to a mill-owner. Quite possibly the fortune had been exaggerated, but she had visited often with her widowed mother, a welcome and fêted guest, even as a child and young girl.

'Show her in, Mrs Judd.' He put his pen back in its holder and rose as Mrs Judd stood back to admit his visitor. He frowned. Perhaps it was the light. The day was gloomy and he'd only lit the lamp on his desk, but he could not reconcile his memory of the lively, well-dressed Miss Woodrowe, who had always had a shy smile for him, with this unsmiling young woman in the drab cloak with its mud-spattered hem. Perhaps he was remembering the wrong girl?

'Miss Woodrowe—do come in. Mrs Judd, tea if you please.'

Miss Woodrowe came forwards and put back the hood of her cloak. Something inside him stilled. Hair the colour of fine sherry, confined severely at her nape, and those eyes, the exact colour of her hair, fringed with dark lashes...this was indeed the girl he remembered. He'd always been fascinated by the matching colour of hair and eyes. But, heavens! She'd been a child when last he'd seen her.

'Good day, Mr Martindale. I hope I'm not disturbing you?'

Girls grew up. He knew that. But—

'No, no. Not...not at all.' What the deuce did one do with a young lady when she called on one alone? 'Er, won't you come nearer to the fire?'

'Thank you.'

He hurried ahead of her and pushed the chair closer to the hearth. It clattered against the fender and he suppressed a curse at his clumsiness. 'You are visiting the Eliots?' he said, and she nodded. 'When did you arrive?' He brought another chair to the fire.

'A week ago.'

That chair clattered on the fender, too. 'A week?' Before he could think the better of it, he asked, 'Why did you not come with your cousins to Alderley the other day for the christening?'

Her chin lifted a little. 'I was not invited, sir.' She began to undo her cloak strings.

'Nonsense.' He waved her explanation away. 'Had Lord and Lady Alderley known of your visit, of course you would have been invited. You were friendly enough with Pippa as children. Here—let me take that.' He reached out and lifted the heavy, damp cloak from her slender shoulders. A faint soft fragrance drifted about her and his senses leapt. He'd forgotten, if he'd ever realised, that she was so pretty. Of course she'd been little more than a child the last time he'd seen her…and now she most definitely wasn't. She was taller, for one thing. Not much, she still only reached his shoulder, but she was definitely taller. Taller, and—his hands clenched to fists on the cloak. Now that her cloak was off, he could see that she'd changed in other ways. She'd…his mind lurched… filled out. Slightly stunned at the direction his thoughts were taking, he hung the cloak on a hook by the fire, fumbling so that he nearly dropped it. Good God! What was the matter with him? Firmly, he banished thoughts that edged towards unruly and turned back to her.

'Will you tell me what I may do for you, Miss Woodrowe?' There. That was better. He sounded more himself. Rational and logical.

She had not sat down, but faced him with her chin up and those tawny eyes full of something he could not quite name.

'I wish you to employ me, Mr Martindale.'

He gulped. He'd been living alone for a while and had a slight tendency to talk to himself, but he didn't really think his mind that badly affected. Or his hearing. 'I beg your pardon, Miss Woodrowe?'

She blushed. 'I need a job. And I understand you are starting a school here in the village, so—'

'Miss Woodrowe,' he broke in, 'is this some sort of silly joke?' He didn't bother to disguise the annoyance that clipped his voice. 'A wager with your cousins, perhaps?' It was precisely the sort of idiotish prank Miss Susan Eliot would think famous. 'You are—' He stopped short of voicing precisely what he was thinking: she was an heiress. And logically an heiress could not possibly need a job.

The blush deepened. 'I'm not joking,' she said quietly.

Something about her voice warned him. And he looked at her properly, looked beyond the bright tawny eyes with their fringe of dark lashes, beyond the disturbing changes in her, and saw her gown.

Alex was no connoisseur of fashion, but even he knew an old, unfashionable, cheap gown when he saw one. And that look in her eyes, as if she were braced against something—as if she faced a firing squad—ripped at him.

'Sit down, Miss Woodrowe,' he said. Even if she didn't need to sit, he did.

Those bright eyes narrowed slightly and her mouth, soft pink, tightened. He cursed himself mentally. What was wrong with him that he could not even couch an invitation politely? Nevertheless, she sat. He sat down facing her.

'Miss Woodrowe…' he began. And stopped. Dash it! This was impossible! How did you ask a young lady what had happened to her fortune?

She saved him the trouble.

'Mr Bascombe, the son of my father's oldest friend, got into debt gambling and used my fortune to try to repair his losses.' She said this flatly, as though it had lost the power to upset her.

'He lost everything. His own money as well as mine. Then he took what everyone considered the *honourable* way out.'

Alex's jaw tensed. To his mind there was nothing honourable about committing suicide to avoid the consequences of your selfishness. 'When was this?' he asked quietly.

'More than two years ago.'

That explained why he hadn't heard. A little over two years ago he'd taken a sabbatical and gone to the Continent for a few months. It also explained the shabby gown and cloak, but—

'And you only came to your uncle's home two weeks ago?'

Her face froze. 'I took a position as a governess.'

Pride. He could understand that, but nevertheless... 'Do you not think it might have been better to come to your uncle immediately?' he asked gently. 'Is he your guardian now?'

Her face blanked. 'I'm one and twenty, sir.'

Of age now, but she had gone out into the world alone at nineteen? His jaw clenched. 'And do you not think it better to remain in his care anyway?' The idea of her fending for herself as a governess! What on earth was Sir Nathan thinking to be permitting it?

'No.'

He cleared his throat, hoping he wasn't going to sound stuffy. 'Miss Woodrowe, even if I thought it proper to remove you from the protection of your relatives, it would not answer.'

'Why not?' she demanded. 'I have had experience teaching—two boys as well as a girl—and it was not for incompetence that I was dismissed—' She broke off, biting her lip.

'I need a school*master*,' he said, tactfully ignoring her slip. 'Not a schoolmistress.' What on earth had she been dismissed for?

She scowled. 'Why? I can teach reading, writing, arithmetic as well as any man would. *And* I can teach the girls sewing and other household skills, such as brewing simples, that would help fit them for service, and—'

'You can't live *here*!' he said.

'Here?'

'In the rectory,' he said. 'The schoolmaster is to lodge here.'

'But the cottage you are going to use has two rooms,' she said. 'I assumed that—'

'No. He will live here,' said Alex firmly. What use was a curate stuck away in the schoolhouse? And why make the poor fellow hire someone to cook and clean for him when the rectory was full of unused bedchambers and an unused chess set?

Miss Woodrowe's brow knotted. 'But, sir, will you not consider—?'

He cleared his throat. 'Miss Woodrowe, the schoolmaster is also to be my curate, you see.'

'Oh. I see.' All the bright determination ebbed and her eyes fell. 'I...I did not realise that.'

Her hands twisted in her lap and his own clenched to fists at what he had seen in her face. She had, he realised, wanted the position. Desperately. Shaken, he said, 'My dear, surely you don't really need such a position? You have a family to care for you, and—'

She rose swiftly, reached for her cloak and swung it around her shoulders, even as he scrambled to his feet. 'I apologise for disturbing you, sir.' Her gaze met his again, shuttered, the soft mouth set firmly. 'Please do not concern yourself any further. Good day to you.'

Alex blinked. He rather thought he had just been dismissed in his own library. Pride goeth before a fall, of course, but this girl had already taken the fall... 'Miss Woodrowe—'

She was halfway to the door and he leapt to reach it first and open it.

'Thank you, sir,' she said politely.

Dignity, he realised. Not pride. A scrap of memory floated to the surface; it had been known that Miss Woodrowe was intended for Sir Nathan and Lady Eliot's eldest son, Tom, from the time they were children. Lady Eliot, he recalled, had mentioned it once. Or twice. She had viewed the match as a settled thing.

'Miss Woodrowe—what about your cousin?'

She turned back, one small hand in its worn glove on the door frame. 'My cousin? Which one?'

The coolness held a warning, but he ignored it. 'Your cousin—Mr Tom Eliot. Was there not…' he hesitated '…some understanding between you?' Tom was a pleasant enough fellow, a little foolish, easily swayed by his mother, but surely a better choice for Miss Woodrowe than working as a governess?

Her eyes chilled. 'Yes. There was an understanding. But it involved my fortune. Not me.' She turned away, chin elevated a notch.

'Miss Woodrowe!' Surely she had not turned her back on her cousin out of pride! 'If you have refused a good man out of wilful pride—'

She stared at him, something odd in her expression. '*Refused* my cousin, Mr Martindale?' Bitterness rimed her voice and that mouth, which he remembered as made for smiles and laughter, curved into a travesty of a smile. 'There would have to be something to refuse first. Tom never actually offered for me. Good day to you, sir. Thank you for your time.'

Alex drew a deep breath and realised that interrogating Miss Woodrowe on the clearly painful subject of her non-existent betrothal to Tom Eliot was not a good idea. Instead he saw her out politely, and went immediately in search of enlightenment.

Chapter Two

Mrs Judd put him right at once. 'Miss Woodrowe, sir? Oh aye. It was well known that she was to marry Master Tom. Lady Eliot had it all worked out from the time they was little. When old Mr Woodrowe died, she was that determined little Miss Polly should come to them, but Mrs Woodrowe refused and Sir Nathan didn't push on it.'

Alex waited. There was never any need to probe with Mrs Judd. Once she was away on village gossip, there was no stopping her. He usually took care not to start her, feeling that, as rector, it ought to be beneath him to listen to gossip. Unless, as in this case, he needed information. Then she was a godsend and he did his very best not to view it as entertainment. In this case, as her daughter was cook to the Eliots, she was the best source he could hope for.

'Course it's all different now.' Mrs Judd rolled out the pastry with great vigour. 'That guardian or whatever he was turned Miss Polly's fortune into ducks and drakes as the saying is. Didn't leave her a feather to fly with, they say.'

She looked up at Alex over the pastry. 'My Nan says Lady Eliot was fit to tie when the news came. Nan expected to see poor Miss Polly any day, but she never arrived. Then word came she'd taken a position teaching.' Mrs Judd snorted. 'Lady Eliot said it was just as well.'

'And Mr Eliot?' Alex's jaw had clenched so hard he could scarcely get the words out. Two years ago. Tom Eliot was twenty-five now. He had been well and truly of age. What had held him back from fulfilling his obligations to his cousin? A girl to whom he had been as good as betrothed, even if he had never actually offered for her.

Ellie Judd banged the rolling pin down on the table and a tabby cat by the fire glanced up. 'Reckon he did just as her ladyship told him. Like Sir Nathan. Less trouble that way.' Mrs Judd sprinkled a little flour over the pastry and rolled it over the raised pie. 'Nan reckons Miss Polly ain't so very welcome at the Manor nowadays.'

Alex gazed unseeingly at the letter he had been writing to the bishop about the proposed schoolmaster. He supposed he could understand the Eliots' outlook, even if he deplored the worldly attitude to marriage that it reflected. Tom Eliot and Miss Woodrowe had not been precisely betrothed, but it had been an understood thing that once she was old enough he would offer and she would accept. It kept her fortune safely in the family and provided a wealthy bride for Tom, easing the burden of finding dowries for Miss Eliot and Miss Mary Eliot.

But with no money the match was seen as unsuitable. He gritted his teeth. The Eliots would not have been alone in thinking that. And it might have been awkward housing Miss Woodrowe, but to let her go to be a governess—that was the bit that stuck in his throat. Two years ago? At just nineteen, dash it! Miss Hippolyta Woodrowe had been cast adrift to earn her keep.

He looked again at the letter.

'…therefore I would be grateful if your lordship could recommend a man to take up these duties as soon as may be in the New Year…'

Miss Woodrowe's determined face slid into his mind.

I can teach reading, writing, arithmetic as well as any man would...

He shoved the thought away. It was important to get a good man into the position. Many people disliked the idea of the parish schools the Church wished to set up, believing it dangerous to educate the poor above their station. The right man, one who could win respect, would go a long way towards breaking down those prejudices. The world was changing. No longer could children be assured of jobs on the estates they were born on. They needed schools to give them a chance.

Polly—Miss Woodrowe needs a chance.

He shoved the thought away. The school *had* to succeed. And if he put a woman in charge, a young lady...a lady's place was in the home, not out earning her living...she was not made for independence...

And what if her home and fortune has been taken from her? What if she has no choice?

Then her family should take care of her!

That was how it had been for his own mother. Memories slid back. He'd been ten when his father died heavily in debt, old enough to realise his mother's grief was edged with fear. Fear she had tried to hide from him as she wrote letter after letter to her own family. He had found some of the replies after her death. Offers to house her—in return for her otherwise unpaid services as governess, or companion. None had been prepared to take her child as well.

Only Dominic's father had offered the widow a home along with her child. Offered to educate his brother's son and provide for him. As a child Alex had taken it for granted. Now he knew how lucky they had been. Not all families could, or would, provide for an impoverished widow and child.

What would have become of his mother if Uncle David had not taken them in?

Miss Polly ain't so very welcome at the Manor nowadays.

He could believe that if they'd allowed her to come asking about the position of village schoolmistress!

His kindly uncle had settled a small annuity on his widowed sister-in-law, providing a measure of independence along with a home.

Picking up the pen, he dipped it in the ink and continued, politely enquiring after the bishop's health and that of his wife. A moment later he laid the pen down, glared at the letter and tore it in two. Mouth set hard, he took another piece of paper, picked up the pen and began, with considerably less care, another letter, this time to his cousin Dominic, Lord Alderley.

He had prayed for the right teacher for the school, and he believed that God always answered prayer. The trick was in recognising an unexpected answer.

Polly pushed open the door of the village shop, glad to be out of the wind again. It sliced through her old cloak straight to the bone. Mr Filbert popped up from behind the gleaming counter. He stared for a moment, then his gnome's smile broke.

'Why, it's you, Miss Polly!'

She managed a smile. Mr Filbert was someone whose manner towards her hadn't changed at all. 'Good day, Mr Filbert. My aunt sent me in for some embroidery silks.'

He blinked. 'Miss Eliot and Miss Mary were here just a few moments ago buying silks for Lady Eliot,' he told her. 'They didn't say anything about your being with them.'

Probably because she wasn't. She'd had no idea her cousins had been planning to visit the village. She could only pray they'd seen her neither entering nor leaving the rectory.

'A misunderstanding,' she said carefully. 'Thank you.'

'They went back to the inn,' he said helpfully.

The already gloomy morning dimmed a little further. Her cousins had heard their mother set her the errand of walking into the village for new embroidery threads and had said nothing. What would have happened if Mrs Filbert had served her and she'd bought the threads again? She forced the bitter, uncharitable thoughts back. Perhaps they hadn't decided to come in until after she'd left. They hadn't passed her on the road, so it wasn't as if they'd had a chance to offer to take her up.

'Thank you, Mr Filbert,' she said. 'I'm sure I'll find them.'

She hurried out of the shop and down the street towards the inn, just in time to see the Eliot coach turning out of the inn yard towards the manor.

'Susan! Mary!' Probably they hadn't seen her…ah, John Coachman had. He was slowing the horses. She picked up her pace, hurrying towards the carriage. Susan frowned, leaning forwards, clearly giving an order. John responded, pointing his whip at Polly hurrying to the coach. Susan's chin lifted, she spoke again, the words indistinct, but her tone sharp… John hesitated, cast Polly an apologetic look and urged the horses on.

Polly slowed to a stunned halt, staring after the departing carriage. Hurt fury welled up, scalding her throat, as she set out for home. The frost had thawed that morning, leaving the lane muddy. By the time she was halfway there, her skirts six inches deep in mud she would have to brush off, she had a new plan. Very well. Her aunt had refused to give her a reference. Mr Martindale had failed her. She braced her shoulders against the biting wind. She would ask Pippa, Lady Alderley, for a reference.

Polly had reached the manor gates before she heard the rumble of wheels slowing behind her. She didn't bother looking around even as the gig slowed beside her.

'Miss Woodrowe. What on earth are you doing?'

The familiar voice sounded furious.

She turned and met Alex Martindale's scowl. 'Sir?'

'What are you doing?' he repeated.

'Returning ho—to my uncle's house,' she amended. A home was where you felt welcome, where you belonged.

His frown deepened. 'But...you're *walking*!'

'I can't fly,' she pointed out reasonably. 'An oversight, but there it is.'

For a moment he stared and she cursed her unruly tongue. Would she never learn to curb it? That was something that other Miss Woodrowe, the *rich* Miss Woodrowe, might have said. In *her* it would have been amusing, witty. In plain Polly Woodrowe it was impertinence.

Then he laughed and it lit the grey eyes which crinkled at the corners in a way that drew her own smile. '*Touché.* Stupid thing to say. May I at least give you a lift down the drive?' He held his hand out, still with that lilt to his mouth. She hesitated, even as her heart kicked to a canter, remembering that his smile had always been just that little bit crooked. There was nothing remotely improper in accepting. Mr Martindale was the rector, and it was an open carriage. For the length of the carriage drive. Except...Aunt Eliot would think her designing, and there would be another row, when she still had not found a position—she quelled a shudder. 'It's out of your way, sir,' she excused herself, ignoring the little ache of regret.

He shook his head. 'Actually, no, it isn't. After you left, I realised that I needed to speak to your uncle about something.'

'Oh.' Oh, dear God. Surely he wasn't going to complain about her? 'I'm...I'm sorry if you were offended that I asked for the teaching position.' Somehow she choked the words out, fought to look suitably chastened. 'There's no need to mention it to my uncle. I won't ask again.'

'What?' He stared at her, puzzlement in those grey eyes. She'd always been fascinated by the utterly black rims, and those dark, dark lashes... 'You thought I was going to complain about you? No, Miss Woodrowe, I was not!' Now he did sound offended.

She opened her mouth to apologise, but he forestalled her.

'Don't,' he said. 'Not one word. Do you hear me?'

She nodded, fuming at the autocratic tone.

'Right. Up you come, then.' That was an outright command.

Seething, she placed her hand in his, felt the powerful clasp of long fingers as he steadied her and helped her up. The horse stood patiently while he flipped the driving rug off his own legs and over hers.

'Sir—'

'Not a word!'

That the Reverend Alex Martindale could sound so angry was a revelation. She sat in silence the length of the carriage drive.

Polly stood quietly while Aunt Eliot railed at her. Once she had been considered an intimate of the family, permitted to use the more familiar *Aunt Aurelia*. Once she had been a welcome guest. Not any more. There was quite a difference between the wealthy heiress of a mill owner and the impoverished daughter of trade.

'The *presumption*! Calling out in that vulgar fashion, in the middle of the street!'

'I thought they had not seen me, Aunt.' She swallowed. Had she given it the least thought, she would have known that any not seeing had been deliberate. Susan and Mary took their tone from their mother.

Lady Eliot ignored this. 'And where is the money I gave you for embroidery silks?'

She wondered what her aunt would say if she handed her a packet of silks instead. 'Here, Aunt.' She took the coins from her pocket and held them out. Lady Eliot took them with a sniff and counted them. She glared at her niece. 'You'll have to go back later. Miss Susan forgot the blues.'

It was the *Miss Susan* that did it…

Polly opened her mouth, fully intending a polite acquiescence.

'No.' It was said before she even knew it was there. She braced herself. It was out and it wasn't going back. Not if she was now supposed to refer to her cousins as Miss Susan and Miss Mary.

Lady Eliot's eyes bulged. *'What did you say?'*

'I said, no, Aunt. I've been once, and I'm not going again. Send Susan.'

'Why you ungrateful, *impertinent*, little—'

Polly let the storm rage about her. Odd how it didn't bother her now, when only a day or so ago she would have been close to tears, wondering how to placate her aunt. Now she simply didn't care.

Alex followed his faintly offended host along the hallway of the Manor.

'I cannot think that Lady Eliot will approve this offer, Martindale,' huffed Sir Nathan. 'Hippolyta has every comfort here, as well as the countenance and protection of her family.'

'Of course,' said Alex. He was half-inclined to make his excuses and leave. Clearly the Eliots were not, after all, trying to shove Polly out the door and he had misinterpreted the situation, placed too much credence in what was, after all, mere gossip. Polly—*Miss Woodrowe* was likely quite happy with her family and had approached him out of pride—not a sin at all to be encouraged, although he could understand her not liking to be beholden.

And if Sir Nathan's nose was out of joint, that was as nothing to Lady Eliot's likely response. At which unwelcome thought he became aware of a strident female voice carrying down the hallway. Someone—apparently a *presumptuous, ungrateful viper*—was in a deal of trouble. It sounded as though one of the housemaids was being dismissed. Sir Nathan, who was more than a little deaf, appeared not to notice anything unusual, but continued along the hallway to the drawing-room door.

Alex hesitated, but Sir Nathan said, 'We shall see what her ladyship says,' and opened the door for him.

'Lady Eliot, here is Mr Martindale with a most extraordinary proposal.'

'...ungrateful, shop-bred upstart—'

Lady Eliot's diatribe was cut off as if by a knife slash.

Alex advanced into the room. Her ladyship sat enthroned in a high-backed chair by the fire, a firescreen embroidered with revoltingly coy nymphs and shepherds protecting her face from the heat. The tea table beside her bore a heavy silver tray with a teapot, creamer, sugar bowl, and a single cup and saucer.

Before her stood Polly, staring at him in obvious shock, and not a housemaid, let alone a miscreant one, in sight.

Alex took a savage grip on his own temper. Lady Eliot had been berating Polly. *Shop-bred. Viper. Presumptuous.*

Hot colour flooded Polly's pale cheeks as she looked at him, yet she held her head high. Embarrassment then. Not shame.

'Mr Martindale—how pleasant!' said Lady Eliot, her voice executing a complete about turn. 'Will you not be seated, and I shall ring for more tea.' The effusive graciousness grated on Alex. Her ladyship turned to Polly with a smile. 'Hippolyta, dear—I shall not keep you now. We may speak later.'

Hippolyta, dear? What had happened to the shop-bred upstart?

'Actually, I should prefer Miss Woodrowe to remain,' said Alex. 'My proposition involves her.'

He barely heard Lady Eliot's shocked *'Indeed!'* for the flare of light in Polly's eyes and the way her soft lips parted. Dragging his wits back together, he continued. 'Ah, yes. That is, you are probably aware that my cousin, Lord Alderley—' he loathed the necessity of making play with Dominic's name, but the devil was in the driving seat here— 'and I intend to establish a village school.'

Her ladyship sniffed. 'He mentioned it at the christening. Naturally, I did not hesitate to offer my opinion.'

Naturally not.

She went on. 'I cannot think it wise. To be encouraging the lower orders to reach above the station in which God has set them must lead to discontent. We must accept the lot to which He has intended us.'

Alex managed not to roll his eyes. She was far from the only one to think that way. Usually persons whose lot God had set in a very fair ground. 'I am rather of the opinion, ma'am, that God moves in mysterious ways and that where He has seeded talent, it ought to be encouraged to flower.'

Lady Eliot looked anything but convinced, and Alex continued. 'While my cousin and I initially intended to employ a schoolmaster, we now think it better to engage a woman.' Dominic had no idea yet that Alex had changed his mind, but Alex was fairly sure he'd explained it clearly enough in the letter he'd sent over before coming here.

His gaze met Polly's and his wits scattered again at the sight of her blazing eyes and those soft, parted lips. Lord! His heart appeared to have stopped and his breath tangled in his throat, while a distinctly unclerical question slid through his mind: what would those lips taste like? Ripe? Sweet? A hot, unfamiliar ache gathered low in his belly. Disturbing—because while it might be unfamiliar, he knew quite well what it was.

He cleared his throat, but the idea twisted it up again. What on earth was the matter with him? He was the rector, for God's sake. Literally for God's sake! He was meant to be an example and shepherd to his flock, not lust after the women in his congregation! He cleared his throat again, this time successfully enough to speak.

'It has come to my attention that Miss Woodrowe—' He let his gaze touch Polly again, felt again the leap of sensation and had to regather his thoughts. 'That Pol—that is, Miss Woodrowe has some experience as a governess and I wondered if she might consider accepting the position.'

'Really, Mr Martindale!' Lady Eliot's nostrils flared. 'What an extraordinary idea! I do not think you can have—'

'Thank you, sir.' Polly's quiet voice cut in. 'I should like very much to discuss it with you.'

'What?' Lady Eliot glared at her. 'Hippolyta, you cannot have considered the implications! And even if you had, you will of course be advised and ruled by those in authority over you!'

Polly's mouth firmed. 'I am of age, Aunt, and in authority over myself. I may be advised by my family, but I will be ruled by my own conscience and judgement.'

'Now, Hippolyta—' bleated Sir Nathan.

'You will remain with your family connections, Hippolyta,' snapped Lady Eliot. 'Just this morning I have received a letter from my cousin Maria, Lady Littleworth. She is still willing to house you as her companion, despite your foolish decision to accept another post two years ago. There is nothing more to be said.' She sat back. 'It would present a very odd appearance,' she continued, clearly not having listened to herself, 'if a girl living under Sir Nathan's protection were to be sallying forth to earn her living as a village *schoolmistress*.' Her voice dripped disdain.

Sir Nathan nodded. 'Very odd appearance. Indeed—' this with an air of clinching the argument '—'tis not possible. How would she get to and fro?'

Alex braced himself. He didn't approve, but he was starting to understand why Polly Woodrowe was so anxious to leave this house on her own terms if the alternative was an unpaid position with Lady Littleworth.

'Naturally the offer includes Miss Woodrowe's accommodation at the schoolhouse if she wishes it.' Hoping Polly could remain with her family, he'd not mentioned that to Sir Nathan earlier and the fellow goggled like a landed trout.

Alex took a deep breath and incinerated every bridge. 'If Miss Woodrowe wants it, the position is hers.'

'Really, Mr Martindale!' Lady Eliot's mouth pinched. 'We cannot possibly countenance such a—'

'Thank you, Mr Martindale,' said Polly calmly. Her face glowed as she turned to him. 'If I may have a key, I will walk into the village tomorrow and decide what will be needed.'

He scowled. The deuce she would. 'As to that, Miss Po— Miss Woodrowe—I have the keys with me now and would be delighted to drive you.'

Lady Eliot drew herself up. 'I must make quite plain that this has not Sir Nathan's approbation!'

Alex bowed to her. 'I perfectly understand that, ma'am.' He turned back to Polly. 'Fetch your cloak, Miss Woodrowe. I will await you in the front hall.'

Polly stared about the second room of the schoolhouse in rising panic. She had not thought. She simply had not thought, had not known. But now the reality of the two-roomed cottage crashed over her like snow falling off a branch.

The schoolroom was in fine order. Neat rows of desks, a cupboard holding slates and other equipment. Books on a bookshelf, a desk for the teacher and a great fireplace. She had seen a huge stack of wood outside. Clearly teacher and pupils were not expected to freeze. The schoolroom itself had been freshly whitewashed and was more than acceptable.

This room, too, had been whitewashed. And that was it. There was nothing in it. Nothing. An alcove to one side, with a wide shelf clearly intended for a bed, was innocent of mattress and bedding. There was no furniture. There was nothing. She swallowed. Even if there were something, she realised with a jolt of shock, she would have no idea how to so much as cook her dinner. There wasn't even a cooking pot in which to cook it, although there was an iron rod, with a hook to suspend a pot, that clearly swung in and out of the fireplace. She had seen such arrangements when visiting women in the village… but a cooking pot would cost money, and she would need a table, and chair to sit on, and bedding and…

And she was not going to give up! She had got the position

and she was jolly well going to keep it. She had some money. Not much, but surely enough to buy a few simple things to furnish this room.

She lifted her chin. 'I will need to—'

'It won't do,' said Mr Martindale. He swung around on her, his grey eyes hard. 'You can't possibly live here! I must have been insane to suggest it.'

Her determination firmed. 'Why not?' All the reasons why not were buzzing frantically in her head. If she could swat them aside, why could not he? 'It…it just needs furniture. A table and chair. Perhaps a settee to sit by the fire. Some bedding and a…a cooking pot.'

His glance skewered her. 'Polly, do you even know how to cook?'

She stiffened. 'Do you?' She tried to ignore the leap of her pulse, the sudden clutch of her lungs at the sound of her name, her pet name, on his lips. For two years she had been *Miss Woodrowe*. Her aunt and cousins insisted on *Hippolyta* now. No one, not one person, had called her Polly since her mother's death. And he shouldn't be now.

'I have Mrs Judd,' he pointed out with a smile.

'And I have a brain,' she said, ruthlessly quelling the little flare of delight at his smile. 'And I can buy a book. And… and ask advice. *Please*.' Oh, curse it! She'd sworn not to beg.

'You'll be *alone*,' he said. 'A young woman, alone.' His mouth firmed. 'I don't like it at all.'

'Well, I do,' she said. 'My uncle is right. I cannot possibly go back and forth from his house.' Better to make the break completely and establish her independence. Aunt Eliot would put every sort of rub in her way. But the bubble of panic rose again. Women were not intended for independence. It was wrong. Against the proper order. Unnatural. She swatted those thoughts away, too. Any number of people had probably thought it against the natural order when King John was forced to sign the Magna Carta. The sky hadn't fallen then either.

Alex frowned, clearly thinking. 'Perhaps lodgings here in the village—'

'No!' Her vehemence was as much at her own cowardice as at his suggestion and she flushed at his raised brows. 'I'm sorry, but I've lived in someone else's home for two years. I…I should like to live by myself.' Being under someone else's roof, subject to their rules and arrangements had galled her. Certainly if she paid board she would not be a dependent, but… 'I should like to try.'

He scowled. 'For goodness' sake, Pol—Miss Woodrowe! It's winter, and—'

'There's a huge pile of wood out there,' she said. 'I actually do know how to light a fire.' The governess had been permitted a fire in her room on Sunday evenings at the Frisinghams', although she suspected this generosity had more to do with prevailing damp than concern for the comfort of a lowly governess. Since no servant had been responsible for lighting it, she had learnt how to manage for herself.

'But by yourself—won't you be lonely?'

She stared at him, surprised. 'You live alone. Don't tell me Mrs Judd holds your hand in the evenings. Are you lonely?'

'That's diff—' He stopped and the wry smile twisted his mouth. 'Very well. Yes. Sometimes I am.'

'Oh.' His honesty disarmed her. But still— 'Well, no. I don't think I will be.' She might be alone, but that didn't mean lonely. She was lonely now, surrounded by people who would prefer that she wasn't there at all, people she had thought cared for *her*. Polly Woodrowe, poor relation and dependant, was a far different creature than Polly Woodrowe, wealthy cousin. But she couldn't explain all that to Alex Martindale—it would sound self-pitying, utterly pathetic. So she said, 'It's different being a guest and family member to being a dependant.'

His brows rose. 'The change in your circumstances is difficult for them, I take it.'

Something in her snapped. 'Difficult for *them*?' She snorted.

'I'm sure it was difficult to discover that the girl you counted on bringing a healthy dowry into the family was ruined! Positively tragic. And…' she was warming up to her subject now, '…if you are going to tell me that it is my *Christian duty* to accept the situation allotted to me by God, with humble piety, then you may go to the devil!'

He blinked and Polly realised what she had said. Oh, goodness. This time she wouldn't have to get as far as being pawed around by the son of the house to be dismissed. This time she was going to be dismissed before she'd even started.

'I was being sarcastic,' said Alex mildly. 'And if,' he continued, 'I had been so mind-bogglingly arrogant as to say that, you'd be welcome to kick me on my way.' He eyed her consideringly. 'You are sure, then, that you want this? There will be no going back, you know.'

She swallowed. 'There is already no going back.' She had already lost her place. In society, in her family. She would have to make her own place.

'I suppose it will be safe enough,' he said slowly. 'Right here in the village. And Dominic owns the cottage, so only a fool with a death wish would cause trouble.' His expression hardened. 'Not to mention having me to deal with.' He drew a deep breath. 'Very well, then. Fifty pounds a year, payable quarterly.'

'Fifty?' It came out as a sort of squawk.

The dark brows rose. 'Not enough?'

This time she picked up the humour in his voice. 'More… more than enough,' she managed. 'I—the cottage will need some things. A table, maybe a chair—if you could advance me a little and take it out of—'

'Certainly not!' He glared at her, grey eyes furious, all humour fled. 'The place will be *fully* furnished and equipped.'

'Equipped?'

He waved vaguely at the fireplace. 'Mrs Judd will tell me what is needed. A…a cooking pot, I suppose. Some utensils.'

He levelled a searching gaze at her. 'Are you quite sure this is what you want? What about Lady Littleworth?'

She swallowed. 'And what will happen when she dies, or decides that I annoy her? She won't be paying me, you know. I've thought it all out. I need to save enough for the future. Perhaps buy an annuity for my old age.'

His jaw dropped. 'Polly—you're twenty-one!'

And one day she would be fifty-one. With no money. Ignoring the little voice of fear, she countered, 'Have you ever met Lady Littleworth?'

His mouth twitched. 'Actually, yes. I take your point. Very well, the position is yours, Miss Woodrowe. When would you like to start?'

Chapter Three

What had she done?

The following Monday, Polly stared at the fire glowing under her cook pot and hoped she wasn't burning her dinner. Mrs Judd had brought along a piece of mutton during the afternoon and explained how to deal with it. It seemed simple enough and the smell coming out of that pot was making her stomach rumble in a most unladylike way. She looked around at the room that was now her home. A table and two chairs in the middle of the room, a mattress and bedding in the alcove, a small cupboard to hold a meagre amount of cutlery and earthenware crockery and here, by the fire, a small wooden settle. She had brought the pillow over from the bed to soften the wooden frame a little and was curled up in the corner of the settle, waiting for her supper.

In the schoolroom everything was prepared for tomorrow when the school opened. Lord and Lady Alderley were coming along with Mr Martindale to speak to the children. A dozen children to start. Boys and girls. She had met most of them after church the day before. Alex Martindale had made a point of it.

Despite the twisting knot in her belly, she thought it would be a great deal better than her respectable position as a governess. For one thing she wouldn't have Mrs Frisingham constantly interfering, making excuses for bad behaviour and vetoing any discipline. Nor would she have the lady's brother-in-law, young Mr Frisingham, lurking in corridors to paw her about and make lewd suggestions. She shivered a little.

She had left the Manor without fanfare. Neither Susan nor Mary had come downstairs to say farewell to her. Only her aunt had seen her off, mouth thin with disapproval.

I dare say it will not take you long to realise the folly of your actions.

Outside the afternoon was drawing in, she had already closed the shutters and blown out the lamp. There was enough light from the fire and she couldn't afford to burn lamp oil wantonly. For the first time in her life, she was alone. Utterly alone. And she had a horrible feeling that loneliness was very close, waiting to pounce.

The knocking on the door made her jump. 'Come in!' she called as she scrambled up from the settle.

Alex Martindale stalked in, a scowl on his face. 'Why isn't the door bolted?' he demanded. The stern effect was rather ruined by a half-grown, black-and-tan setter pup, who rushed across the floor to her, all outsize paws, lashing tail and enthusiastic tongue.

'Bolted?' She stared at him while the pup licked her hands. 'Why?'

'Why?' He looked around. 'Is something wrong with the lamp?'

'No, nothing,' she said. 'Why should my door be bolted? It's barely five o'clock.'

'It's dark!' he retorted. 'Or nearly so. Anyone could come by!'

'Someone just did,' she observed, patting the dog.

'Who?' he growled.

She stared. What on earth had him all on end?

'You, of course,' she said. 'Who else would have bothered?'

'Who else?' he echoed. 'Polly—Miss Woodrowe—any tramp

could come by and see the light. Perhaps decide to find out who lives here.' His mouth flattened. 'And you're here by yourself.'

'Oh.' She flushed. Felt a complete widgeon. 'I see.'

'Thank God for that. Now, will you promise to bolt the door in future?'

All her family's concern had been for how her actions must reflect on them, how demeaning it was. His furious concern for her safety was as warming as the fire itself.

She nodded. 'Yes. If you believe it necessary.' And when she saw the relief on his face she warmed even more.

'Good.' He hesitated. 'I won't stay. I just wanted to give you this.'

He held out a parcel and she took it with trembling hands. 'Thank you.'

He nodded. 'Are you sure you're quite all right here?'

'Yes.'

'And there's nothing wrong with that lamp?'

'No.' She flushed. 'I didn't want to waste oil.'

'Oh.' He looked a little disconcerted. 'I see. Bonny—sit.'

The pup sat, her tail lashing, then, with a sigh, lay down and curled up beside the fire.

'Bonny?'

He smiled. 'An early Christmas gift from Lady Alderley. She thought a dog would be good company.' He eyed the pup dubiously. 'Which is probably true, as long as she doesn't cost me my housekeeper. Mrs Judd is not entirely convinced and nor is her cat.'

Polly laughed. 'But she's lovely. And dogs are good company.'

'True. You're all ready for tomorrow?'

Her stomach twisted. 'Yes. Everything is prepared.'

His head tilted. 'Including you.'

'Yes. Including me.' She hoped.

'No regrets?'

That steadied her as nothing else could have. 'None.' And suddenly it was true. She had no idea how this would turn out, but she had made her choice. The choice *she* had wanted to make. Even if it all came crashing around her ears in the end, for the moment she had her independence and that was golden. If loneliness was the price, then she was prepared to pay it.

'May I open my present?' she asked.

To her amazement, he flushed. 'It's not a present, exactly. Just something I had by me. You might find it useful, that's all.' He scowled. 'It's nothing. Nothing at all.'

Her hands were busy with the string and the paper which came apart to reveal a small, plain wooden box with a key in it. A small posy of inlaid flowers decorated the lid.

'Oh.' Her breath came out on a sigh of delight. Hands trembling, she turned the key and opened the lid to reveal two inner lids with little brass knobs. A slightly pungent fragrance drifted to her and she knew what he'd brought her.

She had to swallow before she could speak. 'It's a tea caddy. Thank you.' It came out as a whisper, all she could manage.

He said, awkwardly, 'It's not a very good one. It's just a hobby. But—'

'You *made* it?' Her hands closed on the little box as emotion choked her. She forced herself to meet his gaze. 'Thank you, sir. It's the loveliest gift I've ever had.'

She lifted one of the inner lids and saw the little wooden spoon, nestled in the tea. 'And you made a spoon, too?' She lifted it out, felt the silkiness of the wood under her fingertips, and swallowed the lump in her throat.

'Two,' he said, his voice gruff. 'One for each compartment.'

Heat threatened behind her eyes as she replaced the little spoon in the fragrant leaves and closed the lid. She wasn't going to cry. She wasn't! Carefully she set the caddy safely on the shelf by the fire with the teapot.

'Thank you, sir.' There, she'd sounded quite steady.

'It's nothing,' he said. The dark eyes watched her and her heart beat a little faster. 'Is everything quite all right, Miss Woodrowe? You are sure you won't feel lonely tonight?'

'Quite sure,' she said, her gaze going to the caddy.

* * *

Alex walked along the village street towards the rectory and his evening Office. Something rested, warm and glowing, near his heart. He'd made the caddy, just the caddy, last summer, intending it for Pippa, but it hadn't seemed quite right for her and he'd set it aside. Seeing it on the back of his shelf the other day after showing Polly the schoolhouse, he'd known why he'd held on to the caddy; it was waiting for Polly. But he'd wanted to make something especially for her, and a tea caddy needed caddy spoons, didn't it? That bare, bleak little room had haunted him while he carved them, but somehow, when he'd seen her face just now as she cradled the gift, the room had seemed full, glowing. Not bleak at all. He clicked his fingers and whistled for Bonny, who was exchanging greetings with the blacksmith's old collie.

Davey Fletcher came out and called his dog. 'Evening, Rector. Your Miss Polly all right, is she?'

'Er, yes.' No point denying where he'd been. *His* Miss Polly? It was natural that he should take an interest in Miss Woodrowe's situation, wasn't it?

'Little bit of a thing to be setting up for herself,' said Fletcher. 'Still, it's a good thing for the youngsters.' He scratched the collie's ears. 'Reckon we'll all keep a bit of an eye on her, eh, Rector?'

The scholars stood behind their desks, faces scrubbed and shining, gazing solemnly at Lord Alderley as he introduced Polly the next morning.

'Miss Woodrowe has agreed to teach you and I know you'll all do your best for her.' He gestured Polly forwards. 'In a way, she is like a Christmas present—one that you'll have all year. We want all of you to learn to read and write, and do your sums so that you can get good jobs and do them well. And now I think if Mr Martindale will finish with a prayer, we'll get out of Miss Woodrowe's way and let her start.'

Alex stepped forwards and everyone bowed their heads

as he spoke directly to God, thanking him for the gift of the children and—Polly blushed scarlet—for the gift of Miss Woodrowe, come at exactly the right time in answer to prayer for a teacher. She doubted that she was entirely what Alex Martindale, Lord Alderley, or even the Almighty for that matter, had had in mind. But here she was and here were the children, and she was going to do her very best for them. No matter that Aunt Eliot and her cousin Susan were standing stiffly at the back of the room with Lord and Lady Alderley. Polly had no illusions that her aunt approved of the situation— Lady Eliot was here because Lady Alderley had an interest in the school and would be present.

Alex finished with the Lord's Prayer and stepped back, gesturing Polly forwards.

'Sit down, children,' she said quietly.

They all sat with a great scraping of chairs.

'Can anyone read or write already?'

Surreptitious glances all round, but one small girl raised her hand.

'Yes?' Polly smiled encouragingly.

'I can write my name.'

At the back of the room Susan Eliot tittered.

Polly didn't bother to look at her, but focused on the child. 'Excellent. It's Maryann Perkins, isn't it?'

The child beamed. 'Yes, miss.' And she spelt her name out painstakingly.

Susan tittered again. This time Polly did look at her. Susan looked back insolently and Polly's baser nature got the better of her.

'Very good. Once I knew a little girl called Susan who took simply ages to learn to write her own name. You'll probably be quicker with your sums, too.' Susan had been the bane of successive governesses.

Susan flushed as Lady Eliot turned an outraged stare on Polly.

Alex Martindale sprang for the door. 'We'll leave you to

it, Miss Woodrowe.' He sounded as though he were trying not to laugh.

Lady Eliot stepped forwards. 'One word, Hippolyta—'

Alex forestalled her. 'No, Lady Eliot. Miss Woodrowe is busy now. I'm sure she will be delighted if you call on her after school.' He smiled at Polly, a warm smile that had her heart doing things it had absolutely no right to be doing. 'Good day to you, Miss Woodrowe. After you, ma'am.' And he ushered Susan and Lady Eliot from the room. Lord and Lady Alderley followed them.

Polly breathed a heartfelt sigh of relief, and, pushing all thought of her relatives from her mind, settled to her task.

By the time half past two came she was exhausted, three more children could write and spell their own names, they could all recite the alphabet, knew their scripture lesson for the day and had started on simple sums and counting. They had finished with a Christmas carol that most of the children knew already, but were more than happy to sing.

In brief moments throughout the day Lord Alderley's words had come back to her: that she was a gift to these children. Certainly her previous pupils had not considered her a gift. Quite the opposite. And perhaps the converse was true; these children were a gift to her. Without them, she would still be in her uncle's house, a resented burden. Now, looking at the children lined up at the door awaiting dismissal, she realised that she had something to give. Knowledge, perhaps an altered future for these children.

'I'll see you all in the morning, children,' she said gently. 'Class dismissed. Off you go.' She swung the door wide, expecting them to make a bolt for it. Instead they trooped out one by one, all of them stopping to say goodbye and thank her.

Maryann Perkins, at the end of the line, explained, 'Rector came to see all our families and said as how one of the best things we could do was to thank you each day because we're real lucky to have you.'

Heat pricked at the back of her eyes. Gifts, it seemed, came in all sorts of unexpected guises.

She had worked out a budget. For food, fuel, and how often she could afford a pot of tea. Coffee was out of the question, but she preferred tea anyway. And she had decided that if she was prepared to re-use her tea leaves, a cup of tea after her class left was perfectly affordable.

A knock came at the back door as she waited for the kettle. Opening the door, she found Alex Martindale.

'Oh.' No doubt he wanted to know if he'd made a crashing mistake or not. 'Come in.'

'No need to ask how it went,' he said, ducking his head under the lintel. 'I met some of the children. They'd all enjoyed themselves and three of them repeated the scripture lesson to me.' He grinned, and her heart somersaulted. 'Caleb Fletcher repeated his sums. Well done.' He put a small pot on the table. 'Jam. Mrs Judd made rather a lot of blackberry last summer.'

She flushed. He was just being kind. It didn't mean anything. 'Thank you.' She loved blackberry jam. 'They all did well. They *want* to learn. Not like—' She stopped.

'Not like your previous pupils?'

She found herself smiling at the twinkle in his eye. 'No. I wasn't a very good governess,' she admitted.

He snorted. 'That I don't believe. In fact—'

Footsteps in the schoolroom had them both looking around as Lady Eliot stalked in. 'Ah. Hippolyta. I must protest—' Her gaze fell on Alex and she frowned. 'Mr Martindale. I cannot think it proper for you to be here with Hippolyta alone.'

'I called to see how Miss Woodrowe had fared, Lady Eliot.' Ice chipped Alex's voice. 'Just as I might call on any of my parishioners.'

Lady Eliot sniffed and looked unconvinced. 'Well, I dare say it doesn't much matter now. And I needed to speak to you as well about that *disgraceful* incident this morning.' She speared Polly with a savage look. 'Poor Susan is *mortified*. I believe an apology—'

'Oh, no, Lady Eliot,' said Alex. And Polly blinked at the bite in his voice. He continued, 'As long as Miss Susan realises how very wrong she was to laugh at Maryann, I am sure no more is needed.'

Polly choked, Lady Eliot's jaw sagged and Alex went on, 'I am sure she understands that to laugh at a child's achievements is not at all the behaviour you expect of her, so we shall say no more.'

The ample, velvet-shrouded bosom rose and fell. Lady Eliot's lips pursed tightly. 'I see. You do not think that making a mockery of her betters–'

'—is any worse than mocking a child?' said Alex. 'No. I do not. And I am not entirely certain why you would consider Miss Susan as Miss Woodrowe's superior.' If his voice had been chilly before, now it could have frozen hell solid.

Hoping to change the subject, Polly said, 'Should you like a cup of tea, Aunt?' Regrettably, she'd have to use fresh tea leaves.

Lady Eliot looked around and visibly shuddered. 'I think not, Hippolyta.' The disdain in her voice brought a stinging retort to Polly's lips. She choked it back somehow and Lady Eliot smiled thinly. 'Good day to you.' She favoured Alex with a chilly nod, 'Rector', and swept towards the door. Reaching it, she turned back. 'Your uncle feels that it would look best if you were to come to us for Christmas and New Year, Hippolyta, despite this foolishness.'

Polly stared at the door her aunt had closed with something close to a bang. She had refused even to think of Christmas, had expected to spend it alone. She wasn't entirely sure that mightn't have been preferable…but, no—the Eliots were her only remaining family. Surely once they realised that she no longer depended on them, that she asked nothing of them beyond being her family…why could they not see that?

*Because without your fortune, you're nothing to them. Only
a shop-bred upstart. Their inferior.*

'Sir Nathan's great-grandfather made his fortune importing
silk,' said Alex meditatively. 'Not that there's anything wrong
with that, of course. I never met your father, but my uncle used
to speak of him as a very good sort of man.'

'He did?' There was a lump in her throat.

'He did. Now, if that offer of tea could be extended to
me—?'

Alex's voice was very gentle. She turned to him and somehow the quiet understanding in those clear eyes calmed all the
hurt rage. If she allowed the Eliots to make her feel inferior,
it would be a betrayal of her father's hard work. Alex's quiet
words had shown her that.

'Yes. Yes, of course it could.' She fetched the teapot to
wash it out, and took down the tea caddy he'd given her. Her
fingers tightened on it, as she consigned her budget to perdition. For him she'd use fresh tea leaves gladly.

To her surprise, Polly found that she settled quite easily into
the rhythm of her new life over the next week and a half. The
children arrived on time each morning and even those villagers who viewed reading and writing with suspicion made her
welcome. Hardly a day went by when some small offering did
not appear either with one of her pupils, or a father dropping
by with something larger, such as the flitch of bacon deliv-
ered by Mr Appleby. 'Give a bit of flavour to a soup,' he said,
hanging it from a beam.

Other parents called, or spoke to her cheerfully in the street.
Pippa Alderley visited after school halfway through the second week and brought several books to lend to her.

'Alex has some you'd like,' she said cheerfully, smiling
over the rim of her mug. 'He brought some lovely sets of en-
gravings back from abroad. Scenes of Venice and Rome.' She
wrinkled her nose. 'He went to Pompeii, too, but he won't
show me those.' She sipped her tea and sighed. 'Dominic re-

fused to take me there when we went to the Continent after we married. He said they wouldn't let me see the ruins anyway. Most unfair, I call it.'

Polly stared, trying to imagine Alex visiting the scandalous ruins of Pompeii. She couldn't quite manage it, so turned her attention back to her guest. Pippa seemed quite unbothered by the less-than-grand surroundings of the schoolhouse. She had spotted the tea caddy the moment Polly lifted it down.

'Did Alex make that?'

Polly flushed. 'Yes.'

Pippa said no more on the subject, but an odd smile had played about her mouth as Polly made the tea.

When she rose to go, Pippa said, 'You'll come for dinner one day, won't you? Alex comes quite often. He can bring you along. He's rather busy just now, but perhaps once Christmas is over?'

Polly flushed. 'If you think he won't mind…'

Pippa looked amused. 'Oh, I shouldn't think he'd mind at all.'

Polly wasn't sure it was a good idea. Alex Martindale called daily, ostensibly to check on the children's progress, and she looked forward to those visits far, far too much. It would be far too easy to let herself dream, believe that those visits and the caddy meant something more than a good man's kindness.

Alex strode back into Alderford late that afternoon, his gun over his shoulder and Bonny at his heels. The sun had set, but scarlet and gold still blazed in the west. He'd made a couple of nearby visits on foot and walked back over Dominic's land.

'Afternoon, Rector.' Jim Benson touched his cap and looked admiringly at the brace of woodcock that dangled from Alex's hand. 'Those his lordship's?'

Alex smiled. 'They were.'

Jim grinned. 'Ah, well. Not like he'll miss them.' He nodded at Bonny. 'Shaping well, is she?'

'Yes,' said Alex, looking down at his dog. 'Very steady. Good nose and a lovely soft mouth.' Which had fortunately now stopped chewing the rugs.

Jim nodded. 'Aye. Looks like she's earning her way.' He touched his cap again. 'I'll be off to my supper. Reckon them birds will go right tasty in Miss Polly's pot!' And with a sly grin, he was off.

Alex stared after him in disbelief. How the deuce had the fellow known the birds were for Polly—Miss Woodrowe? Of course, he'd already given a bird to old Jem Tanner. And yesterday he'd given a brace of rabbits to the Jenkins family... Everyone knew he often gave game to his parishioners, but perhaps he ought not to be calling on Polly quite so often. Not daily, anyway. She was managing perfectly well for herself, after all. Now that he was assured of that, perhaps he could call once, or maybe twice, a week? Just to discuss the children's progress with her.

Pondering this, trying to convince himself that it was a good idea, he approached the cottage, automatically going around to the back door to save Polly having to come all the way to the front door through the schoolroom...

'Out! Out, you brute!'

Something exploded in a white-hot rush in Alex's brain. He had no idea how he reached the door, but he flung it open to find Polly, broom in hand, poking under a cupboard.

A rat of monumental proportions broke from cover and hurtled across the room, Polly charging after it, brandishing the broom. Bonny let out a startled bark as the terrified rodent shot between her paws and vanished in the darkness.

'You let it escape!' panted Polly, clearly furious.

Alex's heart steadied. 'Did you want it for a pet?' he asked, bemused. A rat. God! He'd thought—his stomach churned.

'Of course not!' she snapped. 'I was going to hit it again. Try to kill the wretched thing, so it doesn't come back! It was up there eating my bacon.' And she gestured to a large flitch hanging from a beam.

'You knocked it off?' Somehow it didn't surprise him. According to Greek myth Hippolyta had been a warrior queen, after all.

'Well, of course I did! That's *my* bacon!' Her eyes were slitted with indignation and her cheeks pink. 'Come in and sit down.' Several curls had escaped her loose braid, coiling wildly around her face. They looked abandoned, and—he swallowed—voluptuous, as if they'd curl around a man's fingers in welcome…

Trying to ignore this unprecedented leap of imagination, along with the unclerical leap of his blood, Alex walked in and sat down at the table, placing the woodcock on it. 'Conventional wisdom,' he said, disciplining himself to rational thought that didn't involve half-naked Amazonian warrior maidens, 'dictates that a young lady confronted with any rat, let alone one that size, is supposed to shriek and faint dead away.'

Polly snorted as she closed the door. 'And let the brute nibble his way through my bacon? I don't think so!'

He grinned. He simply couldn't help it. And her eyes answered, brimming with laughter. His heart hitched, his breath jerked in, her name on his lips.

Polly.

Time slowed, stilled, and he rose and took a slow step towards her, quite why he wasn't sure.

Her breath jerked in. 'I'm not a young lady anyway.'

He stopped dead, the spell shattered. 'The dev—the deuce you aren't! What put that maggot into your head?'

'It's not a maggot,' she told him. 'It's the truth. I work for my living, ergo I am no longer a lady.'

Several responses, none of them utterable by a man of the cloth, let alone before a lady, occurred to him. He bit them all back and said, 'I work for my living. Does that mean I'm not a gentleman in your eyes?'

She frowned and he was conscious of a sudden desire to smooth the tiny frown lines away, banish them utterly. 'That's different,' she said slowly. 'The rules are not quite the same for gentlemen, are they?'

No. They weren't. Nor were they always fair, or even sensible. 'You're still a lady,' he said stubbornly. 'Has someone treated you as though you weren't?' Because if they had—his fists clenched in a very unclerical and unchristian fashion. When he'd heard her cry out—his heart had nearly stopped, and he'd been prepared to tear anyone frightening her limb from limb. 'You're still a lady,' he repeated. 'No matter what your relatives may think.'

She leaned the broom back beside the cupboard. 'Maybe. It doesn't really matter. The children did well today.'

He listened as she outlined their progress, forced his brain to concentrate hard enough to make a few suggestions. And wondered if her hair was really as wildly alive as it looked, her lips as soft...

At last he rose to leave, no longer sure he could resist the temptation of finding out. 'I should go. You aren't worried about the rat coming back?'

She grimaced. 'No.'

He didn't believe her, but what could he do about it? He could hardly stay to defend her. The offer hovered on his lips—she could come back to the rectory for the night...Mrs Judd would be there, and— He stopped himself just in time. 'Goodnight,' he managed instead.

She went with him to the door and opened it. 'Goodnight, sir. Thank you for your ideas about the scripture lesson. They were very useful.'

Hearing he'd said something useful about scripture amazed him. He couldn't seem to think at all around her.

'A pleasure. Goodnight.'

He breathed a sigh of relief that was near to a groan as the door closed behind him and he heard the bolts shoot home.

Halfway to the Rectory, he heard flying footsteps behind him. 'Mr Martindale!'

He turned. She was running after him, holding the brace of woodcock.

He scowled. 'Polly! What on earth are you doing? Where's your cloak? You'll catch your death!'

'You forgot your birds.'

She held them out and his hands closed over hers. 'No, I did not. They were for you. Now go back home to the warmth before you catch a chill.'

Before I kiss you.

Her mouth quivered and temptation beckoned. 'You're very kind,' she said softly. 'Thank you.'

He was an untrustworthy scoundrel apparently, because all he could think was how sweet her lips would taste, what it would be like to feel them tremble under his and, if they were at all cold, warm them for her. His hands tightened on hers, felt them tremble as he heard the soft, startled intake of breath…

'Not at all, Miss Woodrowe. Goodnight.' He released her, turned and walked away before he did something about finding out, right there in the dark village street.

Clutching the woodpigeon, Polly stared after the tall, lean figure. Her breath hitched, heart thudding against her ribs. For one startling, blinding moment, she had thought he was going to kiss her.

Chapter Four

Susan called the following afternoon, arriving in the carriage just as the children left. Polly greeted her politely and invited her in. Susan gave the living room a derisive glance, then swung around, a pitying expression on her face. 'You poor *thing*, Hippolyta. I mean, living like this!' She shuddered. 'And you actually sleep in here, too? How *can* you? Really, you must be ready to see sense now. Mama says that Lady Littleworth is still looking for a companion, you know.'

Polly shrugged. 'This is my home, Susan, and I'm perfectly happy here.' She would be even happier if there wasn't that sneaking suspicion that she looked forward to Alex Martindale's daily visits far more than she ought to, that they had somehow become the high point of her day. And not because so often when he called, he had something for her. The woodcock yesterday, a pat of butter, or a small pot of jam that he claimed Mrs Judd had asked him to deliver.

Susan looked disbelieving. 'Happy? Here? But it's so—' She waved her hands about. 'It's so *squalid*! I mean, there's only that frightful settle, or whatever you call it, to sit on, and nothing to do except teach the village children! What on earth do you do in the evenings?'

Apart from wondering if Mr Martindale is going to kiss me?
Polly also refrained from telling her cousin that she went

to bed early to save lamp oil. 'I read. And any mending I do is *my* mending.'

'Oh.' Susan's wrinkled nose suggested that she couldn't think of anything more ghastly. Probably because she had never faced the thought of being Lady Littleworth's companion, or mending the sheets.

'Should you like a cup of tea, Susan?' offered Polly, wondering if she could get away with re-using the breakfast tea leaves.

Susan looked slightly aghast as her gaze fell on Polly's plain, earthenware cups. They were a far cry from Lady Eliot's elegant tea service. 'Oh, well. I shouldn't like to put you to any trouble. It's just, well, Tom is home, you know.'

'No. I didn't know.' She didn't much care, either. She'd see Tom at Christmas and that would be too soon.

Susan gave a conspiratorial smile and said, 'Mama would be furious if she knew what I'm going to tell you, but I thought that it was only fair.' She looked around, as though afraid her mother would pop up out of the floor, and went on. 'Tom thought it better if I spoke to you first.'

Polly stared. 'Tom thought what better?' Surely he didn't regret the way he had behaved two years ago?

Susan patted at her curls. 'Well, you know he's been staying with the Creeds? You remember the Creeds?' Not bothering to let her answer, Susan rushed on. 'He came home yesterday, terribly pleased. And you'll never guess—he's betrothed to Angelica! Mama is in alt, as you may guess!'

For a moment Polly was speechless, but Susan's avid eyes, greedy for the least sign that her barbed news had struck home, stiffened her.

'Oh. That is lovely news,' she said. Susan's slight frown gave her the impetus to forge a smile. 'How nice for them. Aunt Eliot must be delighted.'

Susan stared at her. 'You don't mind, then?'

A little thread of amusement uncurled itself, mocking her. 'Mind? Why ever should I? Please do wish Tom very happy for me. Although I suppose I shall be able to do that for my-self next week.' Christmas was so close now, and never had she looked forward to the festive season less.

Susan recovered somewhat. 'You'll still come for Christmas then?'

'Why should I not?' asked Polly. Was that it? Had Tom wanted her told, so that she might decide not to come, but not had the courage to tell her himself? To hell with him! If he had a guilty conscience, it was his problem.

Susan shifted a little uncomfortably. 'Well, you see, Angelica and her parents are coming to stay. They arrive Christmas Eve.'

Which would make the manor uncomfortably crowded.

'Oh. I dare say I shall only remain a couple of days, then,' said Polly in very cheerful tones. 'You might mention that to your mama for me.'

Susan glared at her and Polly tried hard not to smile. Her sweet little cousin wasn't supposed to have told her anything.

'You know everyone is talking about this, don't you?' burst out Susan.

'About Tom and Angelica?'

'No! About you! About how disgraceful it is that you've done this! You should have gone to Lady Littleworth!'

'And not been paid,' pointed out Polly. 'Instead I have my independence.'

'You would have been *respectable*!' snapped Susan, as if it were a holy grail. She gestured at the room. 'You think only of yourself! It's selfish—living like this, you're shaming all of us!'

'How dreadful for you,' said Polly sweetly. 'Fancy not being able to hide the shame of a poor relation. And, yes, I am afraid that as a woman who must make her own way in the world, I *do* think of myself.' No one else was going to do it for her.

Susan uttered a frustrated noise, turned on her heel and flounced out, banging the door.

With Susan gone, Polly sat slowly on the settle and stared

into the glowing fire. Despite the warmth, a cold emptiness yawned inside her. Fool that she was to have thought even for a moment that Tom might have regretted his behaviour. All he regretted was her lost fortune. If she had married him, how long would it have taken her to see that? To see him for what he truly was? Would she have lied to herself day after day? Year after year? Pretended that all was well? That he was still the handsome, devil-may-care, big cousin of her childhood? How long could she have lied to herself and not become something beyond pity?

With a jolt, she realised that she didn't care about Tom's betrothal. That she had realised a long time ago what a lucky escape she'd had there. A queer thought came to her—if she could turn the clock back, regain her fortune, would it be worth the price of being married to Tom?

Alex winced at the yowl emanating from the basket as he walked through the village that evening. How such a tiny creature could make so much noise was beyond him. And what on earth was he thinking giving Polly—*Miss Woodrowe*, he corrected himself—a kitten without even asking her if she would like a cat. Although he doubted that she would like a cat less than that blasted great rat.

And even a cat would be company for her. He glanced down at the pup trotting politely at his heels. Not as good as a dog, of course, but better than nothing, and a great deal cheaper to feed. Especially if it dined largely on rats and mice. Still, if she preferred not to have the kitten, she could always say so. He didn't much like cats himself, but he thought he could survive one more cat at the rectory if Polly declined.

Serve his housekeeper right! He still wanted to know how on earth Mrs Judd had known he'd visited Polly last night. The dratted woman had asked after Miss Polly when he'd come in, quite as if she had no doubt as to where he'd been, and before he'd known what he was doing, he'd told her about the rat. She'd produced the kitten at breakfast, informing him that it was from the smithy, its immediate antecedents renowned and celebrated ratters.

He should have come earlier, but he'd had to recite the Office and he'd had a sermon to write, not to mention adding up the various parish bills for the month. So there was no question of lingering to talk to Polly now. Quite apart from Mrs Judd's ire if he were late to supper, there was Polly's reputation to consider. There was no doubt that Mrs Judd knew exactly where he was this time. He squashed the flicker of regret.

The little cottage was nearly lost in the darkness, but a faint light crept out from behind the shutters, and the odour of wood smoke and something savoury drifted to him, reminding him that he was hungry. Another yowl from the basket suggested that someone else was hungry. Bonny gave the basket a wary sniff and backed off when it hissed.

Alex grinned. 'Very wise of you.' He'd back a cat, even one this size, against a setter any day. He rapped on the back door.

'Who is it?'

'It's just me. Alex.' Too familiar. 'Alex Martindale.'

Inside the bolts were shot back and the key screeched in the lock. He tried to steel himself, but at the first sight of her, the tawny hair spun to a golden nimbus in the lamplight, heat rose in his blood, and his heart and stomach twisted and clenched. Rather like his tongue.

'Er, Miss Woodrowe.' It was all he could manage. Wonderful. He'd told the woman her own name. He'd never understood that desire could tie a man in knots. Bonny apparently saw nothing in the least awkward in calling at this hour. She shoved past him up the steps and reared up, planting muddy paws firmly on Polly's gown. Nor was *her* tongue in the least affected by shyness as she licked enthusiastically at Polly's hands. Which weren't trying to push her down, but rather were petting the silly creature, rubbing her ears and under her muzzle. His breath shortened and his mind seized. Such soft, gentle hands...

His voice came out as a croak. 'Bonny—down.'

The pup sat, casting a sheepish look up at him, as her tail swept the step.

'It's all right, sir. I don't mind.'

He snorted. 'You will when she's bigger.'

The basket gave another indignant wail.

Polly stared at it. 'Your supper, sir?'

'What? Good God, no!' He held the basket out to her. 'It's a cat, a kitten really. For you.'

Silence spread out around them as she took the basket.

'You brought me a kitten.' There was a queer note of disbelief in her voice.

A stray curl had tumbled over her brow and he had to exert his will against the urge to stroke it back for her. Everything in him clenched as he imagined her silky hair sliding through his fingers, the velvet softness of her cheek under his touch…

Ignoring the rising beat of his blood, he said, 'I thought… it must be lonely by yourself. And the rat yesterday—well, that can't be pleasant.'

'No. Will you come in, sir?'

He shouldn't. Not at this hour. Not after dark when she was living quite alone.

Who on earth is going to know? Apart from Mrs Judd and she seems to like Polly…

He would know and he ought not to do this, but his feet were already over the threshold and she was closing the door behind them. The warmth of the little room enclosed them. Dancing firelight and the fragrance of her supper, her counterpane tossed over the back of the settle with a book propped in the folds.

Don't think of her wrapped in bedclothes!

'Have you eaten?' he asked.

Kneeling down to open the basket, she looked up as she lifted the kitten out. Her smile did odd things to him. 'Yes. A woodcock from last night. It was lovely. Thank you again.' She cuddled the kitten to her, murmuring to it as it batted her

face with a tiny paw. It was a very small kitten, all black and
gold patches laced with white.

'You like cats, then?' he got out. Lord! Her hands cradled
the little creature so tenderly, touching a gentle fingertip to
a ridiculous buff stripe on its nose… He shoved away the
thought—the image, God help him!—of those hands touching *him*. He shouldn't stay, but just being with her, here in the
same room, was a joyous torment. Thank God she still had
the lamp lit. The intimacy of firelight, with her bed there in
the corner… His head spun.

'Oh, yes. But cats made Mama sneeze, so we never had
one. Is it a boy or a girl?'

'Female,' Alex got out. 'Mrs Judd says tortoiseshell cats
are always female.'

She rose and sat down on the settle beside him, the kitten
in her lap. It was content there for a moment, but then, with
a determined squeak, clambered down her skirts and began
to explore the room.

'Another independent female,' he said.

There was a moment's silence. Then, 'Is that so very
wrong?'

'Wrong?' he asked. In a cat? But, no, she was not speaking
of the kitten. Something, someone, had upset her.

'To want to be independent. Is it really so unnatural?' Her
voice was very quiet and full of an uncertainty he'd never
heard in it before.

'I can't see that you had very much choice,' he said. Who
had hurt her? He was conscious of an aching need to reassure
her, to pull her into his arms and just hold her. Perhaps rest
his cheek on that tawny cloud and find out if it really was as
silken as it looked. Just hold her. For comfort, of course. He
groaned silently. Lord help him—he was even lying to himself now. His body, so well disciplined for so many years, was
making up for lost time. Apparently he was not immune to
the sins of the flesh after all.

'My cousin Susan called.'

Ah. No doubt Miss Susan had expressed her mama's opinion of Polly's rebellion. 'Is she well?'

'Very well. We…we were talking about Christmas.' She was bent down, detaching the kitten from where it was climbing her skirts, taking care with each tiny claw. Firelight glinted in the curls drifting around her temple, falling against her silken cheek so that his fingers ached to stroke them back, to tangle in them, tilt her face up to his and find out just how sweet her mouth was.

'I can take the kitten to the rectory while you are with the Eliots,' he forced out, closing his fingers to fists against the beat of temptation in his blood. What the deuce was wrong with him that he could scarcely get himself to act with disinterested chivalry?

She went very still. 'Thank you, sir.'

There was something odd about her voice. As if she were close to tears. 'Polly—Miss Woodrowe, is something wrong? Did Miss Eliot have bad news?'

Her chin lifted. 'Bad news? Not at all. Quite the opposite. My cousin, Tom, is betrothed.'

That brittle voice splintered somewhere deep inside him and all that was left were the most useless, banal words in the language. 'I'm sorry.'

'Don't pity me!'

The words exploded from her, and he bit back everything he would have liked to say. Pity? It was more like rage. Rage that there was nothing he could do to shield her from the pain she must be feeling. Rage that the Eliots, instead of protecting Polly, had cut her adrift. Rage that the world was like this at Christmas when such love was coming into the world that it could barely be contained.

'It's wonderful news,' said Polly, still in that tight, controlled voice. 'My aunt must be delighted. It's Miss Creed, you know. A very eligible connection. She is an heiress.'

This time there really were no words. Instead, he reached out and took her small, cold, mittened hands, and just held them, contained them in the protection of his own. Sometimes words were inadequate things. Touch was better.

She thought if he had not done that, had not enveloped her cold hands in the warmth of his, she could have held herself together. As it was, the gentle strength shredded the threadbare cloak of pride, thawed the frozen place where she had interred all the pain, until her eyes burned and spilled over. She swallowed. Oh, damn! One powerful hand loosened and she wanted to cry out in protest, but his arm came around her and drew her close to rest against his shoulder.

Still he said nothing. No soothing words, no injunction not to cry. Just his solid strength to lean against for a moment, the sort of unspoken sympathy that made the wretched tears flow faster, and his arm about her. She knew he meant only to comfort, but her foolish, wanton body was dreaming of so much more than that. Dreaming of what it would be like if he truly took her in his arms, and not to comfort.

She must be a very wicked girl to entertain such thoughts. Wicked to feel this burn and dazzle in her blood at the gentle clasp of his hand. Wicked to wish that his arm might tighten, that his mouth… Well, it was a sheer miracle that a thunderbolt had not obliterated the schoolhouse with what she was thinking. But then it might have obliterated Alex and she supposed God would not want that.

I'm wicked to think such things.

He snorted. 'I don't think so.'

With a shock she realised that she had spoken aloud.

'Wicked to be angry at injustice and hypocrisy?' asked Alex. 'Well, that makes two of us.' He lifted their linked hands and the grey eyes smiled, full of understanding. 'Linked in the heinous sin of disapproving of the social order.'

'Thank you,' she whispered. *Thank you, God, that he didn't realise what I was really thinking.*

The crooked half-smile—the one that turned her insides

to jelly—twisted his mouth. 'For what? Wanting to kick your cousins into the middle of next week for hurting you?'

He did? Her throat ached.

For being kind.

For understanding.

Her heart full, insensibly eased, she shook her head. 'No,' she said softly, and set one hand on his shoulder, feeling a flicker of muscle beneath the broadcloth. 'For being you,' she said and reached up to kiss his cheek.

For being you. As though he were a gift, when God knew he was nothing of the sort. His heart blazed, and his whole body tightened at her nearness, her fragrance—intoxication itself—and the light touch of her fingers through layers of cloth, the sweetest torment, a burning. The knowledge that she was going to kiss him—only on the cheek, but still the loveliest gift he'd ever been offered.

Then her lips were there, such peach-silk softness, a featherlight caress on his jaw that he should accept as it was meant—but somehow his head had turned—not at all what Christ had meant by turning the other cheek—and his lips had captured hers, his arms drawing her against the burning ache of his body.

Her startled gasp he took gently, even as for one soul-shattering moment she remained utterly still in his embrace. His conscience gave one last, feeble flicker. He must release her, apologise…but her lips moved hesitantly against his and he was lost.

Every nerve, every sinew and muscle leapt to flame as his arms tightened of their own accord, as his mouth returned her shy kiss and took more. Shaken to his soul, he tasted the fullness of her mouth—sweet, so sweet—and her lips parted. His mind reeled, his tongue dipped, found milk and honey, and tasted again and again, while his resolution dissolved, mind and body awash with delight as her tongue met his in hesitant wonder.

This. Just this.

This delight of a woman's body in his arms, her lips and mouth tender under his, and this burning, this singing in blood and bone that could steal a man's senses as surely as any siren.

Desire. His body recognised it and responded, hardening, tightening his arms around Polly, drawing her in to the consuming heat, cradling her closer. And she came, soft and willing, body and mouth yielding, melting against him. One hand found the supple curve of her waist, drifted higher against the swell of her breast and he tasted the surprise in her soft gasp.

Desire. A maelstrom threatening to sweep everything away. Sense, honour, both gone, and reason fast fading. One floundering scrap of reason found a foothold, a touchstone.

Polly. This was Polly.

Somehow he broke the kiss, drew back a little, breathing hard. A little more reason surfaced. He shouldn't be doing this. In a moment he might remember why not…

You're the rector, for goodness' sake!

That hit him like a bucket of icy water. He stared down at Polly, dazed. She looked dazed, too. And her lips were damp and swollen. Pink and ripe. Because he'd kissed her. Even as he looked, all the reasons he shouldn't be kissing her closed in, accusing.

Surely only a complete blackguard kissed a defenceless girl like that? When all she had offered was a sort of sisterly peck on the cheek.

'I…I have to go,' he managed. Because God only knew, if he didn't, where this would end. His gaze fell on the alcove holding Polly's bed and gave him back the lie. He knew perfectly well where it could have ended. That, right there, in that shadowed alcove, was the natural end for such a kiss.

Somehow he forced his hand to withdraw from the fall of her hair, now tumbled around her shoulders. Had he done that? His fingers shook at the silken caress. With even more difficulty he dragged the other hand from her waist.

'Polly,' he whispered. Lord, had he only just seen her? Seen what was in front of him. 'I'm—'

'No.' The luminous golden eyes pleaded. 'Don't apologise. Please, just…just pretend there is a little bit of mistletoe above us.'

Mistletoe? God help them both if he'd had that pagan incentive above him!

He was the rector and Polly had confided in him, turned to him for comfort. He swallowed, brutally aware of aching need. Wanting to cast discretion and propriety, not to mention his vows, to the four winds.

He forced himself to release her and stand up, away from the warmth that was Polly. But his eyes—his eyes remained on her face, lost, and somehow found. Until her gaze fell and scarlet mantled her cheeks.

'I'll…I'll bid you goodnight, sir.'

Polly. Her name lay unspoken on his tongue like honey, as sweet and intimate as her mouth itself.

He swallowed. 'Miss Woodrowe.' He cleared his throat. 'You'll bar the door behind me?' What the hell would he do if she said no? Refuse to leave until she did?

'Yes.'

Thank God.

'Well. Ah, goodnight then.'

'Goodnight, sir.'

Bonny bounded up from the hearth as he headed to the door. He made a mental note that dogs appeared to be very poor chaperons.

Chapter Five

As Polly secured the door, she heard his steps retreating, crunching on the frosty street. With a groan, she leaned back against the door, feeling the bar digging into her back. Her heart still raced and her hands trembled.

She hadn't known a kiss could be like that. Full of wonder and need and delight. She had let Tom kiss her once years ago. He had seemed to enjoy it, but she had thought it horrid. All hot breath and pawing at her breast. This had been quite different. This had been something joyous and right.

Right? What was she thinking? She'd kissed the rector! No doubt there would be a letter dismissing her from her post in the morning. And this time she'd deserve it. Never mind that she'd meant it as a mere peck on the cheek, a…a kiss of gratitude. It somehow hadn't ended up that way. How on earth had she missed his cheek?

Because you wanted to miss it?

Because some wanton part of her had wanted to kiss him, had wanted to feel his arms strong about her.

Her cheeks burnt. At best he'd think her shockingly forward, at worst a depraved hussy…although he *had* been kissing her back. With a great deal of enthusiasm. She pushed that aside. In these matters, from Eve's temptation of Adam on, it was *always* the woman's fault. But how did you explain to a man—let alone a man of God—that it had all been a mistake, that you hadn't really meant to kiss him at all? Or at least not like that. Not like a wanton. Especially when your heart was still pounding and you could still taste him, wine-dark and gentle, in your mouth. When your breasts ached from being pressed against him and your body remembered exactly where those big, careful hands had touched.

God in heaven!

Was that what St Paul meant about better to marry than burn? He'd always assumed that referred to the fires of hell, of sin. Or perhaps St Paul *had* truly considered physical love to be sinful.

Alex's steps crunched through the frost towards the rectory, as his mind spun dizzily. He hadn't known. Simply hadn't known that a kiss could be like that. Like…like an explosion, a beginning and ending all in one.

Better to marry than burn…

'Evening, Rector.'

'Good evening, Davey.' He managed a smile for Davey Fletcher. Prayed the blacksmith hadn't seen which cottage he'd come out of.

'That Miss Woodrowe's a right pretty lass,' said Fletcher cheerfully, patting Bonny as she nudged up to him.

Yes, well. Not all prayers were answered quite as one might like. He knew that.

Fletcher continued. 'My boy, Caleb, reckons she's real nice too, the way she manages all them young 'uns. Teaching them their ABCs an' all.' He nodded. 'Good thing for this village, an' don't you think we're not grateful to you and his lordship for doing it.' He doffed his cap and went on his way, whistling.

Of course, Fletcher probably thought he'd just been discussing the children's progress with Polly. As he should have been.

Instead, he'd been kissing her. And there was only one possible remedy for that. At least, there was only one remedy for him in this situation.

He'd somehow always expected the decision to marry—and the choice of a bride—to be a rational, logical process, just like everything else he'd done in his life. Naturally his wife would be a woman he liked and esteemed, someone he could be comfortable with. But tumbling head over heels in love?

Oh, he knew people fell in love. He'd watched it happen to Dominic and Pippa. It had not looked logical at all. Although perhaps that was just their confusion. The actual result had been perfectly logical. He'd seen that before they had. But still, he'd never thought that it would happen to him. Not like that. But it had. Like a thunderbolt. He dragged in a breath, steadied his thinking, reaching for the calm inner peace he relied on. Just because he'd fallen in love didn't mean it wasn't necessary to at least behave as though he was thinking rationally. More importantly, he needed to behave with honour.

He groaned. Kissing Polly Woodrowe out of her wits was not the action of an honourable man. Not when she had no one to protect her, to guard her reputation, or to advise her.

Of course it would be different if they were betrothed.

Very different.

Kissing her would be quite unexceptionable. As long as he made sure it stopped at kissing. What worried him was that ensuring that it *did* stop at kissing looked like being a problem. He was a clergyman, for heaven's sake!

Apparently he was a man before he was a clergyman. A man who wanted a woman. A woman he liked, cared for and respected. Logically, and thank God he was actually being logical again, that could mean only one thing: marriage.

The next day it was all Polly could do to keep her mind on her pupils and off Alex Martindale. No letter dismissing her had arrived during breakfast, the children all came to school on time and, apart from an awkward moment over Jemmy Willet's arithmetic, the day passed uneventfully.

Until Alex arrived as the children were leaving.

They filed out, greeting him cheerfully as they passed.

Polly listened as he greeted them by name, asking after parents, relatives, little brothers and sisters. He knew these people, she realised. Knew them and cared about them. They were indeed his flock.

And he was probably quite horrified to think that he had placed a wanton hussy in charge of the lambs.

She shut the door behind the children and faced him. 'Mr Martindale, about last night, I'm—'

'Yes. Last night. Miss Woodrowe—Polly—will you do me the honour of marrying me?'

Marriage. In the darkness last night, sleepless in her bed, she had allowed her dreams free rein. And had banished them in the chill light of morning. Alex Martindale could not marry a penniless schoolmistress, whose family did not want to know her.

Surely he knew that?

Apparently he didn't.

He hadn't meant to blurt it out like that, but the mere thought of last night had scattered his carefully prepared speech.

'*Marry* you?' She stared at him as if he'd sprouted an extra head, or possibly horns and a tail.

He cleared his throat. 'Well, yes. I'd like you to marry me.' Rather understating the case, but—

'Why?'

Dash it all! Wasn't it obvious? 'You can ask that? After yesterday?'

She stared. 'This is because you kissed me? You feel honour-bound to offer marriage because you kissed me?'

'No,' he said at once. 'I'm asking you to marry me because I want to be able to kiss you and know I don't have to stop.' Her jaw dropped and he followed up his advantage at once. 'And because I want to kiss you again. Right now.'

Her eyes widened. 'Right now?'

'Yes.'

'But you're…not.'

'No. Because I wouldn't want to stop. And…' he dragged in a breath, cast discretion, not to mention delicacy, to perdition '…because I might not stop.' Oh, God! Now she knew, knew the truth. And she'd think him depraved.

'But, sir—'

'Alex.' He didn't want her calling him sir, or Mr Martindale, or anything else but Alex.

She flushed. 'Alex, then. Don't you see? I'm no sort of wife for you. I've no money. No connections. I would bring you nothing.'

She was biting her lip in a way that made him want to soothe it, kiss away the worry and then bite it himself. Even as the idea of her feeling unworthy infuriated him. 'I'm perfectly well off and my own connections are more than adequate,' he pointed out.

'That's just it!' she said. 'It…it would be most unequal.'

Ah. Here was the rub, then. 'And would that bother you if our positions were reversed?' he asked quietly.

'Not now,' she whispered. 'I've learnt better. But before? When I was wealthy?' Her cheeks flamed. 'Probably, yes.'

Her bone-deep honesty and humility seared him. 'Your aunt would have set the dogs on me, anyway,' he said.

She managed a smile. 'Yes. Warned me that you only wanted my money.'

He snorted. 'Like your cousin?'

She flushed and guilt lashed him. 'I'm sorry,' he said. 'I shouldn't have reminded you.'

She shook her head. 'It doesn't matter. Not now.'

'Then do I have your permission to court you?' he asked.

She blinked. '*My* permission to court me?'

He smiled. 'Who else should I ask?'

Courting was something a gentleman did to a lady. After asking her father or guardian's permission. Only her father was dead and she didn't have a guardian any longer. She had her independence and he had asked *her* permission.

'You want to court me?'

'Yes.' Alex felt that he was on fairly firm ground here. 'It's what a man does when he wants a woman as his wife.' He'd watched any number of courting couples over the years. Then married them. Rather often the christening was significantly less than nine months later in the village and farming community. He slammed a lid back on that pot of thought at once.

'What does courting entail?'

Polly's question had him mentally scrambling. 'Ah, well, I call on you,' he said. 'At respectable hours,' he added hurriedly. 'I can bring you small gifts. Flowers in season.' Please God, by spring they'd be beyond courting.

'That's all?'

He blanked out the image of leaving flowers on her pillow. 'We can walk together.' That should be safe enough for her. It was far too cold for tumbling maidens in the woods.

'That's it?'

'Yes.'

'Are you going to kiss me?'

Polly shut her eyes. She definitely hadn't meant to say that. Well, if anything were needed to change his mind about her suitability as his wife, the realisation that she was indeed a shameless hussy should take the trick.

Dragging in a breath, she opened her eyes to face him.

He was staring at her, wonder in his eyes. 'You don't mind?'

She blushed, shook her head.

'What if—' He broke off. 'You trust me?'

Her turn to stare. 'Trust you? Well, of *course* I trust you!'

'You shouldn't,' he whispered, reaching for her. 'Because I'm not sure that I trust myself.'

His arms closed about her, drew her in to the warmth and safety. For a moment they stood like that and it was enough. The cottage was enough, if it could hold such wonder. Everything in her whole world had contracted to their two bodies. His hard, powerful; the strength in his arms should have terrified her, yet he held her so gently. She looked up, meaning to speak, there were things she must tell him before this went any further. Things that might make him change his mind.

'Alex—' But his mouth covered hers and his kiss silenced her, stole her wits and breath, and ravished her senses.

By the time he broke the kiss and stepped back, his breathing was ragged and her wits were spinning. Those normally gentle grey eyes were ablaze and his hands gripped her shoulders hard.

'Polly, we have to stop this or you won't have a choice about marriage,' he said harshly. 'I shouldn't see you alone like this again.' His hands slid down her arms, so that every nerve danced, and grasped her hands, bringing them to his lips, feathering a kiss over her knuckles. Then he released her and was gone, leaving her dazed and trembling.

Chapter Six

For the next few days Alex stayed away from the schoolhouse unless the children were still there. If he couldn't see Polly alone without kissing her and not wanting to stop, then he had to stay away. For her sake. The last thing he wanted was for someone to catch them and for her to feel shamed into accepting him, or, even worse, for his control to break and his own actions force her to marriage.

So he greeted her in the street after school when she walked down to the Filberts' shop, spoke with her in public after church about the children's progress, walked with her as a small girl, full of delight and chatter, swung on her hand the length of the village street. Polly, he realised in bemusement, was precisely the wife for the rector of a country parish. And, more importantly, she was precisely the right wife for Alex Martindale—the woman he dreamed of and woke up aching for.

The woman he had fallen head over heels in love with.

He finally broke the day before Christmas Eve. Surely he could see her alone for five minutes before she went to her cousins, perhaps even exchange a gentle kiss, without being overwhelmed by lust!

Alex stopped in at the school on his way home from his parish rounds. It was nearly the end of the school day. He could invite Polly to the rectory for a cup of tea. She might even stay for supper. Mrs Judd would be about. They wouldn't be entirely unchaperoned. That would be safer than being with her in the schoolhouse and he could be with her for a little longer. And he wanted to see her in his home. Where she belonged.

He opened the door quietly. Polly was bent over one of the children, explaining something, but she looked up at once, beckoned him in and turned back to the child.

Polly's heart hammered as she explained where the sum had gone wrong, took Sally through it again, setting her a similar sum, and finally patting the girl on the shoulder with a 'Well done' as the difficulty was mastered.

Straightening, she said, 'Time to pack up, class.' There was a scurry for hats, mufflers and coats, the older children helping the younger ones. She didn't look at Alex—Mr Martindale—but watched the children. He had held to his resolve not to be alone with her, walking with her in the street and chatting about the children after church last Sunday.

Once they were sitting quietly again, the children, at a small nod from her, rose as one. 'Good afternoon, Miss Polly!' they chorused, 'And a Merry Christmas to you!'

She smiled. 'And a Merry Christmas to you, class. Line up at the door.'

They scrambled for the door, lining up from youngest to oldest, straight and tall. Still smiling, she walked to the door and reached into her pocket, bringing out a small bag of toffees. 'One each,' she said. 'And enjoy the holiday.'

Grinning and wishing her a Merry Christmas again, the children filed out, taking a toffee each.

As she closed the door behind the last child, Alex said simply, 'I missed you.'

Whatever she had expected him to say, that wasn't it, and her heart leapt. 'Missed me? You've seen me every single day.'

He nodded. 'I know. But it's not the same, courting you in public.'

Not the same as what?

He drew her into his arms. 'Not the same as kissing you,' he murmured, as if she'd asked the question aloud. His lips settled on hers in a gentle kiss that banished every doubt, every fear, and with a soft sigh she surrendered her mouth to him. His arms tightened as the kiss deepened, and she tasted him, warm and dark in her mouth. Shyly she touched her tongue to his, felt his groan of response, the answering leap of desire in her own blood as his mouth possessed hers. Slow, deep kisses, and his hands gentle on her body, reverent as he cupped one breast and her breathing shattered on a sob at the shaft of sensation.

Alex felt, tasted, the soft cry and somehow broke the kiss, shaking, burning, almost beyond stopping. Breathing hard, he rested his forehead on hers. If she didn't accept and marry him soon, he was going to end up stark, raving mad.

'Polly, have you—?'

'Good God!'

The slam of the door and disgusted exclamation had roughly the same effect as a bucket of cold, dirty water. He released Polly at once.

Lady Eliot was staring at them in disbelief. 'If it would not be too much trouble, *Rector*—' her icy tones suggested that he might possibly have forgotten the dignity due to his calling '—I should like to speak to my niece. *Privately.*'

Somehow he steadied his breathing, squashed the urge to recommend that Lady Eliot hie herself to a much warmer address and stepped away from Polly.

He hauled in a breath, one that still tasted of Polly, and said, 'Lady Eliot, I assure you that—'

A small, distressed sound from Polly stopped him. Every instinct bade him tell her aunt that he had made her an honourable offer, that he loved her, wanted to marry her. But—

But she had not accepted him yet. And if he told Lady Eliot, then the pressure on Polly to accept would be immense. If she were unsure of her affections, perhaps still loved her cousin

Tom—an unsuspected green-hued beast inside him growled savagely at the mere thought—then she needed time. Time to be sure of the direction of her heart. No matter that his own heart had found its true north, Polly had forged her independence and he wasn't going to rip it away from her. Polly was more than capable of dealing with her aunt.

So he said, for her ears only, 'As you wish, sweetheart.'

He walked past Lady Eliot with a polite, 'Good day, ma'am', and left.

Polly turned to face her aunt, her cheeks burning. 'Good day, Aunt. How do you go on?'

Lady Eliot ignored this greeting. 'I suppose I am not surprised to find *you* in such a disgraceful situation, Hippolyta, but I confess I had thought better of Mr Martindale!'

Polly drew a deep breath. 'It…it isn't what you think, Aunt! There was nothing—'

'Nothing?' demanded Lady Eliot. 'Hippolyta, you were in his arms and I believe he had been kissing you!' She snorted. 'I am very sure that is *nothing* to a bold piece such as yourself, but—'

'We did nothing wrong!' burst Polly. 'He—' She stopped. She couldn't tell Aunt Eliot that Alex had offered for her. Not unless she meant to accept him. If it became known that he had offered and been refused, it would expose him to ridicule. And she couldn't accept him before she was quite sure he meant it. That his offer did not stem from chivalry alone. She certainly couldn't accept him before he knew the truth about her dismissal from the Frisinghams' employ. If he didn't believe her…something inside her shrivelled at the thought that he might not. After all, she had kissed him first. He might think she was running true to form….

'We did nothing wrong,' she repeated. 'And it is none of your business, Aunt.'

Lady Eliot snorted. 'Well, I dare say, since you no longer reside under Sir Nathan's roof, that you think it none of my business, but I will remind you that your previous effort at entrapping a gentleman ended in scandal and dismissal!' The cold eyes raked Polly from head to foot. 'I assure you that if you bring shame on your family *here*, there will cease to be any welcome for you in your uncle's house! Which brings me to what I wished to say. Perhaps we may go through to your *quarters*.'

Polly opened the door and gestured her aunt through, relieved that she had got up early enough that morning to sweep, dust and clear away breakfast. Even so, she could practically feel the disdain rippling through her aunt as she slowly surveyed the little room, then walked across it, her skirts held high. Humiliated, she saw the room through her aunt's eyes, the single wooden settle by the fire, the pot hanging over the fire, steaming with her supper, the curtained-off alcove that held her bed—the mattress and bedding from the rectory including an old counterpane with the kitten curled up asleep in the middle, the shelf holding cups, plate and bowl, the flitch of bacon hanging from the rafter, and the jars of preserves that her pupils had brought her.

Lady Eliot turned to her slowly. 'You have chosen *this* over a home with your family, Hippolyta? Over a place with Lady Littleworth?'

Not exactly. 'I have chosen to earn my own living, rather than being a burden on my relatives.' And being treated as an unpaid governess-companion-chaperon. Here in this village she was respected, even if her family no longer saw her as respectable.

Lady Eliot cleared her throat. 'I have some news. Family news. Tom arrived home the other day.'

Polly opened her mouth to say she knew. And closed it again. It would be utterly spiteful to give Susan away. The kitten, awake now, clambered down from the bed and scampered across the room towards them.

Lady Eliot continued. 'He has been staying with the Creeds, you know. A very good sort of family. Well connected.'

That went without saying. As did *old money, wealthy.* 'Yes, aunt?' She bent down and scooped up the kitten as one paw dabbed at the temptation of velvet skirts.

Lady Eliot fussed with her reticule. 'Yes, Hippolyta. And I felt it best to tell you that Tom is betrothed to Miss Creed. Naturally Sir Nathan and I are delighted, and of course I have invited Miss Creed with her parents to visit us for the holiday.' Lady Eliot paused for effect. 'They arrive tomorrow and will be with us until Epiphany.' She cleared her throat again. 'Sir Nathan still insists that you must come to us for Christmas, that it would present a very odd appearance if you did not, so I have ordered one of the grooms to collect you in the gig tomorrow morning.'

'Thank you, Aunt.' Polly lifted her chin. 'I should prefer only to stay until Boxing Day.' Clearly Susan had not passed on her message.

Her aunt inclined her head. 'Obliging of you.'

Polly's temper flared. 'Not at all, Aunt.' She gestured to the kitten nestled in her arms. 'I prefer not to leave Speckles for so long.'

Lady Eliot's mouth thinned and her eyes narrowed. 'I see. Very well. I should have thought that the claims of your family—but never mind. Please ensure that you are ready when the groom arrives. There will be a great deal to do and I am sure you would wish to repay your uncle's condescension by being useful.'

Really? You have a claim on me?

The words were there, riding on a surge of fury that threatened to consume her. Somehow she bit them back and escorted Lady Eliot to the door, mouthing polite inanities. Lady Eliot paused on the doorstep and fixed her with a severe look. 'It is, of course, possible that Mr Martindale, as a man of the cloth, may feel obliged as a result of whatever has passed between you to offer marriage, Hippolyta. You may rest assured that his bishop would view such a connection, to a woman of soiled reputation, with extreme disapprobation. Good day to you.'

Her aunt stepped into the carriage and the driver whipped up the horses, who flung themselves into their collars.

Polly slipped back into the schoolroom, closing the door behind her against the bitter wind. Last Christmas and the one before at the Frisinghams' had been dreadful. This one promised to be far worse. She blinked back tears. Crying was a waste of time and she had better things to do than wallow in self-pity. Better to shove it all down inside for now and get on with her chores. She had wood to bring in and supper to finish cooking. Stepping outside, Polly glanced up at the leaden sky. Even as she looked, the first fat flakes swirled down. The kitten mewed, twisting around her ankles. Polly smiled down at it. 'Your first snowstorm, Speckles.'

Christmas Eve dawned frosty and clear on a dusting of snow. Polly came out of her back door carefully. The step was covered in ice. She breathed out and her breath froze on the air. Delighted, she did it again. When she was little Papa had pretended that she was a dragon, breathing fire. Mama had laughed at the idea, puffed out her own breath and joined in her delight when there was snow at Christmas. New life, hope born again. Everyone would be bringing in greenery today to symbolise that life and hope. And dragons breathing fire didn't worry about snobbish aunts, especially on Christmas Eve. She hoped that it snowed at Christmas now for Mama and Papa.

'Mrowp.'

She looked down at the kitten twining about her feet. It dabbed a paw at the icy step and took it back, disgusted.

'No greenery for us today, Speckles,' said Polly. She had to make sure the cottage was tidy and the fire out before the Eliots' gig came for her. She sighed. There just wasn't time to collect greenery, and no point since she wouldn't be here to enjoy it.

A pity, though. There wouldn't be much greenery at the Manor. Aunt Eliot thought such things vulgar. Only for the lower orders. But it was Christmas. A time for being with your

family. Did Mr Martindale—Alex—indulge in Yuletide greenery at the rectory? She'd heard that his cousin, Lord Alderley,
always had the Great Hall decked out, that he'd even married
on Twelfth Night some years ago. Perhaps next Christmas
there would be greenery and joy and—she shouldn't think
about it. Because she really ought not to marry him.

*Why not? Because you have no money? He doesn't care
about that. Because you aren't well born? He doesn't care
about that either!*

You haven't told him why you were dismissed...

Her joy in the morning drained from her. She should have
told him the moment he offered for her. It had been the right
thing to do, but she had been too afraid. Afraid of him not
believing her, turning from her as the Eliots, her supposed
family, had done.

Did she trust him, or not?

She scooped Speckles up and turned back into the cottage.
What a foolish question. Of course she trusted him and, if he
still wanted to court her after Christmas, she would tell him
everything. And then…then if he offered again, they could be
betrothed and perhaps marry at Easter. Her blood quickened
at the thought, heart racing, light and swift at the thought of
a kiss that wouldn't have to stop.

And if he doesn't believe you?

Then she would refuse his offer, even if honour made him
hold to it. To wake up one morning and know that Alex regretted marrying her—lead condensed in her gut—that would
be loneliness indeed.

For now, she would make her breakfast and pack her bag.
Outside in the street she could hear the village waking up,
people talking, children calling to one another.

Joe Turner was the first, arriving straight after breakfast
with a vast amount of holly in his arms.

'Merry Chris'mas, Miss Polly!' His gap-toothed grin
warmed her to the soles of her feet. He walked into her room

and put the holly on the table she had just cleared. 'Me mam says to give you this, and…' he pulled a jar out from somewhere inside his jacket '…this.' He set that on the table, too. 'Plum, it is. From our tree. An' the holly's from the woods. Went out early for it an' brought some extra for yeh.' He wrinkled his nose. 'Prickly stuff, but the berries is right pretty.'

They gleamed scarlet against the dark leaves.

Polly's throat closed. 'Thank you, Joe,' she got out. 'It's… it's beautiful.'

He grinned again. 'Could show you how to twist it together. Makes a nice wreath. Mam does one each year.'

By the time Joe left, a slightly crooked holly wreath was hung up in pride of place over the fire and Polly's heart was light.

Joe had scarcely left before there was another knock on the back door. Opening it, she found Caleb Fletcher and his little sister with a truly staggering amount of ivy in their arms. And a jar of apricot jam. After draping the ivy everywhere they could reach and climb, including around the bed, Caleb said, 'And our mum says as how you're welcome to dinner tomorrow, Miss Polly. We'd be real proud to have you.'

'Thank you, Caleb, but I am promised to my cousins for the holiday.' She said it with very real regret.

He nodded. 'Aye. Mum said you might be, but to ask all the same.'

'Please thank her for me.'

Polly's eyes prickled as the children left. Christmas dinner with the Fletchers, surrounded by greenery, and Christmas joy…no. She couldn't. Not after accepting Aunt Eliot's invitation, no matter how little she wanted to go to the Manor.

By the time Rosie Appleby arrived with sprigs of bay— 'Mam says to use it in stews and soups after Christmas' and a small bay tree in a pot for the coming year—the church clock had struck eleven. Polly blinked. Lady Eliot had been most particular about being ready early because of the Creeds' arrival. After deploying the sprigs of bay, she walked around the side of the cottage with Rosie, the small girl's mittened hand tucked in hers.

'Be you going to your cousins, Miss Polly?' asked Rosie as they reached the street.

'Yes. A little later.'

Wheels rumbled and a carriage came down the village street, drawn by two elegant chestnuts.

'Coo!' breathed Rosie. 'Reckon that'll be Mr Tom's lady?'

If Polly had ever doubted that gossip traveled in a small village, that would have banished it.

'Very likely—yes,' she said as the carriage rolled past, giving a brief glimpse of Angelica Creed. 'Yes, that is Miss Creed.' Her heart sank. In a very few hours she would have to sit down to dinner, with Angelica as guest of honour. She wasn't entirely sure she had enough Christian charity to remember her manners. And then a niggling doubt slid into her mind. Maybe the gig wasn't coming at all?

Rosie let go of her hand. 'Here's Sally Hough, Miss. With bread.'

Sally rushed up to them. 'Did you see the carriage? Mam says as it might be Mr Tom Eliot's new lady!'

'We saw her,' said Rosie importantly. 'It is. Miss Polly says so.'

'Oh.' Sally was visibly deflated. 'Well. I brought some bread, Miss Polly. Mam made an extra loaf and said to bring it over.'

The warm, yeasty fragrance wreathed itself around her. New bread. One of her very favourite things. 'Why don't we take that lovely loaf back inside, you two?' she said. 'We'll cut it and have some with jam.' And if the gig came, then it could just jolly well wait!

Chapter Seven

The gig hadn't come by the time Polly and the two girls had munched their way through two slices of bread and jam each, and the noon Angelus had rung from the church bell tower.

'Getting cold in here, miss,' observed Sally, licking plum jam from the corner of her mouth with great concentration.

'Yes. I let the fire go out because I'm going to my cousins,' said Polly. 'You'd better go home now, girls. Before your mothers wonder where you are.'

The girls rushed off together, hand in hand, waving to Polly. She went back inside and gazed at the cooling hearth. If she lit the fire again the gig would probably arrive just as she got it blazing. Instead, she put her cloak on and sat on the settle. It might be a little warmer there close to the fireplace.

But as the afternoon drew in, and the church clock struck three, Polly's head finally accepted what her heart had known since seeing the Creeds' carriage. It was time and more to light the fire again—the gig wasn't coming. The Eliots dined at three. They would already be seated around the dining table, their grace said, tucking into a splendid dinner, lamplight and candles glittering coldly on silver and glass.

Hurt and fury boiled up and for a moment she hesitated. There was something else she could do—she could walk over to the Manor now and arrive in the middle of dinner, embarrassing all of them.

The gig must have got lost, Uncle. I do hope your groom is all right.

She could hear herself saying it. Revenge sang in her, luring and coldly sweet.

'*Mrowp?*'

She looked down. Speckles was trying to climb her skirts. Succeeding, she arrived at her waist in a triumphant rush. Polly had arranged to leave the kitten at the rectory with Mrs Judd… She looked around at the bare, cold little room. Her reception at the Manor would be even colder.

Shivering, she went to the wood box in the corner for kindling. Her icy hands fumbled with the tinder box, but ten minutes later she had a merry blaze crackling in the hearth. An hour later the little room was warm again, and the last unacknowledged hope that the inconvenience of having to douse the fire would summon the gig had died.

No one was coming now. She doubted that they had forgotten her. At least, Sir Nathan probably had forgotten, but Aunt Eliot never forgot anything. Not unless it was convenient to do so.

With a snort, she collected an onion, turnip, carrot and potato to make soup. Rashly, she cut a larger slip of bacon than usual from the flitch. Before long her pot was simmering over the fire, fragrant with herbs and the bacon. She tossed in a handful of barley and dried peas to thicken it.

Her task complete, she curled up in the corner of the settle with the kitten and one of Pippa's novels, her counterpane tucked about them both, and looked around at her little room. Beyond the shutters darkness had closed in with a lowering sky and the threat of snow. The children had draped the window with great festoons of ivy, the holly berries winked from the slightly lopsided wreath by the fireplace and sprigs of bay and rosemary had been stuck into chinks in the wall.

More ivy decorated her bed, and a pot of rosemary, alive and growing, sat on the shelf with her books and clock. Beside the teapot was the little caddy Alex had given her. And somewhere inside her an icy lump she had not suspected melted in a great rush.

This bare little room held all the love and joy that she could have hoped to find. On this night, of all nights, she knew that a small, bare, unimportant room could hold something greater than the whole world and there was no space in here, or in her, for regrets and the bitterness of might-have-beens. And after all, if she had walked over to the Manor in bitterness and rage, she would not have enjoyed her dinner anyway.

Tomorrow, when she went to church, if Caleb Fletcher's mother repeated her invitation, she would accept. With joy.

Alex walked into his library at six o'clock, having dined at Alderley. Mrs Judd had lit the fire and it cast dancing light into the shadows. He hung his great coat on a hook to dry by the fire. Bonny, snoozing on the rug, looked up, thumped her tail and came to him, shoving her way between his legs and curling around for a pat.

Next year there might be a cat curled up with you by the fire, Bonny-lass.

Next year, please God, Polly would be here with him, filling the old house with her brightness. If she accepted him. That she might not…

Mrs Judd bustled in with a tray, her apron as crisp and white as it always was. 'Thought as I heard you, Rector.' She brandished the tray. 'Mince pies. Made extra. Thought I'd give some to Miss Polly tomorrow.'

'She's with her cousins, Mrs Judd,' he said, quelling the nasty little spurt of selfish jealousy. It was right that Polly was with the Eliots. It was Christmas, when God had given the greatest of His gifts. Love had come down. A better man would pray that Polly might find some measure of peace and acceptance from her family, rather than wishing she were spending the holiday with him.

Mrs Judd's snort was eloquent. 'Well, she's not, then. Didn't send for her, did they?'

'What?' Outrage exploded inside him and he was on his feet before he knew it. 'Are you sure?'

Mrs Judd nodded. 'Those blessed children were in and out of her place all day greening it up for her. All packed and ready to go, she was. Rosie Appleby said as how they saw Mr Tom's young lady go by in a grand carriage, an' Miss Polly was home then. Still home two hours later, and I reckon she's still there because she hasn't brought the kitten—' She broke off. 'And where might you be going, Rector?'

The question went some way to clearing his mind. He realised he'd taken his great coat off the hook. 'To Polly,' he said simply.

Mrs Judd's knowing look was grating, but he let it pass, shrugging into the coat.

'Better take these.' She handed him the plate of pies. 'And this.' The brandy bottle was shoved into his other hand. 'Are you taking that dog?' She eyed Bonny with disapproval.

Alex hesitated as he put the bottle in the pocket of his coat.

'Best to take her,' opined Mrs Judd. 'Gossip do spread in this place,' she said virtuously, 'but no one's going to think nasty thoughts about you paying a Christmas Eve call on Miss Polly with your dog along to play bodkin. No need to mention the brandy.'

The rapping on her door roused Polly from her reading. 'Who is it?' Surely not someone from the Eliots at this hour? And if it was, what on earth would they say when she declined?

'Me. Alex.'

She scrambled up, depositing Speckles on the settle, who gave an outraged mew, and laying down the book.

She opened the door and stared at him.

Snow lay on his shoulders and hair. The foolish man had come out without his hat, muffler or gloves.

'What are you *doing*?' she demanded.

'Probably ruining your reputation if anyone gets wind of this,' he said with a wry smile. 'Would you like a mince pie?' Not bothering to wait for a reply, he stepped past her into the cottage.

Somehow, without her quite knowing how it came about, she found herself on the settle again, the counterpane tucked around her, a mince pie in one hand and a tumbler with a small amount of brandy in the other. Alex was bent down, adding a log to the fire. He'd discarded his coat, saying the cottage was as warm as toast, and she tried not to watch the bunch and pull of his shoulders under his linen shirt. It had to be wrong, watching the parish priest like this.

'Is this a…a pastoral visit?' she asked, taking a bite of the mince pie and nearly moaning in pleasure as the sweetness burst in her mouth.

He considered her question for a moment, adjusting the log. Flames danced and crackled. 'Well, I suppose we could lie and pass it off as pastoral if necessary, but I don't normally take a bottle of my best brandy on pastoral visits. Soup, maybe.'

He glanced up at her as she eyed the brandy in her tumbler suspiciously and he smiled. 'Try it,' he invited. He rose effortlessly, took the bottle and another glass from the shelf above the fire and poured himself a measure. She took a cautious sip and choked as the spirit burned its way down.

'So if it's not pastoral—' She broke off as he sat down beside her.

'What happened to your visit to your cousins?' he asked quietly.

She looked at him. 'You know already. That's why you're here. Did Mrs Judd tell you?'

He nodded. 'Yes. Are you angry?'

'I was.' Honesty compelled her to add, 'I suppose I still am a little. What they did was wrong. But it doesn't matter to me now.'

'Doesn't *matter*?' He glared at her. 'How can it not matter? They're supposed to be your family, and—'

'And they aren't,' she said. Daring, she laid a hand over his, clenched in anger on his thigh. 'Do you know, I've had a lovely day. The children kept coming in with greenery and little gifts. I ate bread and plum jam with Rosie Appleby and Sally Hough, and I put extra bacon in the soup I made for supper.' Under her hand, his relaxed, turned to clasp hers. Her breath shortened as his thumb caressed her palm, but she continued. 'If I'd gone to my cousins I would have missed all that and I'd be spending my evening sitting in the corner of my aunt's drawing room furthest from the fire, feeling miserable and bitter and thinking the *most* uncharitable thoughts about Angelica Creed.' Instead of which she was spending the evening right in front of her own fire, with Alex Martindale holding her hand.

'Come to Alderley with me,' he said quietly.

'What?'

The clasp on her hand tightened. 'You heard me. Come to Alderley. Dominic and Pippa won't mind, and—'

'Alex, I couldn't. I've already—'

'Been invited to your uncle's home?' He snorted. 'And they didn't bother to send the carriage for you? Polly, you owe them nothing!'

'I know, but—'

'Even if they offer you a place in a carriage tomorrow after church—'

'I'll refuse it,' she said.

'You will?' He stared at her, clearly bemused. 'Then for heaven's sake, why not come to Alderley?'

'Because I've had another invitation,' she said. And she told him about Caleb Fletcher. 'So you see, if they issue the invitation again, I should accept. I couldn't possibly not.'

'No. You couldn't,' he said. The wry, crooked smile turned her heart inside out. 'I suppose that's part of why I love you,' he said simply.

Her heart turned right over. 'You…you love me?' Affection, yes. And it appeared he desired her…but *love*?

He blinked. 'Polly, I asked you to marry me. Why would I do that if I wasn't head over heels in love with you?'

There was no answer to that. And at last she admitted to herself why the thought of telling Alex about John Frisingham terrified her—she was in love with him, all the way in love, and if he didn't believe her, she would lose something far more precious than her fortune.

He preached on the subject of love. From his polite apology for possibly repeating things his parishioners had already heard, Polly gathered that a sermon on love was not unusual for him on Christmas Day. He spoke of how all human love was a reflection of God's love. Love for a dog, or cat, or the land, a reflection of God's great love for His Creation. Love for a child, a parent, the love of a man and woman, an expression of God's love for His children. And every gift, gifts to meet a need, to give pleasure, to express love, a reflection and celebration of God's loving gift of His son.

'Every expression of love—verbal, spiritual—' his gaze touched Polly's— 'and physical, is of God. Rejoice in it and be glad.' He named the next hymn and stepped down from the pulpit as the choir took up their instruments.

Caleb Fletcher rushed up after the service, towing his flushed mother through the light dusting of snow. 'Miss Polly!

You didn't go after all! Mam says you can still come to us.'
He grinned. 'Dad says as we'll have a snow fight after dinner, but you can just watch that if you like!'

Polly turned to Hetty Fletcher, who cuffed Caleb's ear
gently. 'Caleb, quiet down, do!' She smiled at Polly. 'We'd
be right pleased if you joined us for dinner, Miss Woodrowe.
Right pleased.'

'I'd love to,' said Polly, delight flaring.

'Oh. Hippolyta, there you are.' Lady Eliot didn't so much
as glance at Hetty as she spoke to Polly. 'Such a to do yesterday with the Creeds arriving. I understand the groom forgot
to come for you.'

Polly dragged in a lungful of air and took a death grip on
her temper, as Lady Eliot continued. 'We were all so busy
that I didn't realise until we sat down for dinner, but—' She
spread her hands. 'Of course the carriages are full now, too,
but I have given clear instructions that—'

'I have accepted another invitation, aunt,' said Polly in the
sweetest tones imaginable.

'—you should be collected in time for dinner and taken
home before supper. What did you say?' She glared at Polly,
affronted. 'Accepted another invitation? And from whom
does this fine invitation come, may I ask?' She cast a derisive glance around the villagers exchanging greetings.

'From Mrs Fletcher,' said Polly calmly, indicating Hetty
beside her. 'And Caleb.' She ruffled the boy's hair.

'Who?' Lady Eliot stared in disdain at Hetty Fletcher. 'Oh,
yes. Fletcher the blacksmith's wife.' She favoured Hetty with a
dismissive nod, and turned back to Polly. 'Really, Hippolyta!
You must not be taking every little thing as a personal slight.
A little thought—'

'Made it clear to me where I'd be most welcome,' said
Polly quietly.

Lady Eliot stiffened. 'Hippolyta, it presents a very *off* appearance for you to be dining with—' she cast another condescending glance at Hetty '—these people, very good as they may be, and—'

Hetty Fletcher snorted. 'Off, is it? Not near so off as them who calls themselves flesh and blood, an' don't bother to collect a girl when they say they will.' A fascinated silence had fallen in the churchyard and Davey Fletcher was striding towards them, but Hetty continued undaunted, her scornful gaze lighting on Tom Eliot, standing with Angelica Creed. 'Nor yet so off as them that make up to a girl when she's got money, but haven't got the gumption to stand by her when she's robbed blind.' Tom's face went crimson.

By now Fletcher had reached his wife. 'Easy then, Hetty love—'

She whirled around on him. 'Don't you gentle me like the horses in your smithy, Davey Fletcher! I speak as I find. Always did.' She patted Polly's hand. 'We got a goose this year. Raised him meself.' She directed a sizzling glare at Tom Eliot and continued, 'Lord Tom Noddy we called him and I'm makin' a nice gravy with his giblets! Best thing for 'em, if you was to ask me.'

Polly nearly choked, wondering just whose giblets were under discussion.

Lady Eliot's colour rose. 'If you imagine your opinion is of the least interest to me, my good woman—'

Mrs Fletcher let out a crack of laughter. 'I'd imagine it's of about as much interest to you as yours is to me and mine. I'll wish you a Merry Christmas, my lady.' She patted Polly's hand. 'You come along soon as you're ready, dearie.' And she favoured Lady Eliot with a nod, turned her back and walked off.

'It's very kind of you, Aunt Eliot,' said Polly politely, 'but I am sure you will all enjoy your Christmas dinner anyway. Do congratulate Tom for me and wish Miss Creed very happy. Good day.'

Lady Eliot swelled. 'And this is your choice?'

'Yes.' She was utterly sure of it. This was her choice and not the least hint of bitterness to taint it. 'Merry Christmas, Aunt,' she said. And meant it. Because she was happy. Deep down, in-the-bone, happy.

Her aunt stared at her for a moment and then, lips thin with fury, stalked away.

'Well done.'

Alex stood behind her. The twinkle in his eye told her he'd heard everything. 'If you go on with Mrs Fletcher, I'll join you there after I've made a couple of visits.'

She blinked. 'But…you're going to Alderley for dinner!'

Alex smiled. 'Not now. I cadged an invitation from Davey and Hetty, so Dominic and Pippa expect us for supper instead. I'm to drive you over in the gig after dinner.' He took her hand in his strong clasp. 'They quite understand. Your baggage is going back with them now.'

Baggage? What baggage?

She looked across the churchyard at Lord Alderley and Pippa, who smiled back. She wondered what it was that they quite understood. Rather more than she did, she suspected.

That intense happiness remained with her all through dinner. *Mama and Papa would have enjoyed this.*

The laughter, the homely fragrance of the dinner, the bright faces around the table. The whole Fletcher family, from Davey's father down to a newborn niece, was there and a number of friends, besides herself and Alex. It had been like this when she was little. Papa had often invited friends and even employees to join them for the day. She remembered him laughing at the head of the table, teasing Mama about the size of the goose he was carving… Sometimes, if the frost had been hard enough, they had skated after dinner, flying along the ice, Papa and Mama holding hands…

She had thought all this lost to her for ever, but perhaps it wasn't. Looking up, she found Alex's dark gaze on her, full of understanding.

This could be ours. All of it.

Snowballs whizzed through the air after dinner. Being an only child, snowball fights were not something she was at all familiar with...although it looked as though Alex was. She blinked as Caleb caught him in the side of the head with a well-aimed snowball and fled, shrieking with glee, as the rector scooped up snow, threatening dire retribution.

He came back, laughing and brushing snow from his shoulders. 'We'll have to go in a moment,' he said. 'The light will go soon and it's likely to snow again.'

'It's been lovely,' she said wistfully.

'Yes,' he said. 'A little different from the Eliots, I dare say.' A smile tugged at the corner of his mouth.

'Just a little,' she agreed.

'I particularly appreciated Lord Tom Noddy's giblets,' he said, grinning openly.

'Aunt Eliot didn't,' said Polly. 'She'll never speak to me again!'

Alex chuckled. 'Sadly for you, my love, she'll have to. Politely, too. As my wife, she won't be able to ignore you.'

Polly's breath caught. 'Alex, I haven't—you need to think. Your family—'

'They like you very much, if you hadn't noticed,' he said.

'As the village school mistress, perhaps, but—'

'As Polly Woodrowe,' he corrected her. 'Do not confuse my cousins with your cousins!' He gave her a little shake. 'What's happened to my independent, unnatural Miss Woodrowe?'

His.

She took a trembling breath. She was such a coward not to have told him the truth...

'Alex?'

'Yes?'

His smile tore at her. 'Do you...do you skate?'

The smile deepened. 'Badly. We'll find some skates at Alderley.'

Chapter Eight

Supper at Alderley was not as rowdy as dinner at the Fletchers, but it was no less joyful. Pippa's father, Philip Winterbourne, was there, doting on his grandchildren and regaling them all with tales of his travels. Alex had always liked the old man enormously. He no longer travelled as widely as he had once and now made a point of visiting his daughter each Christmas.

'Making up for all the Christmases I missed when she was a little slip of a thing,' he explained to Polly. The shrewd eyes didn't miss much and Alex caught them on his own face, considering. The old fellow gave him a knowing smile and raised his glass. 'To Christmas, past, present and future.'

Next Christmas... Alex smiled at Polly as he raised his glass and drank. They all did, and then Dominic lifted his yawning daughter into his arms and said, 'Someone's bedtime, I think.' He stood carefully and carried the child out, Pippa's setter, Ben, at his heels.

Beside him Polly covered a yawn. She flushed. 'I'm so sorry. It was just little Emma's yawn started me off—'

Pippa laughed. 'If you're tired, I'll take you up. Don't feel you must stay up if you'd rather not.'

'Well…'

Alex rose and held out his hand. 'Come. I'll see you to the stairs.'

* * *

Next Christmas, Alex thought, as he bade Polly a chaste goodnight at the foot of the stairs under Pippa's admittedly benign gaze, he would be escorting Polly upstairs himself. He hoped.

As it was, he shut his eyes. It was probably a very good thing he had no idea which bedchamber Pippa had given Polly.

'Are you feeling quite the thing, Alex?' asked Pippa. One look at her amused face told him that she knew exactly what he was feeling.

'Quite well.' He smiled at her. 'I'm going to the library. When you see Dominic, you might tell him there was something I wanted to ask him about.'

Pippa smiled. 'Of course. I'll send him down.'

He felt a complete idiot and Dominic was probably going to roast him mercilessly. But who the deuce *but* Dominic could he ask for advice on such a subject? He loosened his cravat with restless fingers. Polly Woodrowe had turned his well-ordered life inside out in every way imaginable. And in ways he hadn't imagined—because he'd never imagined *wanting* a woman like this.

Oh, he'd felt desire before. But he had never acted on it in any way. At all. Not since he'd kissed Daisy Simpkins from the village when they were both sixteen, and he'd only done that because Dominic had dared him.

He'd gone up to Oxford knowing that he was going to take Holy Orders. It was what he'd wanted and he'd willingly accepted all the implications of that. He'd thought that he must be suited to the celibate life, or some such nonsense. He'd even viewed the wall paintings at Pompeii with what could pass for scholarly curiosity.

Now he knew better. It was because he hadn't known Polly as anything but the guarded heiress promised to Tom Eliot. What was consuming him now didn't pass as curiosity, let alone scholarly.

He shut his eyes.

Dominic walked in. 'Ah. There you are. Pippa said you wanted my advice.'

Alex turned away, so Dominic wouldn't see the colour heating his face. 'Something I need to tell you first. I'm sure you're wondering why I asked for Miss Woodrowe to come.'

'Beyond her family treating her badly?'

'Yes. Beyond that.'

'I can see you want to tell me.' It sounded as though Dominic was trying not to laugh.

Alex swung around. 'I'm in love with her.' He hadn't meant to blurt it out quite like that. He'd had a great many sensible things to say about the advantages of getting married and what a sensible girl Polly was. That he liked her, respected her and thought she would make a good wife.

Dominic's grin broadened. 'Congratulations. She's a charming girl. When is the wedding to be?'

Alex cleared his throat. 'She hasn't exactly accepted me yet.'

'Well, congratulations, anyway,' said Dominic cheerfully. 'She seems like an intelligent sort, of course she'll accept.' He strolled over to the side table that housed a brandy decanter and poured two glasses. Alex accepted one and took an abnormally large gulp. It burned its way down.

'So what was the advice you wanted?' asked Dominic, leaning on the edge of his desk and sipping his brandy. 'I seem to recall you had to clean up the mess I made proposing to Pippa.' A reminiscent grin tugged at his mouth. 'Lord, what an idiot I was! Don't tell me you need me to return that favour?'

Alex tugged at his cravat, felt a flush burning over his face. 'Not exactly. She has got some maggot in her head that she isn't the right sort of bride for me, but—' He could deal with that. Time. Love. He had both. And whatever else was bothering her, well, she would tell him about that when she was ready and he would be able to reassure her and that would be that. But what really had him in a panic…

Dominic waited, sipping his brandy, a booted foot swinging idly. 'Something else bothering you, then?'

That was one way to put it. 'I'm a virgin,' he said baldly.

Dominic's eyes widened and the boot stilled. 'I take it you aren't looking to me to rectify that?'

For a moment Alex was speechless. Then— 'Curse it, Dominic! I'm serious! What if I mess it up?' His throat closed. 'Disappoint her? Hurt her?' There—it was out. The thing that terrified him above all others.

And Dominic was watching him with that dratted odd smile on his face. 'I didn't have that to offer Pippa,' he said quietly. 'And I felt as though I ought not to touch her, that I wasn't fit to come to her.'

Alex's breath escaped. So he did understand, but— 'Not quite the same. At least you knew what you were doing.'

Slowly Dominic nodded. 'Yes. But the price of that... I don't think you really wish there had been some other woman, do you?'

Another—? '*No.*' The answer was there and out before he'd even thought about it. There was only Polly.

Dominic's smile deepened. 'Hmm. Then your problem is no problem at all. All you have to do is love her. All of her. With all of you.' He sipped his brandy meditatively. 'A re-reading of the Song of Songs might help. Sometimes I can't believe they left it in the Bible, and there are always those volumes of yours from Pompeii. However...'

He got up, walked over to one of the bookshelves and reached up, bringing down two volumes. 'Here. You may find these of some practical use, but really, all you have to do is take your time and love her.'

Alex drove Polly home to Alderford on New Year's Eve. Dominic and Pippa had urged them to stay longer, but he declined for himself and Polly did too. He had said no more to her on the subject of marriage, but trusted to the welcome she had been given to assure her that his family considered her a more-than-acceptable bride for him.

Leaving the gig with his groom and collecting the kitten from Mrs Judd, Alex lifted Polly's valise and walked her down to the schoolhouse. Her room was positively frigid, and, ignoring her protests, he bundled her up in the counterpane on the settle to keep warm, and set about lighting the fire for her. Pippa had provided a basket of food, but he put the kettle on the hob and made a pot of tea.

He brought her a cup and smiled as she curled her hands around it.

'Warmer?' He'd see about a closed carriage now that he was to marry.

'Much,' she said.

He sat down beside her. 'Is it too soon to ask you again to marry me?'

Her hands trembled on the cup. 'No, but I need to talk to you.'

That didn't sound good at all.

She went on. 'There is something I have to tell you. Something that might make you change your mind.'

Cold leached through him. He could imagine nothing that could make him change his mind, unless... Was she going to tell him there had been someone else? Perhaps Tom Eliot? They had once been as good as betrothed. He took a deep breath. It would be understandable. She had cared for Tom, would have had no reason not to trust him and give herself. A shudder ripped through him. He could forgive her that mistaken trust. It would be a great deal harder to forgive Eliot for betraying her... He swallowed.

'So tell me, sweetheart.'

She shook her head. 'Tomorrow.'

He wanted to push her, put it behind them and reassure her that it made no difference, but he nodded slowly. 'Tomorrow, then. After which I will ask you again, you'll say yes, and we'll announce our betrothal at Alderley on Twelfth Night. Agreed?'

'Agreed,' she said softly. He reached out and she laid her hand in his.

Alex found the letter beside his breakfast plate the next morning. He turned it over, recognised the crest on the seal and groaned.

'Stomach ache, sir?' Mrs Judd bustled in with the eggs and bacon.

'Not yet,' he said and dropped the letter beside his plate again. He'd deal with a letter from Lady Eliot all the better on a good breakfast. Lady Eliot's letters all followed the same pattern: a protestation that she was the last to interfere or pass judgement, but that she considered it her Christian duty to call his attention to the disgraceful behaviour of one or other of his parishioners.

He helped himself to bacon and eggs liberally, in the meantime mulling over his plans for the day. He needed to visit a couple of outlying farms with sick parishioners. If he took the gig rather than riding, then Polly could come along. He made a mental note to ask Dominic's advice on buying a suitable horse for Polly. A nice little mare. They could stop in at Alderley on their way home.

Mrs Judd came back in with the coffee. He smiled. 'Thank you, Mrs Judd. Er, I suspect I'll be stopping at Alderley tonight.' Dominic and Pippa would very likely demand that they stay to supper and insist that they remained for the night.

The housekeeper nodded. 'Aye, sir.'

Footsteps sounded in the hall. Alex looked at Mrs Judd in surprise. 'Who else is here?'

Mrs Judd shook her head. 'No idea, but—oh! It's your lordship.'

Dominic strode into the room. 'Morning, Mrs Judd. Is that your coffee I smell? Excellent.' He pulled out a chair and sat down.

'Would you like breakfast as well?' asked Alex.

'No, thank you. I've had breakfast,' said Dominic. 'Just not enough coffee. Ah, thank you.' Mrs Judd had handed him a cup and saucer from the sideboard. He poured a cup of coffee and sipped it.

Alex frowned. Dominic occasionally appeared at breakfast, but only if something urgent needed seeing to. 'That will be all, Mrs Judd. Perhaps you could ask Symons to have the gig brought around in an hour.'

'Aye, sir.'

As soon as the door closed behind her, he looked at Dominic. 'Something wrong?'

Dominic subjected him to a very careful look. 'I thought so, but—' He broke off, staring at something on the table. 'Ah. Read your post, Alex.'

Puzzled, Alex picked up the letter, broke the seal and unfolded it. 'It's only from Lady Eliot,' he said, as he began to read. Yes, Lady Eliot in her usual form…*my Christian duty*…

He read further and his eyes widened.…*behaviour unbecoming to your calling*…a little further and…*stemming from the disgraceful appointment of a woman whose virtue must be questioned*…

'*What?*' Somehow he was on his feet, the letter crumpled in his fist. 'That—'

'Bitch?' supplied Dominic helpfully.

'Yes! That and—'

Dominic's brows rose as Alex described Lady Eliot in terms that would have shamed a sailor. He didn't think he'd ever seen his cousin quite so angry. He'd certainly never heard him swear.

'I take it your letter is as offensive as mine?'

'*Yours?*' Alex swung around, all guns blazing. 'You received one, too?'

'Excellent as Mrs Judd's coffee is, I've got coffee at home. I came to show you this.' Dominic reached into his pocket, pulled out Lady Eliot's letter and offered it.

Alex strode over and snatched the letter, scanning it rapidly. Then he looked up. 'Dominic, she's written to the bishop!'

Dominic shrugged. 'That doesn't really matter. Your living is in my gift. He can't dismiss you, although I suppose he could defrock you.'

Alex stared at him. 'You think I'm furious about that? That she's implied I seduced Polly? That I am unfit for my position?'

'Rather more than implied,' said Dominic mildly.

'I don't give a…a *damn* what she says about me,' snarled Alex. 'It's what she's saying about Polly!' He waved Dominic's letter and adopted a censorious and somehow prurient tone. '*Encouraging improper, lewd behaviour in the Rector… entertaining a man*—no doubt she means myself!—*in her room at unseemly hours of the night…her name already a by-word after dismissal for attempting to intrigue her employer's brother…*and it goes on!' He looked up from the letter. 'She wants the bishop to force us to dismiss Polly!'

'I'll admit, I'm more curious about the *lewd behaviour* on your part,' said Dominic lazily. 'Not to mention the *unseemly hours of the night* bit.'

Alex snorted. 'I kissed her, dammit! And some busybody must have told her that I called on Polly late Christmas Eve!'

Dominic wrinkled his nose. 'Kissed Lady Eliot?'

'Polly, you idiot!' And there had been nothing unseemly about any of it!

'Oh. Well, that's all right then. Here, drink your coffee before it gets cold.' Dominic pushed Alex's coffee towards him. 'If you'd been kissing Lady Eliot I would have been worried. Alex, it's not that bad. I've invited the bishop to stay.'

He'd judged that announcement badly. Alex choked on the coffee.

After a solid thump on the back, Alex managed to get the coffee back on course and speak coherently. 'You *what*?'

'Invited him to stay. For Twelfth Night. And the Eliots. I wrote to them before I came down.'

Alex's jaw dropped.

'Pippa seemed to think it was the best strategy,' said Dominic cheerfully. 'Pity about the Eliots, but they are her family I suppose.' He shrugged.

'Dominic, Polly and I were going to announce our betrothal on Twelfth Night!'

Dominic took that in his stride. Pippa had suspected things were moving fast. 'Excellent. Congratulations. Pippa said to bring Miss Woodrowe back to Alderley to stay for a few days. That should squash any gossip, especially if you're here. Finish your coffee while we plot this out properly.'

He found Polly curled up in the corner of her settle. She looked up as he came in and he knew at once that Lady Eliot's spite had struck here, too. He was across the room in three swift strides, crouched down before her with her cold hands safe in his.

'Polly Woodrowe, if you even think of letting this come between us, I swear I'll put you over my knee and…' His voice trailed off.

Her hands trembled in his. 'That business at the Frisinghams'—that was what I was going to tell you about today, but—'

'I know. But you can tell me now if it will make you feel better,' he said.

She let out a shuddering sigh. 'I should have told you the truth when I applied for the position of schoolmistress. Why they dismissed me.'

He said nothing, just lifted one small, cold hand to his lips, felt her fingers tremble and melt against his mouth. Slow heat surged through him in mounting waves. It was all he could do not to haul her off the settle into his arms and kiss her, kiss away the pain and sadness.

'Don't,' she whispered. 'I…I can't think when you do that.'

Well, that made two of them. Instead he pressed her hand to his cheek. 'Just tell me, love.'

'Mr Frisingham's youngest brother came to stay. He'd been in trouble at Oxford. Barmaids in his rooms, I think.'

Alex snorted. 'That sounds familiar.' Most young gentlemen spent more time at Oxford on extra-curricular activities with barmaids than on their studies.

She nodded. 'He seemed pleasant enough at first. Polite. Held doors open for me. Then he started turning up in odd places where he must have known I'd be alone. Or he'd pass me something and make sure he touched my hand. Or just… touch me.' She shuddered. 'He grabbed my…my bottom once. Said something about—' She stopped, scarlet. 'I shouldn't say such a thing to you.'

He fixed her with a glare. 'Because I'm going to marry you, or because I'm the rector?'

'Both,' she said.

He sighed. 'Polly, I'm still a man and being the rector doesn't make me a eunuch. Our marriage is definitely going to be consummated and I'll probably grab your bottom, too!'

'If you must know,' she replied, her cheeks flaming, 'he said it was sweet and juicy!'

He took a deep breath and reached for control. 'Hmm. Leaving aside young Mr Frisingham's accuracy of observation—' Polly's jaw dropped and he smiled, despite the searing urge to find young Frisingham and tear him apart '—there's still the matter of his bad manners.' His voice hardened, he simply couldn't help it. 'He's lucky that there are fifty miles of bad roads between us and that I have too much to do this week to ride over and administer a thrashing.'

'A thrashing?' It came out as a squeak.

'Beat him up,' explained Alex.

'But you're a clergyman!'

He shrugged. 'I have my share of unchristian impulses. Sometimes I even act on one. Did Mrs Frisingham catch him with his hands on your bottom?'

'No. She caught him coming out of my room,' said Polly

very quietly. 'I...I didn't invite him in.' Her eyes met his, pleading for understanding...

Something in him went very still. 'Polly, sweetheart.' He swallowed, not sure he could say it for the murderous rage choking him. 'He didn't—'

'No,' she said swiftly. 'But he tried. So I grabbed a poker and screamed. Which brought Mrs Frisingham along in time to see him leave, straightening his cravat.'

'And naturally,' said Alex, every vein iced with fury, 'he blamed you. Claimed you enticed him?'

Polly nodded, not saying anything, and he settled her more closely against him. There was really nothing more to say, he supposed. With a sigh, she relaxed against him. His arms tightened and he breathed the fragrance of her hair. She fitted perfectly, warm and soft in his arms, close against his heart.

'I was an idiot not to tell you, wasn't I?' said Polly at last.

'You did tell me,' said Alex. 'Just now. When you were ready.'

'After Aunt Eliot told you and I had no choice.'

'After your aunt couldn't mind her own business,' he said. 'You weren't going to accept my offer *without* telling me, were you?'

She shook her head. 'No.'

He pressed a kiss to her hair, breathed its fragrance. He was silent for a moment. There was more. Much more. At last he said, 'What you said last night, about something that might make me change my mind—well, I wondered if perhaps you and Tom...when you were betrothed—' She wriggled around to stare at him, and he flushed, ashamed even to have thought it. 'I didn't care. At least, I did, but I understood. And I can assure you, even if that bas—Frisingham, that is—*had* forced you, or even just seduced you, I'd still love you and want you as my wife.'

'You would?'

The shock and wonder in her eyes shook his heart. 'Casting the first stone is not numbered among my many sins, Polly love.' He scowled. 'Unless Frisingham comes in range. For him I'd make an exception.' He'd probably throw the second and third stones for good measure.

For a moment she just stared at him. Then she said, very softly, 'I love you, Alex Martindale.'

For a moment he absolutely could not speak. His heart was too full and that simple declaration had just changed his world. For the first time he realised how afraid he had been that she did not, perhaps, *love* him, but liked him well enough to accept him anyway.

'Then should I ask you again to marry me?' he asked at last.

'Do you need to?' she asked softly.

'Apparently not,' he said. He kissed her gently instead, groaned as the soft lips parted, and tasted her deeply. Releasing her mouth, he whispered, 'Tell me you got in one good hit with that poker.'

Something between a sob and a laugh escaped her as his lips found a sensitive place beneath her ear.

'Two,' she confessed.

'Good girl.' And he returned his attention to her mouth.

Chapter Nine

The bishop arrived at Alderley shortly after breakfast on the sixth, shook Dominic's hand in the Great Hall and introduced his wife, an apple-cheeked lady with soft silver curls under a cap. 'Very kind of you to invite us, Alderley.' He looked around smiling at the decorations. 'Well! I see you know how to keep Christmas here. Now, where's young Martindale?'

Alex came forwards. He'd had a brief note from the bishop saying they'd *discuss matters* at Alderley. Nothing more. He didn't know if the old chap had believed Lady Eliot's libel or not, but since the letter hadn't referred to it, he'd decided to answer it in person.

The bishop shook his hand vigorously, beaming. 'Well, well. Good to see you, my boy.' So maybe he wasn't in danger of being defrocked. The bishop continued. 'Now, you know I had a letter from Aurelia Eliot, I dare say.' He grimaced. 'Thank God it's you dealing with her most of the time and not me! Dreadful woman! Anyway, where was I?'

'Aurelia's spiteful letter, dear,' prompted his wife. 'She always did have a nasty tongue.'

'Oh, yes.' The bishop cleared his throat uncomfortably. 'Most unpleasant. Couldn't believe you were behaving badly over this Miss Woodrowe, of course. And I understand the school is a great success.' The shrewd old eyes twinkled.

'Took a most unchristian pleasure in writing to tell her so, too. Now, where is the girl? This her?' He looked straight at Polly, who blushed.

Alex drew Polly forwards to present her, and the bishop gave her a careful look. 'Hmm. Well, ticking off Aurelia Eliot was fun, but I believe marrying you two will be a great deal more enjoyable. Didn't need Alderley's letter to tell me you were courting!' He took in their stunned expressions, and said, 'That was what it was all about, wasn't it, boy? You were courting and the Eliot harpy got her stay strings knotted over it?' He scowled. 'Dare say she wanted you for that totty-headed daughter of hers.'

Alex choked as the bishop's wife said, 'For heaven's sake, dear!'

The bishop looked a little shame-faced, but said, 'Anyway, when you two are ready, just let me know.' He looked around the hall and said thoughtfully, 'Of course, I'm here right now, you know, and...' The bright old eyes travelled hopefully from Polly's face to Alex.

'Sir, you'd marry us now? Today?' managed Alex.

'With the greatest of pleasure,' said his lordship promptly. 'A bishop's got to be useful for something, even if it's only granting a marriage licence.'

'Sweetheart?' The endearment went no further than Polly's ears as Alex turned to her and her heart stumbled at what she saw in his eyes.

'You're sure it's not too soon?' she whispered.

The bishop snorted. 'Of course he's sure, girl.' He turned to Dominic and Pippa. 'Suggest we leave Martindale to convince her, Alderley, while your good lady finds some Christmas cheer to warm our old toes while he's doing it. Draughty things, carriages.' Chatting cheerfully, he lead the way from the hall.

Alex drew her into his arms. 'Polly love, there's no need to wait. It's all right here, just waiting for us. Our love. Our lives.'

He glanced up. The Christmas wreath was right above them, a few mistletoe berries still on it. A pagan tradition, he supposed, but he bent his head and kissed her anyway.

The wedding took place just before noon in the village church. Somehow word had gone around—Alex suspected Mrs Judd—and the church was packed with his parishioners. A message had been sent to the Eliots and they sat stiffly in their pew, the Creeds beside them. Lady Eliot looked as if humble pie were not at all to her taste.

The bishop performed the service with a positively scandalous enthusiasm, enumerating the reasons for matrimony with great vigour and clarity. It didn't help that Dominic leaned forwards to murmur, 'Did you read those books?' He had, of course, but just glared at his cousin and resisted the temptation to tell him to shut up.

A great number of people crowded into the Great Hall at Alderley afterwards for a wedding breakfast that merged into a Twelfth Night celebration.

He meant to leave quietly, slipping out of the place with Polly, without anyone noticing.

It didn't work at all.

The bishop shook his hand happily on the front steps. 'I'll wish you a goodnight, boy.'

The wink sent heat surging across his cheek-bones.

'Thank you,' he said, but the bishop had turned his attention to Polly, bussing her heartily on both cheeks, and whispering something that sent colour flying to her face as well.

'You make sure he takes good care of you, child,' he continued, holding both her hands between his.

'I will, sir,' Alex assured him, wrapping Polly's cloak around her.

Dominic enveloped him in a bear hug. 'Keep those books as long as you like, Alex.' His grin was wicked.

Alex cleared his throat.

'What books?' asked Pippa curiously.

Dominic's grin turned even more wicked. 'I'll explain later.'

'Books?' asked Polly, as Alex handed her up into the gig.

He made a pretence of checking the harness. 'Just some books Dominic lent to me.'

Stars blazing above, they came into the village at a slow trot, the horse's breath steaming in the cold brightness. Polly snuggled close against Alex—her husband. This night of all nights, coming home was right. The dusting of snow cast its own starlit glimmer, enough to see by and this was where they belonged, where they should start their married life... her train of thought broke.

'There's a lantern lit on my doorstep,' she said, straightening. 'I mean, my old doorstep. What on earth is that doing there? And the chimney is smoking!'

Alex steadied the horse. 'Odd. I'll take Buttons around to the rectory stables while you go inside and then I'll check.'

'We'll check,' she said.

He raised a brow. 'The *obey* part didn't last long.'

She just smiled and he laughed. 'Very well, but it's cold.'

Alex's groom came out, wished them happy and took the gig and horse. 'We're just stepping around to the schoolhouse, Jim,' said Alex. 'Someone's left a lit lantern on the front step. It should be put out.'

'Oh, aye,' said Jim, not sounding at all surprised. 'Best take a look inside, Rector. Never know what them rascally young'uns'll get up to.'

Inside, the cottage was warm as toast and a veritable forest of greenery festooned the little room. Setting the lantern on the table, Alex stared around. A bottle of his favourite wine and two of his best wine glasses stood on the table. A counterpane he was fairly sure was out of his spare bedchamber had been added to the bed. A large loaf of bread, still warm, a pat of butter, a pot of jam and a bowl of eggs also sat on the table. Someone, he concluded, probably several someones, was giving him a very broad hint.

He hesitated. Surely he should take her home to the rectory? But he'd fallen in love with Polly in this room. What could be sweeter or more fitting than for their marriage to start here? Besides which, he wasn't entirely certain he could be trusted to get her as far as his bed in the rectory…

Polly gazed around the little room that had been her home. 'They've…they've prepared it for us,' she said softly. 'Like a bridal bower.' And left the lantern outside to ensure they investigated.

'Shall we stay here, love?'

His deep voice shook a little, and, her heart leaping into her throat, she turned to him, suddenly nervous.

He seemed to know.

'Polly, nothing has to happen tonight if you don't want it to—'

Oh, but she did want it. It was just… 'I don't know what to do,' she confessed. 'Not really.'

He came to her, took her hands in a gentle clasp. 'Then we'll find out together.'

'Together?'

His smile was rueful, tender. 'Sweetheart, you won't be the only virgin in that bed.'

For a moment she didn't understand, and then— 'Oh.' She blushed. 'You haven't—?'

'No.' His hands tightened and he lifted hers to his lips. 'I haven't. For better or for worse, I'm entirely yours.'

Candlelight and warm, fire-lit shadows wove and danced around them as, with soft murmurs and whispers, clothes were discarded, falling unregarded until she was trembling in his arms, clad only in her chemise. His shirt was gone and his chest grazed her breasts, a shuddering pleasure. One large, gentle hand shook on her hip, trailed fire up over her waist and found an aching nipple through the soft linen. She gasped as he caressed it and he stole the sound from her lips with a searing kiss, swinging her up into his arms and walking to the bed to lay her in it.

He watched her as he finished undressing, his gaze hot, turning her bones to honey. Her breath shortened as he pushed off his drawers and slid into the bed with her, pulling the covers over them. For a moment he held back, just gazing at her, and she did not know what to say, what to do. And then she realised. There was nothing to say. Only something to do. Daringly, she sat up, hauled off the chemise and held out her arms. Heat darkened his eyes and he came to her in swift urgency, taking her mouth in a fierce kiss that took everything and promised more.

The world burned in a bright crucible, remade in fire as he felt her soft breasts crushed against him, tasted her need and passion. His hands stroked and explored. Lord! How could skin be so supple, so silken? His fingers shook as he stroked a peaked nipple and he bent his head to taste, to lick and suck gently. Her body arched against him and her soft cry nearly unmanned him as her fingers dug into his shoulders. So many sweet places asking for his possession. His hand slid down, over her hip, pressing between her thighs, finding a heated welcome.

She gasped in shock, stiffening, and he stopped at once, breathing hard. Fear streaked through him. If he'd frightened her, shocked her, he didn't think he could bear it.

'Polly...'

'I don't know how to please you,' she whispered.

Please him? If she pleased him any more he'd probably die. But— 'Touch me,' he murmured. 'Just touch me. Anywhere. Everywhere. And let me touch you the same way.' If he was going to burn he might as well do it properly.

'Yes.'

He gritted his teeth as her hands moved, explored, a curious finger stroking his nipple so that he groaned. A tentative kiss and lick that nearly shattered his precarious control. He hung on to it and slowly, very slowly, slid his hand back to the springy curls between her thighs. Again she stilled, but then as he stroked gently and took her mouth in a tender kiss, her thighs opened and he found her.

Hot. Damp. And so very soft.

'Alex?'

His name had never sounded so sweet. He kissed her deeply, feeling her response in a liquid rush on his fingers, finding a spot that brought a sharp cry to her lips and had her hips surging against him, seeking more. Shaken, near to breaking point, he gave it to her, loving her until she was crying and twisting against him.

'Polly.' Her name was a ragged groan. 'Sweetheart, I don't think I can wait any longer.' He ached to possess, to be possessed in turn.

Her lips brushed his jaw. 'Then do not.'

And in the end it was the sweetest, most natural thing in the world. At his gentle urging, her thighs parted eagerly on a sigh he drank from her lips and he was there. Pressing into the loving welcome of her body. His senses reeled at the tight heat caressing him, the silken feel of her body cradling his, her breasts against his chest, the taste and scent of her, and he fought to make this moment last for both of them.

And then he felt it, her body's innocent resistance, and the slight jerk of pain at his threatened entry, heard her breath catch. He hesitated, shaking, burning, and she cried out, her hips pushing up against him and his body answered her plea, taking her with a swift, gentle completeness.

And they shall become one flesh. He shuddered, lost in wonder. He didn't know where he ended and she began, if he had taken her or given himself. He didn't even know if it mattered. They were one. She lay trembling beneath him, her body yielded and he was all hers. Nothing else was, or could be. Here, in this bed, he had everything.

Carefully, his blood burning, he began to move and discovered there was more to have. Far more. The soft gasp of her breath, her body in harmony with his, blood and bone in perfect union as he loved her to the depths of his soul and found the well of giving to be infinite as her love poured back. And there was the earthly joy of flesh sliding against flesh, his body inside hers, held tight and sweet, her frantic sobs that echoed the pounding of his heart, her mouth clinging to his. He could feel the end coming, bearing down on him in bone-shaking glory, but she was still moving, pleading, needing more of him. With a groan, he slid his hand down between their bodies, found the sensitive nub above where they joined, and pressed. She cried out, her body convulsing about him, and he was there with her, the world broken and ablaze as consummation took them.

Polly awoke, realised she was alone in the bed, and that, judging by an over-enthusiastic rooster, it must be nearly dawn. Rolling over, relaxed and sleepy, she saw Alex, gorgeously, wonderfully naked, putting a couple of logs on the fire. She watched, wondering if the bishop would be shocked to know what a wanton the Rector of Alderford had married. Probably not, she decided. He'd had a distinctly worldly twinkle in his eye as he wished Alex a goodnight…as he'd whispered to her that he had no doubt of it at all…

Alex turned to come back to bed, back to her, and her breath caught as he smiled at her. He looked…not sleepy at all, but extremely wide awake. He got into the bed, pulling the covers snugly over them.

'Fortunately,' he said, as he took her in his arms in a far-from-sleepy manner, 'it doesn't matter whether that was a nightingale, a lark or just Bill Fenton's misbegotten rooster—we can stay right here and enjoy ourselves.'

'We might,' Alex murmured some time later, 'have made a Twelfth Night baby.' They lay cosily in bed, listening to the world come alive outside in the village street, and Polly was the warmest, sweetest weight imaginable in his arms.

Her breath caught, even as she blushed scarlet. 'That is a very improper thing to say,' she said, rather unconvincingly.

'Nothing improper about it,' he assured her. 'Twelfth Night is a traditional time for renewing fertility and tumbling maidens. Not in the woods like May Day, of course, too cold for that. But…' he glanced up at the greenery swathing her bed '…I note that someone has brought the woods to us, so it will probably work just the same.'

'And that,' she said severely, 'is a very wicked, pagan thought.'

He grinned down at her and stole a kiss. 'It is indeed.' He kissed her again until she was squirming pleasurably against him. Lifting his mouth from hers, he noted that her eyes were thoroughly dazed. 'Remember those books Dominic mentioned? I borrowed them from his library,' he told her, caressing the silken curve of one hip.

'Oh? What sort of books?' she asked, wriggling against him in a way that guaranteed his insanity. 'Like the ones Pippa says you have from Pompeii?'

He choked. 'Not quite,' he murmured against her lips. 'But they were certainly full of wicked, pagan suggestions.' His mouth drifted lower, finding the sweet, frantic beat in her throat. 'All about how to tumble maidens. The sort of things a rector shouldn't even know about, probably.'

'No,' she whispered. 'But since you do…'

He rolled on to his back and lifted her over him. 'Since I do…' he agreed.

* * * * *

Finding Forever at Christmas

—

Bronwyn Scott

Dear Reader,

There's so much to love about Christmas! I love presents. One of my favorite sayings is that good things come in small packages, and that is certainly true with Finn and Catherine's story, which is packed full of presents.

First, it's a story about coming home, which is a powerful theme for a lot of us. Catherine is home after five formative years in Paris, and she is coming back a "grown-up." Finn has returned after pursuing his scientific ambitions in the Caribbean. Both are wondering if home is a place that suits them anymore or if they've outgrown it. If so, where do they belong now?

The second present in the story is for regular Bronwyn Scott readers. You'll never guess who Finn teams up with in the Caribbean! Regulars will recognize Viscount Wainsbridge right away from *A Thoroughly Compromised Lady*. If not, this would be a perfect chance to give yourself a little Christmas present and read it. Jack and Dulci's wild adventure won't disappoint.

The third present wrapped in this story is the first glimpse at the brand-new series Rakes Who Make Husbands Jealous! In Finn's story, you get to meet his younger brother, Channing Deverill, who has an interesting pastime. He runs an all-male escort service in London on the sly—the League of Discreet Gentlemen. What Channing is actually doing at the Christmas Party with Lady Alina Marliss, only time will tell—look for that exciting new series, starting with *Secrets of a Gentleman Escort,* in January 2014. Drop by and visit the blog for updates at www.bronwynswriting.blogspot.com.

Merry Christmas,

Bronwyn Scott

DEDICATION

For Max and Lara and their family, just because. Who would have thought when we became friends thirty-three years ago at a young-writers' conference (let's emphasize *young,* we were twelve, after all) it would have turned out like this? Actually, I'm not surprised at all. You're writing papers on Hebrew vowels and I'm writing romance novels and, yep, that sounds about right. Love to you all.

Chapter One

December 21st, 1838

She was home! Catherine Emerson knew it the moment she stepped into the foyer of Deverill Hall as assuredly as she knew her own name. The hall was just as she remembered it: the long oak staircase draped with winter pine, boughs laden with red-satin bows and ropes of gold beads; she breathed deeply, taking in the sharp tang of the outdoors brought inside. It might possibly be her favourite scent. Five years had been a long time to be away.

Of course this wasn't really *her* home in the truest sense. Her home was two miles away, where she lived with her mother and father—quietly. The 'un-quiet' of the Deverill household was one of the things she loved the most about it. It had been a marvel of her childhood to know a family with not one, but *four* children in it. Nothing had ever been quiet about Deverill Hall.

To prove it, a loud scream of delight echoed from the top of the stairs, 'Catherine!' Rapid footsteps tapped down the steps in a flurry of brightly coloured skirts, announcing the arrival of the Deverill girls. Catherine smiled. Some things never changed.

'Alyson, Meredith!' Catherine was caught up in their embraces, all three of them laughing and talking at once. They'd been inseparable in their youth. In the summers she'd practically lived here, running the fields, riding the grass tracks. She'd been such a regular companion, she'd had her own room, even her own pony, then a mare when she'd outgrown good-natured Henry.

'Look at you! How sophisticated you've become!' Meredith exclaimed, stepping back to take in her ensemble, a deep forest-green carriage dress, cut tight and form fitting in the latest fashion. 'A white fur muff, too! It's just exquisite, Catherine. Paris agrees with you.'

'And engagement agrees with you.' Meredith's pale cheeks were aglow with colour, her blue eyes lit like candles. She looked positively beautiful. 'I am so happy for you and for Marcus.' Meredith engaged! It was almost too much to take in. She was glad Meredith had written and given her time to adjust to the news.

'Alyson has news too.' Meredith elbowed her younger sister and gave her a sly look. 'You should tell Catherine.'

Alyson, the shyer of the two, blushed. 'Nothing is for certain, but Jameson Ellis has been calling on me since the summer. I believe he will speak to Father while he's here for the Christmas festivities.'

'Oh, how wonderful.' Catherine smiled, but inside she felt a little piece of her hopes crumble. Both girls to marry! Where would that leave her? She'd been gone and the world she'd left behind had changed. Catherine looked up at the staircase, her sense of homecoming diminished. She'd come here wanting to catch up. But instead everyone had moved on.

She'd known where she belonged in the old world—here at Deverill Hall with her friends, her second family. She wasn't sure where she belonged in the new. Would there even be room in that new world where she had to share her friends with husbands and babies and whole new families? It wasn't that she was jealous or that she begrudged the girls any of their happiness, it was just that she'd rather wrongly and unrealistically thought everything would have frozen in time, waiting for her to return.

Alyson tugged at her hand, excitedly. 'Finn and Channing are both home.' She dropped her voice to a conspiratorial whisper. 'Finn's latest mistress threw a diamond necklace at him. Apparently, she didn't like her parting gift.'

'We aren't supposed to know…' Meredith laughed '…but it's hard not to. Finn's got a cut, just there.' Meredith tapped a finger along the lower part of her cheek. 'Come on, Catherine. The boys will die when they see you!'

Or she would when she saw them, Catherine thought, very aware her pulse had speeded up at the prospect. More specifically at the prospect of seeing *him*, Channing Deverill, the younger brother and bane of her childhood—the secret subject of her adolescent longings. She wasn't certain exactly when her feelings for him had changed. But one summer day he'd smiled at her from across the picnic blanket and she'd been lost. Then the fantasy had taken hold. She was going to marry him and for ever be a part of the Deverill household in the most legal and permanent way possible. She had it all planned, right down to the dress—she'd wear her grandmother's wedding gown and he'd wear a blue morning coat that showed off his eyes. There would be flowers, lots of flowers.

As for Finn, she supposed he was still his dark, dour self. It was no surprise his mistress had thrown a necklace at him. She'd probably done it to get his attention. From what Catherine remembered, Finn was more interested in his botany than anything else. Whenever the five of them had gone on summer picnics, it had been Channing who entertained them with wild stories. Finn would wander off and come back with pockets full of samples, spouting Latin phrases as he laid his treasures out on the blanket. Then again, Finn had been five years older than she at a time when a few years' difference in age had seemed to be a chasm.

The girls drew her into the formal receiving room, their arms twined through hers. The room was full of neighbours and friends and holiday cheer, the mantel hung with an impressive pine swag, a huge fire sending out a welcome warmth from the hearth. 'Look who we found in the foyer!' Meredith called out.

All eyes swivelled Catherine's way, many of which she recognised, but only one pair held her interest. Catherine searched the room until she found Channing's blue eyes. His face split into a wide grin at the sight of her. Her breath caught as he advanced through the crowd, gently shouldering a path past groups of visitors and guests gathered in conversation about the room. Her memories of him had not done him justice. He was all lean, golden grace. His body moved with a loose-limbed confidence and he was far more handsome than she recalled. Five years had allowed his features to mature; the planes of his face bore a sharp elegance that erased the last traces of boyishness just as she hoped the last five years had erased the last of her gawky adolescence.

She'd imagined this moment for ages: Channing seeing her, *truly* seeing her for the first time as a woman. It was the stuff of fairy tales, the one thing that made her five years away worthwhile, knowing when he looked upon her next she'd be as poised, as well dressed as the women he associated with when he was up in London. She wasn't supposed to know, but he had quite a reputation in town for being a lady's man. Seeing him like this, she had no trouble believing it. Who wouldn't want to dance with such a fine man or be seen on his arm at the opera?

Catherine favoured him with a warm smile and held out her hands as he neared. She would show him she could be a credit to him. She'd seen the great operas in Paris. She could carry on intelligent conversation in French and English about their storylines and composers.

'Good Lord, Cat, is that you?' Channing took both her hands and kissed her cheek, appreciation evident in his eyes. He was indeed impressed by the transformation. But she would not be too easy to catch. Men liked a challenge up to a point. Her friend, Vivienne, in Paris, had taught her that. Catherine did not hesitate to offer a gentle reprimand.

'*Catherine*. You know I prefer Catherine,' she corrected. Growing up, she hadn't cared for any of the derivatives that went with her name. But Channing had never divined that.

'You look beautiful.' His eyes twinkled at her, making her feel like she was the only woman in the room. 'Welcome home. Come and meet everyone. I'll introduce you.' He gave her his arm and just like that he was forgiven. The fairy tale was beginning. She was on his arm, touring the room, meeting old friends. Catherine's hopes rose. Maybe there would be a third engagement to announce before the holidays were over.

Finn Deverill returned to gazing out of the long window overlooking the snow covered garden. The excitement of Catherine Emerson's entrance was ebbing as people fell back into their conversations. She hadn't noticed him. He was used to it. Most people didn't when Channing was nearby. While he was the serious, older brother, Channing was the younger, extroverted brother, full of charm and wit. 'Never mind,' one of his great-aunts had told him when he was growing up. 'He's not the heir. He needs all the charm he can get. You have the earldom to speak for you.' Then she'd patted him on the knee in consolation.

The problem was he'd like to speak for himself. There'd been several young ladies over the years who'd been vastly interested in his title, but none who'd been interested in *him*. Finn rubbed his cheek absently. If his mistress had understood that, things might have ended differently, better. They still would have ended, though.

It galled a bit that Catherine hadn't noticed him. She'd been part of his boyhood. He would have thought she at least would have noticed him. He'd certainly noticed her and in ways he'd not anticipated.

She'd swept into the room between his sisters like a Christmas flame. The years had tamed her carroty riot of hair into a smooth cascade of deep auburn, twisted elegantly into a knot at her neck beneath that jaunty hat on her head. Time had brought feminine curves to the stick-straight slimness of her once-boyish form. A man's hand would fit comfortably, *perfectly*, at the notch at her waist, to say nothing of how a man's mouth might fit over those kissable, pink lips or how his other hand might cup the swell of a breast presented so enticingly in that form-fitted jacket of forest-green merino.

Christmas flame, indeed! Catherine Emerson had become a temptress. The idea shamed him as soon as he thought it. These were not thoughts worthy of one whom he'd viewed as a sister most of his life.

Still, it was a difficult claim to dispute and one that went beyond her looks. She'd acquired a certain grace. She exuded energy and good will as she moved through the room on Channing's arm, chatting briefly with each neighbour and relative by turn. Some she knew, some she did not, but her warmth didn't distinguish. It was genuine and thorough for each person she met.

Finn remembered that about her. She'd been devoted to wounded and stray animals, always bringing home a bird to be mended. Once she'd brought home a stray dog from the village and begged him to set the pup's leg. It had been silly, but he'd done it after she'd followed him around all afternoon and nagged him with a tenacity that would have done any little sister proud.

The pair of them were making their way towards him now, a stunning combination of flame and gold. Channing bent to her ear and whispered something that made her laugh, her face turning up to his. Finn's gut clenched. The look on her face was unmistakable. She *wanted* Channing. 'Wanted' might be too intense a word, but he'd been accused of being too intense a man in the past. Intense things were common to him.

'There you are, dear brother. What are you doing over here by the window? Surely there aren't any flowers to see at this time of year, not outdoors at least. Inside, there is one, however.' Channing smiled at Catherine. 'Our Cat has blossomed. Have you greeted her yet?'

Finn stifled a grimace. Channing knew very well he hadn't. 'Welcome home, Catherine.' He kissed her cheek, breathing in the scent of her: fresh peaches and a hint of vanilla, to subdue the potential heaviness of the scent. 'Ah, Apocynaceae, plumeria in winter, what a wondrous perfume.' Finn murmured. 'You always liked Mother's plumeria.' The beautiful blooms never left the hothouse, but Catherine had liked their vivid colours and tropical smells.

'You remembered!' Catherine beamed and he felt uncommonly proud of himself for his simple answer. 'People always guess peaches, but no one guesses what flower is used. I've heard plumeria also smells like coconut.' She nudged Channing. 'You thought it smelled like roses.'

Finn laughed. 'He thinks everything smells like roses.'

Channing took the ribbing in his stride. 'As you can see, he's the same old Finn, still has his nose in the flowers.'

A stir across the room at the door caught their attention, as another guest entered, a lovely blonde dressed in royal blue with a white fox fur thrown around her shoulders. Channing tossed him a quick meaningful glance and excused himself. 'I'll leave you two to catch up while I greet our latest arrival.'

If Catherine thought Channing's departure abrupt, she was still gracious about relinquishing him, but not before Finn noted the fleeting disappointment in her eyes. 'Who is she?' Catherine asked brightly, moving to stand by him at the window. It was a good vantage point, really, from which to take in the room or the outdoors depending on one's mood.

'That is Lady Alina Marliss. She is Channing's special friend for the holidays.' Finn didn't say more. He owed Channing his privacy. If Channing wanted to share his latest venture in London, he would. It wasn't Finn's job to do it for him.

'Is there an understanding between them?' The cool look on Catherine's face confirmed his information had been construed in a certain way, certain assumptions made. He knew what she was thinking. Well, if that wasn't quite accurate, that was Channing's problem too. There were merits to being forthcoming about one's activities. Channing would learn that soon enough.

'I'm not aware of the details.' Finn replied obliquely. He turned his attention out the window, away from the room, hoping she'd do the same. 'Tell me about Paris. Did you find it to your liking?'

'It was wonderful.' She smiled out into the gardens, keeping her response neutral and vague. 'But it wasn't here. It wasn't home.'

He understood that feeling all too well. There was something magical, something comforting about being home even while there was a stifling, restless side to all that comfort, too. Lately, he'd been feeling the latter.

'And you? I heard you spent some time in the Caribbean with an expedition?'

Finn looked down at her, caught in the warmth of her smile as she looked up at him, aware that she was spending an awful lot of her time studying the little cut on his cheek. He echoed her words even if he didn't mean them in exactly the same way. 'It was wonderful, but it wasn't home.'

He found himself telling her about the highlights of his trip: the new flower he'd found, the amazing colours of the rainforest, the plethora of bugs that had occupied his campsites. He'd not meant to get carried away; he knew what most people thought of his scholarly pursuit. It was time to change for supper before he realised how much he'd told her, the drawing room starting to empty as ladies drifted off to exchange carriage ensembles for evening gowns. The whole time, her eyes had been fixed on his in rapt attention, not the usual polite attention he was used to, and he'd simply kept talking, saying anything that came to mind to keep that gaze on him.

His mother moved towards them, a young man and woman in tow, clearly a brother and a sister from the genetic similarities stamped on their features. 'Finley, this is Lady Eliza Dewhurst and her brother, Lord Richard. They've only just arrived. They were delayed a little by snow on the roads. I am hoping you will be so kind as to take Eliza in to dinner later.'

Finn would have groaned if he could. His mother had made no secret of her high hopes for Lady Eliza, the daughter of a marquess. Certainly she was pretty enough in a blonde, pink-cheeked way common to many pretty English girls. But beyond that, he could tell already she simply wasn't his sort.

Lord Richard bowed to Catherine. 'Miss Emerson? If you would do me the honour this evening?'

Catherine gave him a small curtsy, the sort due to a marquess's younger son. 'It would be my pleasure.' She said the words as if it really would be. And maybe it would, Finn thought. At least the young man wouldn't spend the evening talking about bugs and plants. Finn focused his attention on Lady Eliza, but he was only partially successful in his efforts. His critical mind wasn't ready to leave the topic of his reaction to Catherine Emerson's return. His response was most unexpected and surprising. It was three days until Christmas. It made him wonder what else the festivity had in store.

Chapter Two

It was always the same. Whatever the festivity had in store for him, change didn't seem to be a part of it, Finn concluded after dinner. Counting this year, he had twelve years of adult memories as evidentiary proof to support the claim. He surveyed the post-dinner scene from his place at the drawing-room mantel beside his father; all the usual company were assembled in all their usual spaces on sofas and chairs around the room. Mrs Moffat, the vicar's wife, had sat on the cream sofa for at least a decade that he knew of, and probably longer. Old Mrs Anderson *always* sat next to Mrs. Moffat and old Mrs Anderson had *always* been old. Finn couldn't recall her ever having been young.

There would be cards and the young ladies would take turns at the pianoforte, playing quiet carols as background music to the evening. Then there would be his mother's special spiced cider and gingerbread to go to bed on. There was comfort in the knowledge that it would always be this way, but there was dissatisfaction too. Nothing changed and it made him restless.

Oh, certainly there were some variations on the theme. This year it was Lady Eliza his mother was foisting on him. Every year, a different girl, but it was still the same 'foisting ritual', as he'd come to think of it. It would be that way until he settled for one of them.

'What did you think of Lady Eliza?' his father asked quietly, correctly guessing the direction of his thoughts, if not their timbre. 'I think she was quite taken with you at dinner.'

'Or my consequence,' Finn replied drily.

His father shrugged. 'She's the daughter of a marquess, Finn. I doubt she thought twice about it. Consequence is her due. If anything…' he chuckled '…we're a come down for her, being only lowly earls.' But it was a jest only. Everyone knew what a fine catch the Deverills were; the title was old and the coffers were deep.

His father sobered a bit, his voice low. 'I know you're restless, Finn. You're at that age. Every man in this room over thirty-five has been through it. You're twenty-eight now; you've reached a point in life where you have to work out if you're restless for something, or someone.' His father's eyes strayed to where his mother stood chatting with guests. 'For me it was someone.'

Finn knew his father spoke the truth. After thirty years of marriage, four children and the chaos of a full home, his father had not once looked at another woman. Growing up, love and fidelity had never been in doubt in their household. Finn did not think he could find that devotion with Lady Eliza.

Finn took out his pocket watch and checked the time. He showed the watch face to his father. 'The games should begin in five, four, three, two and one.' They chuckled together because, as if on cue, Finn's mother began organising people around the card tables into equally matched groups. 'Just like clockwork.' Finn snapped his watch shut and put it back in his waistcoat pocket.

His father gave a little laugh. 'I must go and do my duty. Your mother is saving a chair for me. Mrs Anderson and I will try to take it easy on the novices.'

Finn looked about the room, making sure everyone was engaged in cards or conversation if they preferred not to play. All but one seemed happily occupied. For the first time that evening, Catherine sat alone in a quiet corner. The little group that had originally been drawn about her had moved off bit by bit. She'd been dazzling at dinner. The young marquess's son had been quite taken with her and yet, whilst Lord Richard might be of an age, he appeared far too young for her against the Parisian polish of her time abroad.

For the evening, Catherine had changed into a gown of deep turquoise, more green than blue, that showed off her hair and eyes to their best, the deep vee of her neckline showing off more than that. Next to her, Lord Richard's glossy blond locks had looked positively adolescent.

'No cards?' Finn approached the sofa.

Catherine shook her head. 'I wanted to sit back and watch everyone.' She sighed, her eyes dreamy and far away, nostalgic perhaps. 'So much has changed, I wasn't ready for that.'

Finn squeezed into the space next to her on the two-seat sofa. Whoever had designed these cosy numbers mustn't have been a very large man. 'We're at odds then. I was just thinking how nothing had changed. Every year it's the same people, a little greyer in some cases, a little older in all cases. All of us here in the same place, eating the same foods, playing the same games.'

Catherine gave a light laugh, a hand coming down gently on his arm, the most natural of gestures. 'Oh, Finn, I think that's what is called a *tradition*.' She lowered her voice slightly. 'And I missed it, every last minute of it while I was gone. Don't misunderstand, Paris is a fabulous city full of culture and art and intelligent people. My great-aunt showed me everything, we met everyone. I lacked for nothing, not in friends or any creature comforts. But no matter how elegant or refined Christmas was in Paris, it wasn't Christmas *here*. I came back for those Christmases only to find that they are gone.'

Catherine looked down at her hands encased in pristine white gloves that travelled to her elbows. She fiddled with the sparkly bangle about her wrist. Finn could tell by the fidgety motions the disclosure had meant something to her.

'They're not gone.' How strange that he had been wishing

they were gone or different somehow, while she'd been wishing for the opposite. 'We're all still here.'

'But Mrs Moffat's daughter is married and has a baby. Meredith is engaged. Alyson has a beau. Mrs Anderson...'

'Is still old,' they both said in unison, laughing together.

'See, everything is still the same.'

'Well, perhaps.' Catherine conceded with a smile, mischief roaming in her eyes as they glided over the cut on his face, or maybe not. Maybe he was too sensitive about it. 'Except that cut on your cheek. That's definitely new. How did you get it?'

Ah, he wasn't going to escape. 'Would you believe me if I said my valet cut me while shaving?' Finn tried. The whole episode had been painful.

'No.' Her eyes were full of laughter and he knew she knew the truth.

'I'm going to get Meredith for this.' Finn blew out a breath, but he wasn't really angry. He shook his head and gave a little groan. 'She told you.'

'I'm sorry.' Catherine sobered. 'It must have hurt.' He knew, too, that she meant it in all ways, not just the physical.

'It did, but we didn't suit.'

'Does that mean you don't have anyone special?'

'No, hence Lady Eliza.' Finn gave a wry smile. 'My mother will not stop until I've picked one.'

'I'm surprised.' Catherine cocked her head to one side. 'I would have thought you'd be the first. I rather suspected I'd come home and find you married with a baby or two.'

'Why is that?' Finn asked softly, staring back. How had he never noticed the flecks of blue in those green eyes before? It was those flecks that gave her eyes the impression of being sea-green, instead of mossy.

Those eyes had lured him in momentarily. He wished he hadn't asked. With anyone else such a question would be far too intimate to ask and he wasn't sure he wanted to know the answer. Please don't let it be because of the title, he thought, or because all he was capable of was doing his duty as opposed to mustering any depth of affection. Too many people had thought that in his past.

'It's who you are, Finn. Your family is important to you. It stands to reason you'd want to have a family of your own,' Catherine answered.

'Some day,' he answered. She was right, of course; family *was* important. He loved his sisters and his brother even though he often disagreed with Channing's approach to life. 'Speaking of family, how is yours? I trust they'll be along in a day or two.' It might be better to steer this conversation back to safer ground.

'Tomorrow. My father's nearly done with his latest book. It's a treatise on local crop-rotation methods. He interviewed every farmer in the area for it. But you probably know that,' Catherine added hastily.

Finn nodded. 'I do know. I was interviewed for it, too.' He liked the quiet, scholarly Robert Emerson. The two of them could talk for hours about things that would put the average person to sleep within moments. But that didn't mean Robert Emerson was dull. He had a way about him of pulling people in, putting them at ease just by being himself. Perhaps Catherine had got that particular talent from him.

'And Lady Eliza, does she share your devotion to family?' Catherine persisted, clearly unready to let the prior subject drop.

Finn shook his head. 'I don't think Lady Eliza shares much of anything with me.'

'Ouch!' Catherine made a mock grimace. 'Was she as bad as all that? I thought she seemed passable.'

'Oh, she was,' Finn put in quickly. 'She just wasn't for me.' There'd been a lot of women who just weren't for him. 'I suppose you could say I've wanted something that's not yet been available.'

'Or someone?' Catherine replied astutely, her words not all that different from his father's, but she was no longer looking at him, but out over the guests. Finn could guess who her eyes sought, but finding it wouldn't make her happy. Suddenly he didn't want Catherine to find Channing, didn't want her to see him fawning over Lady Alina Marliss and her delectable charms.

Finn rose, blocking her view of the room. 'Come with me, I have an idea.' Everyone here were old acquaintances. No one would think twice if he stepped out of the party with a long-time family friend.

They slipped out of the drawing room, her hand in his as they made their way along a darker corridor. 'Where are we going?' Her skirts were gathered in her free hand to keep up.

He tossed a smile over his shoulder. 'Take a smell, you know where.' Finn held the door open to the darkened kitchen. Cook would be having a short break before she came back to prepare the tea cart at eleven.

'Ah, the cider's on the stove already.' Catherine breathed deeply and so did he, taking in the cloves and cinnamon.

Finn rummaged through the cupboards until he found two mugs. He poured a ladle full of cider in to each mug. 'You can't tell me *this* has changed since you left.'

Catherine sipped, hands wrapped around the mug. 'Not at all. Mmmm. This is good.' She grinned at him over the rim. 'Do you suppose there's any gingerbread?'

Finn whipped a white cloth off a plate in the centre of the long work table. 'Right here.'

Catherine took a bite of the hard biscuit and its icing. 'Perfect. No torte, or mousse, could be as good as Deverill cider and gingerbread.'

Finn took a bite too. 'Do you remember the year all five of us sneaked down to the kitchen and ate gingerbread until we were sick?'

Catherine groaned. 'I do. I thought I'd never want to eat gingerbread again, but apparently I was wrong because we were back at it the next year.'

'And the year after that. I suspect we had a little help from Cook by then.' It had become a Deverill children's tradition to sneak into the kitchen and gobble gingerbread and cider the opening night of the holiday house party. After that first year, Cook had discreetly seen to it that they were well supplied.

'Are you ready for our next stop?' Finn took her hand and they were off again into the dark corridors of the hall. He stopped at the back door and shrugged out of his evening coat. 'You'll want this. It's still snowing outside.'

'Outside?' Catherine wriggled into Finn's evening coat. It held his heat and it smelled like him—apples and spice. She pushed up the sleeves to free her hands. Was Finn really that big? His shoulders were enormous if the coat was anything to go by.

'There's someone I want you to meet.' Finn looked down at her feet. 'If we're fast, we might be able to salvage your slippers.'

They sped across the snow-dusted lawn towards the barns, snowflakes twinkling in their hair like wet diamonds. To-morrow there'd be several inches on the ground if it snowed through the night. Finn pushed aside the stable door and she stepped inside. It was warm and full of the smell of hay and horses. She instantly knew who they'd come to see. 'Druid!' Catherine set off down the aisle, skirts held high.

She stopped in front of a stall containing a white mare. 'Druid, it's me.' The mare nickered and stuck her head over the stall door. Catherine stroked her long nose. 'I can't be-lieve she's still here.' She heard the quiver in her own voice.

'Of course she's still here.' Finn came up behind her, offer-ing the mare a treat. 'She turned nineteen this autumn. She's not young, but she's got years of riding left in her, probably even a fence or two. She's been well taken care of.'

'I remember the day we brought her home,' Catherine said wistfully. She'd been so very touched the Deverills had got her a horse to keep at the stables. It had been like an unoffi-cial declaration of membership into the family.

'I remember the day she tossed you in the stream.' Finn laughed.

Catherine elbowed him in the ribs. 'You would remember that.'

'And I remember the day you took your first jump on her, the old hedge by Anderson's farm,' Finn said more seriously.

Catherine turned to face him. 'It's good to remember.'

A little smile played along the seam of Finn's mouth. 'There's someone else who wants to see you.' He gave a little whistle and Catherine's mouth went slack. Out of the tack room came a shepherd, more grey than brown in his coat. He walked with a bit of a limp, but his eyes were alert and his ears were pricked up at attention.

'Hamish!' Catherine held her hand out to the dog. 'He's still walking after all these years.' She smiled. 'Perhaps you missed your calling. You should have been an animal doctor.'

She studied Finn. 'You've been generous tonight.' He'd always been generous in his own quiet ways. He was the eldest, but he'd made time for them all, joining them for picnics, no doubt forced into the role of chaperon by his parents. But he'd never complained. She'd not been lying when she'd said family was important to him. He'd been a good brother to them, yet tonight, standing here in the barn, his jacket draped about her, she didn't feel as if she was with her brother, but with a friend, a *good* friend. It was an entirely new way to see Finn. Tonight he didn't seem so dour, so serious.

'I wanted you to see not everything changes. Much is as you left it.'

Druid took that moment to nudge her rather roughly in the back. Catherine stumbled most ungracefully into Finn, her nose colliding with his chest. 'Easy, now, maybe that cider was stronger than I thought,' Finn joked, gripping her arms to steady her.

'It was Druid! She pushed me with her nose,' Catherine protested with a laugh, but she could feel her cheeks flushing as she looked up at Finn. Such close proximity had never bothered her in the past, but tonight she was acutely aware that she wore his coat, that it smelled of him, all spice and nutmeg and apples, that his chest where her nose had been crushed was a plane of muscle beneath his shirt. No wonder it hurt.

She rubbed at the side of her nose. 'Ow, your chest is hard.'

Finn laughed, but didn't release her. 'You'll live.' Something warm sparked in his dark eyes and that warmth transformed his whole face. The austere cut of his jaw, the straight line of his nose, the set of his brow were suddenly alive. There was nothing dour or withdrawn about *this* man, so unlike the polite statue that had greeted her in the drawing room upon her arrival. She'd seen signs certainly, when he'd talked of his science, but now the man was in full evidence. His dark head tipped, his lips parted and for a fleeting moment her heart raced at the thought: he is going to kiss me. Finn Deverill is going to kiss me. But he didn't and the moment was gone as quickly as it came.

'We'd best be getting back.' Finn stepped away. 'We wouldn't want to miss the best part of the evening—a second round of cider and gingerbread.'

But Catherine thought she might have already missed the best the evening had to offer, which was an entirely ridiculous conclusion because her fairy tale didn't involve Finn Deverill, it involved his brother.

Chapter Three

December 22nd

The sleighs were waiting in front of Deverill Hall after a jolly breakfast featuring every early morning delight imaginable: shirred eggs, sausages, fried potatoes, toast, Cook's famous cinnamon buns and smoked salmon, no doubt caught in the cold rivers of the countryside. Catherine thought she might burst out of her clothes, but that didn't stop her from heaping her plate high in celebration. No one in Paris did breakfast like a proper English household.

Afterwards, full and happy and ready to embrace the elements, which weren't all that dangerous—the overnight snow had stopped and the skies had cleared, leaving the day perfect with blue sky over head and crisp snow on the ground—the guests made their way outside where the countess was organising everyone into sleighs.

'Catherine, over here.' The countess gestured. 'You can ride with Meredith and Marcus.'

That was the plan at least. How she ended up with Channing and Lady Alina was a bit of a social mystery. No sooner had she put her foot on the rung of the sleigh to join Meredith then Channing had called out from his sleigh, 'Mother, Catherine is to ride over here with us. I haven't seen her the entire time and I want a good visit with her.'

Catherine could see the idea didn't please the countess. A little furrow formed on her brow as she mentally tried to rearrange the seating to accommodate the change, but Channing was faster. 'Mother, Alyson and Ellis can ride with Meredith and Marcus instead.' Channing held out a hand to her before his mother could argue. 'Come on, Cat, I'll help you in.'

'*Catherine*, please,' she said softly, gripping his gloved hand and stepping in.

They were joined eventually by Lord Richard because the countess abhorred uneven numbers the way nature abhors a vacuum, but it hardly mattered. Channing had invited her of his own accord to ride in his sleigh. Surely that signified as interest.

Channing made the necessary introductions, settling lap robes for the ladies. It gave Catherine time to study Lady Alina, who was undeniably stunning and unique with her platinum-blonde hair and blue eyes, almost as blue as Channing's. She looked like the queen of the frost and she was dressed like it too in a habit of bright blue the same shade as the dress she'd worn yesterday.

'It's my signature colour,' Alina said somewhat coolly when Catherine commented on how well it suited her.

'Our Catie is just home from Paris. She can tell you all the latest fashions from the Continent, m'dear.' Channing patted Lady Alina's hand, but he was looking at her. She could almost forgive him for the abbreviation of her name. Almost.

'Catie?' Lady Alina caught it immediately, her gaze shifting from Channing to her and back again. Catherine didn't think anything got past her.

'I prefer Catherine,' Catherine said hastily.

Channing dismissed her comment with a wave of his hand. 'No one named Catherine actually goes by it. They're Caties or Cats or Cathys or even Kits,' he protested good naturedly as the sleigh took off behind Meredith's.

'Channing's right.' Alina offered coyly, an arm sliding through his almost possessively. 'You need a nickname, something distinctive to set you apart.' Channing? She called him by his first name? Catherine had never heard any woman do that. Surely Channing would correct the familiarity. It should be Mr Deverill. Her heart sank. She called Finn and Channing by their first names because it was expected. She was as good as family. But this platinum-haired woman had no such claims.

'I must disagree,' Catherine said, wanting to be argumentative. She didn't much like this special guest of Channing's. 'Many great women in history have used their full name: Catherine the Great, Katherine of Aragon, Catherine de Medici, Catherine Parr, Catherine of Valois.' Catherine drew a breath and tossed Channing a flirty smile. 'None of them, I assure you, was ever addressed publicly as Cat.'

Channing laughed and held up his hands in mock surrender. 'You have me there. I couldn't argue either way. I haven't heard of half of them. Catherine of Valois? Are you sure that's a real person?'

'That's because you always wheedled out of your lessons.' Catherine was starting to enjoy herself as the sleigh runners sped over the snow to the lake.

'Catherine of Valois married Henry V. If I remember correctly, she was considered a beauty in her day.' Lord Richard entered the conversation with his nervously wrapped compliment clearly intended to come to her aid. Catherine felt badly for having left him out. She'd almost forgotten he was there.

She turned a beaming smile in his direction to make reparation for her neglect. 'Do you enjoy your history, Lord Richard?'

'Yes, very much so,' he replied, but Catherine saw the beginnings of infatuation in his eyes and heard the unspoken message. She would have to tread carefully here with his feelings. Her interests lay elsewhere—in fact, they lay just across the seat from him and she could feel Channing's eyes on her as the sleighs pulled up to the frozen lake. The lake on the Deverill property could always be expected to be solidly frozen by Christmas. She couldn't recall a year it wasn't. The skating outing was a traditional highlight of the Christmas party.

Catherine loved to skate. Her own skates had been carefully packed earlier that morning and she was eager to get them on. There was the general hubbub of getting skates distributed and laced and then she was on the ice, sailing across the smooth surface. Catherine executed a turn and nearly collided with Channing.

He steadied her. 'Sorry, thought you saw me coming. Come skate with me?'

'Where's Lady Alina?' Catherine looked over Channing's shoulder, half-expecting to see the frost queen materialise.

'She's not skating.' Channing gestured towards the shore where a large pavilion had been set up for those who wished to watch the skating. Lunch would be served there later. Channing held out his hands, crossed at the wrists. 'Do you remember this?'

She did. Catherine crossed her hands too and gripped his. 'We were the only ones who were any good at it.'

'Do you think we still are?' Channing was laughing, a wide grin on his face, his blue eyes dancing as he began to spin them. They used the tension of their arms to spin faster. Catherine threw back her head, the blue of the skies whirling in a blur as they spun. She was going to be dizzy when they stopped, but she didn't care. Right now she was skating with Channing on a perfect winter morning and he had come to her. He'd even walked away from the frost queen, at least temporarily.

They began to slow. Halting gradually did help the dizziness factor. By the time they stopped, a crowd had gathered about them, clapping and cheering. The children clamoured for a try. 'Spin me, spin me! Show me how.' Channing gave her an apologetic shrug, but he wasn't disappointed in the attention. He grabbed up one of the children and began explaining how to do it.

Catherine smiled and followed suit, working with a little girl in a red coat, one of the Moffat grandchildren. Perhaps there would be another chance to talk with Channing later. Soon, they had the whole lake trying their spin.

'You must be getting tired. You've been at it for an hour,' a low voice said at her ear. It was Finn. Her body seemed to tense at his presence.

Either by plan or by accident, she hadn't seen him all morning, not even at a distance, although she'd assumed he was somewhere in the crowd. Perhaps there was a reason he hadn't sought her out. Perhaps he was as discomfited as she about the moment in the stables. She'd tried not to think about it overmuch. It was silly really. It had lasted mere seconds and she might have even imagined it had happened at all. Had he thought about it too? Catherine shook her head. 'Dizzy maybe, but not tired. I could skate all day.'

'Good, then you can come take a turn with me.' Finn tucked her arm through his. 'Nothing fancy, just gliding.' His breath came out in little puffs.

'Where have you been?'

'Organising things behind the scenes. I came down earlier with the servants to make sure the lake was safe and the pavilions were set up.' That explained why she hadn't seen him at breakfast or as they'd all bundled into sleighs.

'I found something this morning.' Finn guided them towards a spot in the lake where it veered off from the main body, back in to the forest.

'I love how still everything is in the winter,' Catherine whispered, taking in the absolute quiet of the woods.

'Be very quiet and look over there,' Finn whispered back, his breath at her ear. 'Right past the trees on your left. I don't dare raise my arm. I don't want to frighten them.'

She saw them right away. 'Oh' was all she could manage.

A doe and her new fawn were tucked in the copse on a warm bed of fir boughs. Their grey-brown coats made them nearly invisible against the trees.

'The fawn can't be more than a few days old,' Finn said. 'It's early, most fawns aren't born until closer to spring.'

Catherine shot Finn a worried look. 'Will they be all right?'

It was cold, food was likely to be scarce. Spring seemed a long way away from December.

Finn chuckled and eased them out of the little frozen estuary. 'They'll be fine. I'll have the gamekeeper watch for them and leave out extra grain.'

They skated out, but they didn't go back to the lake. Finn had another surprise waiting. 'Guess what, the upper part of the river froze.' Finn propelled them further away from the skating party until they were out of sight and the winter silence surrounded them, broken only by the rhythmic click and slice of their blades.

The river was breathtaking, its icy beauty entirely untouched. They stood in the middle of the frozen river, taking it in: blacks and greys and whites and a hint of blue where the sun overhead hit the ice. All about them winter's palette was at its finest. Snow was piled on dark branches. In the distance, a lone hawk cried.

'It's like we're the only two people in the world,' Catherine breathed. Even her voice sounded hushed as she looked up at Finn. Lord, he was tall! She was forever looking up at him to make eye contact. Tall, and broad. She'd never considered his shoulders until last night.

A thought struck her. 'You're a winter person.'

Finn's brow knitted, but she could see the comment amused him. 'What does that mean?'

'You're like the winter; you're dark and quiet, yet there's a lot going on beneath the surface that one doesn't see unless one knows where to look.'

'And you know where to look?'

'Yes, but it sounds like you're fishing for a compliment,' Catherine scolded playfully.

'All right, assuming I am, what else makes me a winter person?' Finn smiled.

'You have winter's colours. You're dark—your hair and eyes are like those branches leaning out over the river.'

Finn chuckled. 'At least you didn't say my hair was grey.'

'Dark is mysterious and winter is mysterious,' Catherine pressed on, defending her position, entirely aware there was mystery in the air now. Something was changing between them. She was alert to every aspect of his body, to the breadth of his shoulders, the dark depths of his eyes, of his hand where it rested on her waist as it had so many times before. But never like this.

She began to babble, trying to bring back the safe Finn, the Finn she knew and thought she understood. 'As for me, I'm a spring person. My red hair, my green eyes, all spring.'

'You're a veritable *rainforest* of colour,' Finn corrected.

'Is there lots of red and green in the rainforest?' She tried for humour in hopes of regaining some neutrality. The conversation was definitely charged with dangerous undertones— dangerous because she didn't necessarily understand them. They'd taken her at complete unawares.

Finn's face cracked into a smile that broke the austere planes of his face. 'There are shades of red so vivid, so intense, they deserve words we haven't invented yet. There's turquoise, too, and teals and blues. It's not just the colours though, it's the plants, the animals, the sounds. Oh, Catherine, you can't believe how rich it is.'

But she could believe it if Finn's passion for the subject was anything to go on. She could almost imagine the trees alive with colourful birds, the air full of new sounds, and vivid sights everywhere the eye turned. 'How different it must be from here,' she managed to say, feeling a little foolish. She'd thought she'd come home educated and sophisticated from Paris, that she'd seen the world. In actuality, she'd seen a city.

Finn had seen places and things that sounded like fairytale beings come to life.

'It is different. But rainforests are dark places too.' Finn's smile faded and his face became serious again. 'We explored places where the tree canopy was so tall and so dense sunlight could not filter down to the ground. It was perpetual night.'

That she could not imagine, but it made her shudder none the less. It was also another reminder of all Finn had seen and done. To wander in a land such as the one he'd described was almost beyond comprehension. She knew people explored, of course. She'd just never known someone personally. Finn had had incredible adventures, seeing far-off lands and things most men would never see in their lifetimes.

'Perhaps I was wrong,' Catherine ventured softly, her eyes focused on her gloved hand encased in his and laying against his chest. 'Perhaps you are more like a rainforest, with your depths and your secrets. I don't think people really know you at all, Finn Deverill.' She certainly didn't, or hadn't until this little glimpse. If she'd known him, she'd never have thought he was dull. There wasn't a boring bone in Finn's body. No man could do what he'd done, seen what he'd seen and remain two-dimensional.

He squeezed her hand. 'The people who count do.' He gave her a smile and she felt the warmth of realisation sweep her. He counted her among their number.

'I'm most unusually wrong. You're not a winter.' The moment had unnerved her and she was babbling again, desperately out of her depths. 'Now, Channing's a—'

Finn shook his head slightly. 'I don't want to hear about Channing.' That was when it happened. Finn's gloved hands came up and took her face between them. This time there could be no mistake, no sudden retreat. This time, he kissed her. His mouth covered hers, taking full possession, and she welcomed it. Her body knew what to do and her mouth opened to his, her arms about his neck, her body moulding to his, all of her suggesting this intimate gesture was most welcome.

There was not one kiss, but a series of kisses as their mouths learned one another, tongues exploring tentatively at first, then more confidently finding their way and yet there was something leashed behind the encounter that yearned to break free, yearned to claim more. A fire was kindling low in her belly, a delicious heat running through her veins. She could feel the press of his form, the manly contours of him even through their layers of clothes.

Kissing Finn Deverill was extraordinary. Kissing Finn Deverill was impossible.

He must have realised it the same instant she did. They sprang apart by implicit consent. They stared at one another with mixed expressions: horror warring with amazement. She fumbled for words, but Finn found them first.

'I am sorry. I was overcome by your beauty and the moment. We should forget this ever happened.'

They weren't exactly what a girl wanted to hear after the most earth-shattering kiss she'd ever received, but Catherine nodded, knowing that her nod was already a lie. She doubted she would ever forget the day she kissed Finn Deverill any more than she'd forget the day she'd discovered just how fascinating he really was.

Chapter Four

Finn sipped his brandy, feet balanced on the fender of the fireplace in the library. A warm fire and a fine brandy might create a more comfortable setting for contemplating what he'd done, but they couldn't change it. He'd *kissed* Catherine. Devoured her was a more accurate description. What had he been thinking?

That was the problem. He hadn't been thinking at all. He'd been *feeling*, something he seldom allowed himself to do. Feelings weren't good for science. But he was thinking now, when it was too late. Even so, the solitude of the library was failing to provide him any valid answers to his thoughts.

Normally, this was the place he came when he thought about his work, his flowers, his plants. Tonight, all he could do was think about Catherine. He thought about how she'd looked, so vibrant with her auburn hair and deep-teal-wool skating costume with its skirts short enough to let her skate with ease. She'd been a splash of vibrant colour against the stark beauty of the winter landscape. He thought about how she'd felt in his arms, how she'd *wanted* to be in his arms. There'd been no reticence about her. Her arms had gone about his neck, her body had pressed willingly to his, her breasts soft against his chest.

Arousal was stirring again. He had to stop thinking about

it! Suffice to say, she'd liked his kiss, more than liked it, and so had he. *That* was the problem, the only problem in an otherwise perfect day. He and Catherine had skated back to the party and judiciously avoided one another the rest of the day, although that hadn't stopped him from watching her.

The rest of the outing had gone off without any trouble. Lunch had been a delicious assortment of cold meats and hot soup. The guests had enjoyed themselves. No one had twisted an ankle, or cut a leg with a blade or any of the other small crises that can plague a skating party, although Finn had prepared for all contingencies.

It was a good thing the rest of the day *had* been so carefully planned because he wasn't sure he could have dragged his attention away from Catherine. Finn had found it deuced difficult *not* to seek her out with his eyes and what he'd seen had infuriated him.

Channing had invited her to sit with his group at lunch and had taken her back out on the ice for one last spin. Channing had taken her up in his sleigh for the return journey. And Channing had walked into the drawing room upon their return with Catherine on one arm and Lady Alina Marliss on the other. Well, he couldn't have them both. Finn would see to that. He was going to have a long conversation with Channing.

About what? Finn's more logical side prompted. His anger was irrational when one truly examined it. He was angry because his brother was being nice to an old friend? He was angry because his brother skated with Catherine when she'd skated with almost everyone from children on up? His anger made no sense except for the niggling phrase that pounded in his brain: *she's mine.*

That's why he was angry and that was irrational. Catherine Emerson was *not* his. Not in that way, not in any way. For all he knew, she was simply home for Christmas and would return to Paris in the New Year.

A knock sounded on the library door, but the door opened without waiting for a response. 'I thought I might find you here.' Channing stepped into the room. So much for thinking the house-party guests would be too busy changing for dinner to give him a moment's privacy to sort through his thoughts. However, if he meant to have that discussion with Channing, there seemed to be no time like the present.

Channing seemed uncharacteristically hesitant. 'I need to talk to you.' Channing paced the room, stopping every so often to distractedly play with an object.

Finn sat back in his chair and waited. When nothing was forthcoming, he offered a prompt. 'Is there a problem with Lady Alina?' Whatever was bothering Channing was serious—Finn had seldom known his brother to be at a loss for words.

'Yes—no—not directly. The problem is with Cat.'

'Catherine. She likes to be called Catherine.'

Channing halted his tour of the room and faced him. 'Oh, not you too. Next you'll be telling me about Katherine de Medici.'

'Do you even know who that is?'

Channing threw up his hands. 'No, but *that* is not the point. I saw you kissing her today. Alina and I happened to come upon the two of you.' Channing seemed to have recovered his powers of speech now that he'd got started. 'By the saints, Finn, you were all over her. I could hardly tell where one of you ended and the other began!'

'We were supposed to be alone,' Finn retorted, well aware that his answer wasn't anywhere near good enough. He was still trying to wrap his head around the fact they'd been spotted and by Alina Marliss of all people.

'Being alone or not doesn't excuse it,' Channing said with surprising authority. The shoe was so seldom on this foot it made Finn wonder. He thought of all the attention Channing had lavished on Catherine today, of the way Catherine had looked at Channing in the drawing room just yesterday and an uncomfortable idea came to him.

'Why are you so interested? I doubt we'd be having this

discussion if you'd discovered me kissing Lady Eliza.' He was a grown man and he was entitled to his privacy. Goodness knew he'd protected Channing's privacy often enough.

'I know you, Finn, and you'd *never* kiss Lady Eliza.'

'But apparently I would kiss Catherine Emerson and hence the conversation?'

'You *did* kiss her and you knew I liked her, you knew!' Channing sounded positively petulant.

Finn stiffened in his chair under the barrage of Channing's accusation. 'I knew no such thing. You have a female guest here. Lady Alina is the recipient of your attentions.'

'She is a business arrangement and you knew that too.'

'I'm the only one who knows it. What do you suppose Catherine thinks of Lady Alina's presence? She asked, you know.' It was Channing's turn to be affronted.

'What did you tell her?'

'I told Catherine you had an understanding with Lady Alina.'

Channing's face went red. For a moment Finn thought they might come to blows. 'Bastard,' Channing growled in low tones.

'I assure you I am not.' Finn was feeling surly. He wanted to hit something even if that was Channing's perfect face.

'You knew what she'd make of that answer. You deliberately made it seem as if I were not an eligible Parti.'

'Channing, you are *not* an eligible party,' Finn argued. 'I answered as you wanted. I protected your privacy. If you don't like it, you can tell Catherine the truth, that you run a gentlemen's service in London.'

'I can't do that.' Channing sighed and pushed a hand through his hair, some of the anger leaching out of the encounter. 'What are your intentions towards her?'

Finn shook his head. 'And I can't tell you that.' He hardly knew himself. It had only been a handful of hours since the kiss, only a day since her return to their lives. His actions at the lake had surprised him. He'd not planned to kiss her, just as he'd not planned to nearly kiss her in the stables. Today, he had not let the opportunity go. He only knew that he was drawn to her. She was beautiful and she looked at him like he mattered in the way a man should and not as a future earl. She listened to him. Those traits alone were worthy of his consideration or maybe they were merely signs of his desperation. He would not know unless he pursued this avenue. A good scientist tested his variables.

'Then we're at an impasse,' Channing said wearily. He looked as if he wanted to say something else. His mouth worked, but no words came. He simply left the room.

Finn swirled his brandy in its snifter, idly watching the firelight play across the amber surface. When he'd thought of the impending festivities, this scenario had never crossed his mind: he and his brother quarrelling over a woman and that the woman would be little Catherine Emerson, their childhood friend. Finn tipped his glass sideways to catch the facets of light. Yet, as distasteful as the situation was, he was not willing to cede the field to Channing. Who would have thought it would come to this?

'The king has come!' Catherine yelled in good fun and everyone sitting in the circle of chairs scrambled to exchange seats. Catherine scrambled with them, shrieking and jostling to edge Meredith out of the last chair.

Tonight, Channing was the game master and the young people had the drawing room to themselves for parlour games while the older guests had adjourned to the music room for quieter activities. The room was alive with energy and the games were starting to take the edge off the day's events, or rather *the* event.

What did that kiss mean? Mistake or not, something had prompted it and the almost-kiss in the stables. These two thoughts had tumbled around in her head all afternoon and she was no nearer an answer. Perhaps Finn and she should talk, but Finn had made himself scarce, retiring with the older guests after dinner. He wasn't too old for the games. Marcus and Ellis had joined them, after all. But instinctively, she knew why Finn hadn't come. The kiss had messed everything up. And yet it was beyond her how something so wondrous, so glorious, could be so off-setting.

There was one last round of change seats and Channing called out a new game. 'It's time for our finale, Throwing the Smile.' Channing paused with a grin, waiting for everyone's attention. 'Only this time, we'll mix in a game of forfeits.' There were oohs and nervous giggles as Channing explained the game. 'Marcus will start. He will stand in the centre of the circle and try to make someone laugh. Then he'll wipe his smile off his face and give a "straight look" to someone in the circle. If they smile, they have to pay a forfeit, instead of sitting out.' There was an excited outburst of talk at the announcement. Channing raised his hand for silence. 'As game master, I've decided what the forfeit will be. Do you all see the mistletoe ball hanging in the doorway? A Christmas kiss will be the forfeit. Are we ready?'

The game was under way amidst laughter and much commotion debating who had or hadn't smiled. Marcus struggled, needing three rounds in the centre before Meredith took pity on him when he threw her a stare and she smiled back. 'I can't have anyone else kissing him, can I?' she'd joked, dragging Marcus to the mistletoe ball, but it was Marcus who swept her into his arms with a dramatic kiss worthy of Drury Lane. Then Ellis kissed Alyson and the point of Channing's game became obvious not long after. The forfeit rule was designed to let suitors claim a kiss or perhaps more covertly for would-be suitors to announce their intentions in a fun, entertaining venue.

The circle began to shrink as people sat down with the ones they'd caught throwing a smile, even though the rules hadn't required it. There were few people left. Catherine wondered who she'd have to kiss—maybe nice Lord Richard, who had so far resisted the stare, although several of the girls had tried, no one trying harder than Jenny Brightly. Or maybe Channing. Lady Alina had pleaded a headache after dinner and gone to her room. Catherine's pulse began to race. Channing had made it a point to spend time with her today after she'd returned from the river with Finn. But it had felt different, awkward almost.

A part of her felt disloyal to Finn although there was no reason for it. She'd spent time with Channing before. Her conscience made short work of that argument: *Yes, when you were ten years old, when you were nothing more to him than a little girl with carroty hair and he was nothing more to you than a grubby boy*. This was different. Still, why not spend time with Channing? Finn had told her to forget about the kiss. Besides, Channing was her fairy tale, he'd always been her fairy tale. He was fun and exciting and today at the lake proved it. Didn't it? They'd spun in playful circles, but it had been Finn who had truly excited her with his talk of unseen lands and dark forests where the sun never reached the earth.

Channing can't even remember to call you by the right name. Well, everyone had their foibles. It was a very little thing, really, as foibles went. Finn had his foibles too, always talking about things in Latin. She wondered what Finn would call a kiss in Latin. The thought brought a smile to her face.

No, don't smile! But her warning to self came too late. She was smiling and Channing had caught her.

'Time to pay the forfeit, Cat.' Channing was grinning, others were applauding, some even whistling. The crowd was getting rowdy as the evening neared its end.

Under the mistletoe ball, Channing tipped her chin up. 'Make it a good one, Cat.' It was said in fun, but something else glimmered in Channing's eyes just before his mouth caught hers. He wanted this kiss—some important test rode on this for him.

This was it, the dream! Channing was kissing her, had sought her out for this kiss on purpose. She waited to feel something, anything. But nothing came. She supposed the kiss was technically proficient as kisses went. It wasn't wet or sloppy or chaste. But in the end, it was just a kiss under the mistletoe, only a forfeit from a parlour game, and it left her surprisingly unaffected. Unfortunately, it hadn't left everyone as unaffected as she.

Chapter Five

Finn had slipped in the back of the room and he was angry, seethingly angry. Catherine knew it right away as soon as she spotted him, standing with his arms crossed. She didn't think anyone else noticed, though. He was one of those sorts who just got quieter and grimmer the angrier he became. Like the day he'd had to climb up the apple tree in the Deverill orchard to get her down after he'd warned her not to climb the tree in the first place. But Channing had dared her and she *never* backed down from a dare.

Her eyes met Finn's briefly through the crowd. She flushed and looked away, feeling a prick of guilt as if she'd been caught doing something illicit, as if she had *betrayed* Finn. Such a feeling was ridiculous. Why should she feel guilty? It was a parlour game, a silly forfeit. Everyone else had done it. Even if it had meant something, that should be all right too. Just because Finn had kissed her first didn't mean he had any rights over her. With that kind of logic, it meant Billy Fisher should feel jealous since he'd kissed her once at a birthday party in the village when they were thirteen. Billy Fisher had definitely been 'first' long before Finn's devilish kiss on the river.

Catherine could feel her own fury start to simmer. Why should he be angry at all? *He'd* declared the kiss was a mistake in the first place, something that should never have happened. A horrid thought occurred to her. Had Finn been as unaffected by their kiss as she had been by Channing's? Was that the reason he wanted to forget it? He'd been disappointed? She certainly hadn't been. How awful to be the only one. Her thoughts leapt back to Channing, who still had his hand on her arm. Had he alone been affected by their kiss? She tossed him a bright smile so he wouldn't feel badly if that was the case. Perhaps he wouldn't know.

Finn surely hadn't known, otherwise he wouldn't look so quietly thunderous at the back of the room. The guilt swamped her again. She could only imagine how it *had* looked: Channing's golden head bent to hers, Channing's hand cupping the sweep of her jaw. It had probably *looked* quite stunning to the viewer if it had borne even half of Channing's usual grace. But it had meant nothing.

Finn was the first of the adults to arrive, the music room crowd heralding the coming of the tea cart, her parents among them. They'd come over in the afternoon while everyone was still at the lake. Her father sidled over to Finn and Finn's expression seemed to soften. They bent their dark heads together, engaged in conversation, Finn bringing up his hands every so often to make a point. She wondered what they were talking about. Her father had always liked Finn, always said he had a good head on his shoulders.

'You're staring,' Channing said at her ear. He hadn't left her side since the kiss. Apparently his test had been passed. But not hers.

'I was just wondering what could be of such interest to the two of them.' Catherine shrugged, looking at Channing as if seeing him for the first time. He was unquestionably handsome, but what else was he? He hadn't sailed the tributaries of the Orinoco, or walked the depths of the rainforest. Tonight, Channing Deverill came up lacking by comparison and by extension—so had the dream.

'Flowers or crops would be my bet.' Channing laughed, entirely unaware of her inner thoughts. 'Not exactly topics of scintillating conversation to the rest of us. I guess it is good they have each other to talk to.' He smiled, his blue eyes glinting with a hint of mischief. 'Speaking of conversation, there's something I want to talk to you about.' He led them apart from the crowd, over by the window. Finn's window, although it was silly to think of it that way. It was anyone's window really. No one owned that space.

'What is it?' Catherine asked, a bit breathless, but not for the reasons she'd imagined at the prospect of Channing pulling her aside.

'Will you save me a waltz tomorrow night at the Yule Ball? I have it on good authority from my mother there will only be three.' He made an exaggerated moue of disappointment. 'I told her there should be more; everyone dances the waltz these days. But she's surprisingly old fashioned when it comes right down to it. Anyway, I wouldn't want yours to be filled up before I could ask.'

'Of course I'll save you one.' She favoured him with a warm smile. Was that a flicker of relief? Was the handsome and sought-after Channing Deverill *relieved* that she, Catherine Emerson, daughter of the local gentry, had accepted a dance? It was enough to make her think the world had turned upside down. But she was not naïve and there was one question she had to ask.

'What about Lady Alina?'

Channing's smile faded ever so slightly. 'There are three waltzes; I couldn't possibly dance all of them with her, could I?' he answered with a glibness that didn't quite match his expression. 'Besides, I want to dance with you. You left for Paris before we could have a proper dance together.'

Catherine couldn't argue with that. She'd been fifteen when her great-aunt had sent for her. She'd not been old enough to attend the local assemblies and more grown-up parties. 'I would be glad to dance with you then, as long as I'm not upsetting Lady Alina.'

'Don't worry about her. It's not what you think.' Channing

paused, appearing to debate something in his mind. 'She's been out of society for a while. You could say I'm helping her reintegrate.' Channing's voice dropped, his pressure on her hand tightened. 'She has no claim on me that matters, Catherine, nothing beyond the duties required of being a good host.'

The implied message was staggering. Catherine rummaged her brain for an appropriate response. What was it her friend Vivienne, who had never lacked for male attention, had always used? Ah, she had it. 'Then I am most honoured,' Catherine said softly.

Channing raised her hand and kissed her knuckles. 'It is I who am most honoured.' His blue eyes held hers for a long moment. 'Now, if you'll excuse me? I need to see to the guests. Mother will skin me alive if I dominate the prettiest girl in the room while old Mrs Anderson goes languishing for lack of tea.'

Finn was gone when she looked around the room. He was no longer standing with her father when she went to join him and her mother, nor was he with anyone else, although Catherine sensed she wasn't the only one hoping to spy him. Lady Eliza seemed to be looking for him as well. Catherine sipped her cup of tea, thinking Finn might reappear after running some hosting errand for his mother. Finally, when it became apparent he wasn't going to come back, she broke down and asked, 'Was Finn feeling unwell?'

Her father shook his head. 'He had some things to see to in the library.' In the library? In the middle of a house party? Only her father would not find such an excuse odd.

Catherine couldn't help but ask the most obvious of questions. 'What things? What could be so important Finn had to see to them right now?'

'*Lord Swale,*' her mother corrected softly, but Catherine didn't miss the insistence in her voice. Catherine stared at her mother, not quite digesting the comment. *Who? Oh, Finn.*

'You're not children any more, Catherine. It's not seemly to use his first name. He's the heir.'

'He's always been the heir,' Catherine said testily simply for the sake of argument. What did that have to do with anything anyway?

Her mother gave her a reproving look. 'You're grown up, it's different now.'

Catherine smiled an apology. She was just being peevish and it wasn't fair to take it out on her mother. 'I'm tired from the long day outdoors. I think I'll go up to bed. I'll see you in the morning.' She kissed her mother on the cheek.

'Sleep well, darling. I hear there's shopping in the village tomorrow for last-minute Christmas presents and the ball tomorrow will make a late night.'

'I will.' And she would sleep just as soon as she paid one last visit to the library.

Finn stared into the fire, a book open on his lap. He hadn't read a page of it. In fact, he hadn't done much of anything since he'd come in here. He simply couldn't stand to be in the same room as Channing, watching him woo Catherine. More than that, he couldn't stand to watch Catherine smile back at his brother as if she welcomed those attentions.

There was no 'as if' about it. Finn had seen the way she'd looked at Channing that first night. He'd seen the way they'd laughed together today on the lake, spinning in those ridiculous circles. And he'd seen the way they'd looked together when Channing had kissed her under the mistletoe ball.

Finn rather wished he hadn't seen *that*. But he had and they had looked beautiful together. Then Channing had led her aside and they had talked and Channing had kissed her hand. Finn hated that move of Channing's, who had been perfecting the art of hand kissing for years. His brother once told him he had a way of doing it where his eyes lingered just over the tops of the knuckles because women thought it was irresistible. Had Catherine thought that? Had she liked Channing's mistletoe kiss? More importantly, had she liked it *better* than his?

That last thought was not well done of him. It reeked of jealousy and for no reason. He'd kissed women before and there'd been no need for validation. The door to the library opened a crack and a form slid inside in a susurration of gold-tissue skirts and matching slippers. This was the second visitor today. His private lair was becoming deuced popular.

'There you are!' Catherine's voice was a loud whisper. 'I wondered where you went when you didn't stay for tea.' Her voice was full of false cheer. She was nervous. There was some consolation in that unless she was nervous because she'd come to tell him bad news. In this case, bad news was defined as anything he didn't want to hear. Finn managed a smile and manners. He gestured to the empty chair beside his. He set aside his book and gave Catherine all his attention, which wasn't hard to do. She'd had it before she'd entered the room.

'Channing's asked me to save him a waltz,' Catherine began, taking extra time to settle her skirts. She didn't meet his eyes and that 'bad news' scenario was definitely spot on. He no more wanted to hear about waltzing with Channing than he wanted to hear about the plague.

'Your mother has requested *three* waltzes for the ball.' She did look at him then, a little sideways glance and a quick half-smile on her lips, lips he'd kissed. He was afraid he would spend the rest of his life looking at those lips and thinking of that kiss. That one moment had now succeeded in dividing a lifetime into before and after.

'I'm sure yours will fill.' Why was she telling him this?

Her gaze was more direct now. She turned to face him in her chair, the firelight catching her hair and turning it the most wondrous shades of flame. 'I'm sure they will too. I am certain Lord Richard will want one and that leaves just the other left.' She paused and drew a deep breath. His usually confident Catherine was flustered, at least slightly. The next words came out in a rush. 'I'm wondering if I should save it for you?'

He should hit himself in the head with the book he'd been pretending to read. He'd been obtuse. The man who'd sailed to the far side of the world and sought out indigenous plants never before seen to the English eye had missed this simple inquest. She wanted to dance with him. She'd sought him out. She'd only told him about Channing in order to propel him into action. When he hadn't taken the hint, she'd been forced to be more direct. If she hadn't been sitting right there watching, he'd have given his forehead a good smack. Now all he could do was reply in a fashion that wouldn't embarrass them both.

'I would like that very much. Thank you for thinking of me. Do you think you might save me the opening quadrille too?' Then he added hastily, 'Unless it's already spoken for?'

Catherine gave a little laugh. 'No, as far as I know, it's still the custom to mark one's dance card the night of the ball.' An awkward silence sprang up. 'Are you going into the village tomorrow? My mother tells me there's a shopping expedition.'

'I haven't decided yet. There are preparations for the ball that might demand my attention.' *Ask me to go. I would come if you wanted it.* He simply didn't want to go and watch Channing's pursuit of her.

'You should come.' It wasn't quite worded exactly as he wished but it was a start.

'Why?'

Catherine smiled. 'Because the shops are full of Christmas treats and because I want you to, Finn.' She clapped a hand over her mouth. 'My mother thinks I shouldn't call you that.'

'Call me by my name?'

'Yes. She thinks I should call you Lord Swale because we're not children any more.'

'But we are still friends, aren't we, Catherine?' He couldn't imagine calling her Miss Emerson at this late date and he knew he could not tolerate Catherine of all people calling him Lord Swale. He didn't want to be a viscount to her.

She reached between their chairs and squeezed his hand. 'We'll always be friends, Finn.' To tell the truth, that wasn't precisely what he wanted to hear. He couldn't imagine being only her friend at this late date either. They'd crossed an invisible line today and there was no going back, not for him.

The conversation lagged awkwardly and she reached for the book he had left on the table between their chairs. 'Is this what you were reading? *Botanicals of the Rainforest*?' Her eyes perused the cover, coming to rest on the small gold letters at the bottom. 'You wrote this?' There was awe in her voice as she opened the cover.

'It's from my expedition with Viscount Wainsbridge, he and his family have permanently taken up residence in British Guyana to oversee British interests there.'

'You needn't be so modest, Finn.' Catherine smiled at him over the pages. 'My father writes books and I know good work when I see it. Are these your drawings as well? You're a talented artist. I'm impressed.'

It felt uncommonly good to be praised. 'Channing doesn't appreciate the book.'

Catherine smiled and turned another page. 'Channing thinks all flowers smell like roses.'

They both laughed then. It wasn't meanly said and it occurred to Finn it had been ages since he'd had an inside joke with someone. That the person he should have one with was Catherine spoke deeply to him in a frightening but fundamental way.

'Tell me about this.' She held the book out to him, pointing to a peculiar flower.

'That's curare. It's a deadly plant, actually. One wouldn't guess it. It looks more like a weed than anything else. All the tribes have their variation of curare poison. We found out the hard way.'

Catherine tucked her feet up under skirts. 'Well? Aren't you going to tell me about it?'

Finn waved away the suggestion with a hand. 'You don't want to hear about it.'

'Yes, I do.' Catherine passed him the book. 'Tell me.'

'All right,' Finn acceded, but secretly it was no hardship to tell her. It felt good to have an audience. His family listened to be polite. 'Jack and I had been out for three weeks and we were deep in the rainforest, and five miles out from our current base camp.'

'Jack?'

'Viscount Wainsbridge,' he explained. 'We were set upon by natives who believed we were trespassing. Set upon isn't quite the right word, we were ambushed. We never heard them coming. The natives move with enormous stealth and silence. One moment Jack was standing beside me and the next he was down. A tiny dart had hit him in the arm and the curare, the poison, worked that fast. The natives use it on their darts.'

'What happened?' Catherine was enrapt.

'I took out my pistol and fired into the bushes. The noise scattered them. They weren't prepared for gunfire. It gave me time to get Wainsbridge up. We took refuge in the bushes. There was no way I could outrun an unseen enemy with a wounded man on my shoulders. I hid us as best I could, primed my pistol and waited until dark. *Then* I made a run for it, dragging Wainsbridge with me every step of the way. He reacted badly to it—apparently he'd been hit with it once before. We had an antidote at camp, however, and he recovered, but it was a near thing. I didn't know it at the time, but if we'd waited much longer he would have been beyond the antidote.'

'You walked through the rainforest for five miles carrying a full-grown man?'

'Dragged him part of the way—I didn't say it was a pretty remove.' Finn chuckled.

'But you saved him at your own expense.' Her eyes shone with admiration. 'You're an uncommonly good man, Finn.'

'I didn't do it to be a hero, Catherine. I did it because it was right.' Finn shut the book, a little uncomfortable with the shine in her eyes. Is this what he wanted? Catherine Emerson to fall in love with him? Or he with her? Maybe it was too late to think he had any choice in the matter. In any case, it was too late to be caught in the library with her.

'Shall I see you to your room?' They rose together and Finn picked up a lamp to light their way. But when they reached the library door, Finn stopped. He couldn't leave this room without knowing where he stood with her. If there was no going back, there was only going forwards. Finn set down the lamp. 'Catherine, wait.'

She turned, finding herself between him and the wall of the door. There was nowhere for her to go. He bracketed her with his hands braced on either side of the door. Her breath caught. He could see the pulse-spot at the base of her neck leap ever so delicately, her sea-green eyes widen in desirous anticipation. She was not opposed to this.

He kissed her, hard and insistent, his mouth slanting over hers with determination. This kiss was different than the one at the river. That kiss had been about surprise and exploration. But this was about claiming, about wanting. And it wasn't enough. They were both breathless when they pulled away.

Catherine's eyes held a challenge as they searched his face, his eyes for some explanation. 'Don't tell me that was another mistake. Once I might believe but not twice.'

'That was no mistake.' And just to be sure, he kissed her again.

Chapter Six

December 23rd, the day of the Yule Ball

'You are so lucky!' Jenny Brightly trilled as a group of them tramped through the snow to the village for shopping the next morning. Catherine smiled patiently. Jenny was eighteen and pretty and a bit man crazy but one could hardly fault her for all her exuberance. 'If Mr Deverill had kissed *me* under the mistletoe I would have swooned. I just know it!' The other girls with them agreed.

'Do you think he means to court you?' Another girl, Amanda Hardwick, put in.

'Hardly.' Catherine dismissed the idea with a wave of her mittened hand. 'We are old friends and it was just a game.' The air was crisp and the grey sky overhead promised a cold day.

'I don't have any old friends who kiss like that!' Amanda gave a dramatic sigh. 'Are you sure he doesn't mean to court you?'

Catherine laughed away the notion, but she wasn't sure there wasn't some truth to it. After yesterday, she wasn't certain of anything, except she was glad Alyson and Meredith had opted to come down in the sleigh rather than walk. Such conjecture about their brother and their best friend would be upsetting? Awkward? Both? She wasn't sure what their reaction would be.

The village came into view, looking picturesque, as they started down the slope. Snow clung to the church spire and was piled in thick layers on the roofs of the shops. Catherine changed the topic of conversation to shopping.

In the village, Meredith and Alyson were waiting to drag her away from the group. 'Mr Waters has a new shipment of ribbons in just for Christmas!' Alyson exclaimed excitedly, pulling her into the 'emporium', the village's pride and joy.

The emporium was warm and crowded with shoppers. It was hard not to be sucked into the Christmas spirit. 'I don't need any ribbons,' Catherine protested with a laugh after Alyson's fifth attempt to get her to purchase a length of dark-green ribbon.

'Yes, you do. You need to meet people. Young men in particular,' Alyson replied, selecting another length, this one in a blue. 'It's been three days and you haven't met anyone but Lord Richard.' Alyson made a pouting moue. 'You'll never meet anyone if you spend all your time with Finn, always talking about his plants.'

'Well, you never know,' Catherine answered, reaching for a length of emerald green to distract Alyson and hoping her face didn't give her away. It was bad enough Alyson had noticed she had been spending time with Finn.

'Oh, that emerald green will look lovely on Christmas day.' Alyson frowned. 'But it doesn't match your gown for the ball. You have to get something to match for tonight too.' She went back to the length of blue, talking the whole while. Meredith, Catherine noticed, had gone silent and was studying her intently. Did Meredith guess?

Catherine didn't have to wonder long. She and Meredith were alone outside, waiting for Alyson to finish her business at the milliner's, when Meredith brought up the subject. 'Where have you and Finn been sneaking off to? Alyson might not have noticed, but I have. Marcus has. He commented on it last night.'

Well, Marcus and his powers of intuition could go hang. It certainly put her in a difficult position. She'd confess all to Meredith if there was something to confess. But at this point, she hadn't any idea what to say. *Finn and I have fallen in love?* No, she couldn't say that. It wasn't true. Was it? Did people fall in love in a matter of days? 'We went to the barn. I wanted to see Druid and Hamish.'

Meredith raised a censorious eye brow. 'That explains the first disappearance. Were Hamish and Druid at the lake too?'

Catherine felt a moment's panic. How much had they seen? How many people had noticed them leaving? 'Finn wanted to show me an early fawn.'

'And?' Meredith prompted.

'That's all,' Catherine bluffed—she hoped it was convincing.

'You looked a bit unnerved a moment ago. Seeing a fawn doesn't match the reaction.'

Perhaps it wasn't Marcus's powers of intuition she needed to fear. Catherine bit her lip. 'It's complicated. I can't really explain it.' Not even to herself.

Meredith's eyes flashed in triumph, dark eyes like Finn's. '"It" means there's something then. I thought so,' she said with an air of mystery.

Catherine reached out a hand and gripped Meredith's wrist. 'Please don't say anything.'

Meredith smiled softly and covered Catherine's hand. 'Of course I won't, but you'd better stop keeping secrets. My best friend and my brother. Who would have thought?'

Catherine shook her head, her words rushing out as she spied Alyson coming out of the store. 'It might not be anything, Merry. It was only a couple of kisses. They just sort of happened. They don't have to mean anything.' Then she blushed, her cheeks hot in spite of the cold. Had she really said that?

Catherine expected Meredith to tease her. Instead Meredith leaned close and whispered, 'Don't disappoint me. You know Finn better than that. Do you really think he does things that have no meaning?'

She *did* know Finn better than that, Catherine realised. Perhaps that was what had been bothering her about their kisses. He could say they were a spontaneous venture, but she didn't believe it because it simply wasn't his nature. They did mean something, but what exactly? Was that the reason he hadn't come on the expedition at the last minute? She'd thought it was settled last night.

The thought stayed with her the rest of the day as she picked out little gifts for the family. She had other things packed in her trunk that she'd brought from Paris, but she'd wanted something small to set at their plates for dinner. There were ribbons for Alyson and Meredith, an orange for their father who had a passion for the citrusy fruit and a small, carefully carved chocolate swan for their mother and hers. And that left only Finn. In earlier days, she'd have got him peppermints. But that was before he'd kissed her, before she'd kissed him back and her body had gone all hot and trembly in his arms until all she could think about was him, until all she could *want* was him.

Besides, what would he think if she gave him peppermints *now*? Would he think he had bad breath? She'd never known kissing to be this complicated before. Kissing redefined everything. At least Finn's kisses did. It was probably noteworthy to point out that Channing's kiss had not altered the speed with which she'd decided on his gift: the usual pistachios.

It was another hour before she decided on something. By then, the sky was overcast and glowering. Sleighs had come down from the house to carry the merry shoppers home with their packages, but they were gone by the time Catherine arrived at the meeting spot. Only one sleigh remained, a small two-seater with Finn at the ribbons. 'Where is everyone?' Catherine looked around, a little nervous. How many people would have noticed this special attention? He'd not come on the excursion, but had driven down specifically for her.

'They've gone on ahead. I told them I'd wait for you. Everyone is in a hurry to dress for the ball.'

He helped her in, his hand strong and firm at her elbow.

'You said you'd come today,' she said once her packages were stowed safely at her feet and Finn had arranged the lap robe to his satisfaction.

'I had work to do.' Finn climbed in beside her, his leg resting against hers in the small space. 'A ball takes a lot of manpower to put together.'

'You work a lot. First, the skating party, now this.' He had his other work too, always writing articles or working on his research. Who knew what other responsibilities he had regarding the estate? He'd been the responsible one growing up too. It was no surprise he'd turned out this way—so serious, so hard working. 'Don't you ever have fun?'

'My work is gratifying. It's a special source of fun.' Finn reached for the reins, but Catherine was faster. She snatched them and shouted to the team, slapping the reins on their backs for good measure, 'Get on!'

'What are you doing?' Finn raised his voice to be heard over the wind.

'Going for a sleigh ride!' Catherine called back, tossing him a triumphant look as they sped over the snow. New flakes began to fall, lighting the greying landscape in the magical dusk. It was a thrill of a ride. They sailed over rolling hills, the speed heady and exhilarating. Catherine shot a glance at Finn beside her, his face a study of surprise and then a smile and then a great, loud laugh as they took a snowy corner. The brisk wind hit her face and she gave a shout of pure delight.

She pulled the horses to a halt near the shelter of the woods, her breath coming out in panting puffs from the excitement. 'I haven't driven like that since…since last winter!'

'Last winter?' Finn sat back in the seat. 'I suppose I should be thankful this was a regular skill of yours. Where did you learn to drive like that?'

She let the reins go slack and leaned back with him. She laughed. 'We have snow in Paris too, you know. My friends and I would have sleighing parties in the Bois de Boulogne outside the city. My great-aunt has a friend who has a château and we'd visit quite a lot if there was snow.' Catherine gave her hair a toss, swinging it over one shoulder. Finn shifted in his seat.

'Do you miss your friends in Paris?'

'I do, but I like being home and being with my parents. My friends and I will write and Paris isn't so very far these days. I will see them again.'

'Do you mean to go back?' His dark eyes were serious once more.

'Only to visit.' She smiled and rapped him on the arm. 'Are you eager to get rid of me so soon? It's been three days and already you're packing me off.'

'No, I'm merely trying to discern your plans.'

Why? she wanted to ask. Catherine felt as if any false step here would prevent Finn from saying what was on his mind. They were dancing around something here. She kept her answer vague.

'I hadn't thought of any beyond getting home and celebrating Christmas.' *And marrying Channing and being part of the Deverill clan for ever.* That particular plan sounded a bit childish now in retrospect. 'I'll help my father with his research, of course. He always needs help organising his material.' Catherine shrugged. 'The usual, I suppose. There will be church meetings and ladies' circles. Perhaps we might go down to London for part of the Season. What about your plans? Do you have any more expeditions planned to the Caribbean?' She could see him already at the head of an expedition, sailing down uncharted waters, so strong, so alive.

'I don't know. Maybe. Viscount Wainsbridge would like

to have me map a new river for him, but I'm not sure I can get away. There is a lot to do here and Father is relying on me more and more.' There was a battle waging there. She could see hints of it in his eyes, no matter how blasé he tried to sound. The earldom had long been a conflicted issue for him. It was the conditions that disturbed him the most, the idea that his father would have to pass for him to achieve the ends to which he'd been raised. He was in no hurry to inherit and yet such waiting must be stifling for a man like him. He wanted to *do* something with his life, not sit around waiting, not when there were new worlds to explore.

'Channing could help while you're gone.'

That earned her a stern look. 'Channing will be in London. He spends most of the year there now with his, ah, new business venture. Besides, I wouldn't want to miss the girls' weddings. They're both bound to be married by this time next year.'

'It's all right to do something for yourself, to want something just for you, Finn,' Catherine offered tentatively.

Even if it's you? She had no idea how utterly beautiful she looked—the picture of health, bright and vibrant against the white of the snow. His body recognised such beauty instantly, although he wished it wouldn't. Finn shifted once more in his seat. 'It's complicated.' *Like our kisses.* 'The balance between duty and desire is not necessarily something that can be explained.' Again, much like his reaction to her.

Finn picked up the ribbons. If he didn't do something soon, he'd end up kissing her again. There was no question of doing more than kiss, not out here in the snow even if he wanted it to be otherwise. It was far too cold to start taking off clothes. He called to the horses, setting them in motion, but another idea had been set in motion. His brain wouldn't let go of a naughty train of thought—tonight, at the ball, perhaps? It wouldn't be too cold then and there'd be all sorts of places to sneak off to, all sorts of people *not* paying attention. It would be one time when it would be good not to have people notice him. While Channing was dazzling everyone, he could be whisking Catherine away to a secluded library.

To do what? Seduce her? He might be serious, but he wasn't a monk. He knew very well from first-hand experience what went on in dimly lit libraries at balls when no one was watching. But seduction was just one step away from marriage. Finn knew very well that seducing Catherine could not happen without the benefit of marriage to follow. She was the daughter of an old family friend, his sisters' best friend and his own friend as well.

'Watch out for the tree!' Catherine called at the last moment, covering his hands with hers and pulling on the reins. The sleigh swerved around a thin birch tree sticking out of the ground just in time.

Catherine laughed. 'What are you thinking about that has taken all your attention?' She playfully yanked on the reins. 'Let me drive home and you go right ahead with your thoughts.'

'You might think twice if you knew what they were.' Finn gave her a wry smile and relinquished the ribbons. It wasn't often a lovely woman drove him around with her hair hanging down her back, snowflakes tickling her nose. In fact, there'd never been a time that he could recall.

Chapter Seven

'You've been spending a lot of time with Lord Swale.' Catherine's mother stroked the brush through her hair and Catherine met her mother's gaze in the mirror of her dressing table. She wasn't fooled by the casual tone. Whenever her mother called Finn Lord Swale, something was afoot.

Catherine shrugged, trying to make light of it. It had been hard enough to explain to Meredith today. She couldn't imagine making sense of it to her mother. 'He brought me home from shopping, that's all.' There was no need to mention the skating expedition. Her parents hadn't even been there for it.

'He brought you home considerably later than the other sleighs,' her mother added.

'I was late. He was kind enough to have waited for me.' *Definitely* no need to say anything about racing the sleigh, their quiet talk in the woods or Finn's disclosure about his future.

Her mother set aside the brush and met her eyes in the mirror. 'At the end of the day, he's a viscount. Some day he'll be an earl, Catherine, and you'll still just be you: the daughter of well-respected gentry with a baron for a relative somewhere in the family tree. You're well born, but not high born, whereas Finn Deverill is both.' She paused. 'What I am trying to say is that he can't marry you. I have it on good authority from the countess herself that they fancy a match between him and Lady Eliza.'

The daughter of the marquess, someone more suitable for a man of Finn's station, a viscount waiting to be an earl. Her mother was implying something else too—a warning perhaps that a lord might dally and flirt where he liked without making promises. It was hard to imagine Finn as such a man. Then again, Lady Eliza was here. He'd taken the marquess's daughter into supper, but he'd been kissing *her*.

Was this what he'd meant by the balance of duty and desire? In the woods, she'd thought he'd been talking of the Caribbean and his work versus the responsibilities of the earldom. In reality, he might have been talking about her balanced against his duty to marry well. Family was important to Finn. He would not let them down with an indiscreet match. He'd indicated as much today. It wasn't in his nature to pick his heart over his head.

'He's a friend, nothing more.' Catherine managed a smile even though a small piece of her was breaking inside. Maybe not even a small piece. It might very well be a large piece. Catherine had to concede, her mother's logic made too much sense. Finn had not once alluded to their kisses beyond calling the first a mistake. He'd made no promises, no claims in words and he wouldn't. No matter how angry he was over Channing kissing her under the mistletoe ball, he was going to court Lady Eliza Dewhurst of the adequate bosom and the more-than-ample pedigree because it was the right thing to do.

Her mother kissed her cheek. 'I don't want to see you hurt. It's better to head these things off before they become confusing.' In other words, before they become dangerous, before the rashness of youth and hot blood took them down a path only one of them could afford to travel. Catherine thought it might be too late for that. Oh, there was no physical damage done. She knew the real damage her mother alluded to. One couldn't come of age in Paris and *not* know. But emotions, *her* emotions, were engaged and she rather thought Finn's were, too, even if he would deny them.

'Now, darling, we need to get dressed. It won't do to be late to the ball when we don't have to go any further than downstairs.'

All she had to do was go downstairs? Catherine thought. She might as well go to the moon. Going downstairs was proving to be nearly as difficult. She stared at her reflection in the vanity mirror. Was a dalliance all Finn saw when he looked at her? Did he look at her and see a nice but unsuitable girl? Her mother had meant well with her blunt speech, but now Catherine had to face the opening quadrille with Finn and her newborn doubts.

No, she wasn't going to think of it that way. Catherine put her mental foot down. She'd been looking forward to the Yule Ball and she had a beautiful gown she'd been saving for the occasion. She wasn't going to let a warning about Finn get in the way of that. Forewarned was forearmed. She would dance with Finn and with Channing and with the other young men present and that would be that. Except perhaps with Channing. She'd spent precious little time with Channing today. With her mother's warning tucked in her mind, tonight might be the perfect opportunity to return more fully to her original intentions.

The maid came and helped her finish her preparations, fussing with Catherine's simple hairstyle and helping her slide into the frothy gown of white silk and lace. 'Oh, miss…' the girl sighed appreciatively as she tied the wide blue sash about Catherine's waist '…you look an absolute treat. The gentlemen won't be able to keep their eyes off you!'

Catherine smiled and studied the gown in the long mirror. The bodice, done *en coeur*, left her shoulders bare, the delicate fall of lace veed to the centre of her bosom, drawing the viewer's eye downwards to the tight-fitted waist and the gentle, natural curve of the full skirt over her hips. The skirt would bell out nicely, but not obtrusively, when she danced.

The style was simple, but the fabrics were of the finest, the tailoring of the latest preferences from the fall of lace at the bodice draped à la Sevigne to the silk-de-chine scarf she would carry for effect. The ensemble was perfection.

Catherine slipped her feet into matching white slippers, an enormous luxury. She wouldn't get more than one night out of the delicate shoes before they would look dingy. But her great-aunt had insisted and bought them as a farewell gift. The image in the mirror smiled.

By the time Catherine joined her parents in the receiving line her resolve had returned.

And was immediately tested.

Finn stood at the ballroom door alongside his mother and father, greeting guests who'd been invited along with the house party, looking resplendent in dark evening attire. His jacket was cut tight across his shoulders, emphasising their breadth, and tapered at the waist to show off the trim, masculine line of him, long legs and all. His hair, walnut-dark like his father's, gleamed in the light, his jaw stern. But his eyes! Oh, his eyes were like liquid chocolate, warm and seductive all at once. It was his innate sincerity, Catherine thought, that created the look. She wanted to fall into them. Surely, any woman would want to. Funny, how she'd failed to notice such charms until now.

'Good evening, Mr Emerson, Mrs Emerson,' the countess gushed sincerely. 'Catherine, dear, you look stunning.' Finn's mother smiled warmly. 'The girls are already inside waiting for you. Finn, doesn't Catherine look lovely?'

She felt Finn's eyes on her as she curtsied to the earl, trying to act formal and informal all at once as if nothing was out of the ordinary. It was odd enough to curtsy to the earl, who was like a second father to her, to say nothing of feeling Finn's not-so-neutral gaze while she did it. But the proprieties must be observed on such occasions. Both the countess and her mother were sticklers on that account. Familiarity bred complacency and complacency bred slovenly behaviour.

'I thought you might miss our dance,' Finn said once she reached him. He offered her his arm. There was to be no reprieve then, no time to drift over to visit with Meredith and Alyson and let her senses settle. 'The sets are starting to form and you'll want to see the ballroom.' He bent close to her ear conspiratorially. 'Mother has outdone herself this year.'

Catherine felt herself start to relax. Decorations were a safe topic and they conjured up a host of memories. The countess used to let the children have a sneak peek at the ballroom every year before the guests arrived and they were shooed up to the nursery. 'I remember the year your mother had the poinsettia theme.' The columns had been draped in white swathes of fabric and the niches throughout the room had been filled with vases of the imported plant. The effect had been simple and stunning.

'Euphorbia pulcherrima.'

'I beg your pardon?'

'That's the Latin name for poinsettia. It means the most beautiful of the euphorbiae. It has other names, too, like lobster flower, the flame flower.' The low timbre of Finn's voice, private, intimate even though they were in a crowd, created the impression the flower wasn't all he was discussing in terms of beauty. A delightful shiver went through her, although she knew better than to allow such a reaction. Her mother's warning haunted the recesses of her mind. But she had no time for warnings as Finn ushered her inside the ballroom. A little gasp of awe escaped her as she took in the decorations of white and silver—and was that ice? It was. They perfectly mirrored the weather outside and created the ideal winter scene inside.

'It's a winter fantasy,' Catherine breathed.

'That's exactly what my mother calls it—her winter-fantasy ball.' Finn chuckled. 'I'll tell her you approve.'

'It's beautiful.' And it was. She could hardly take it all in. White gauzy fabric spangled in silver wrapped the columns, white hothouse roses adorned the niches in tall, elegant gold-and-silver urns. Even the ceiling was decorated, hung with giant glittery silver snowflakes and long crystals that simulated icicles. But the *pièce de résistance* was the orchestra dais set up at the top of the ballroom, where bunting held with navy-blue bows denoted the orchestra and two giant-swan ice sculptures graced each end like bookends. The effect was stunning and drew the eye down the length of the ballroom.

She and Finn took their place at the head of their set with three other couples and the dance began. 'Our first dance together,' Finn whispered with a smile as they began the opening figure. *'Le pantalon.'*

'The trousers,' she said, trying to keep her mind on the dance. They were the lead couple so they danced the pattern first. It was difficult though when her eyes wanted to watch Finn and trousers was the very last thing she should be thinking of, especially his.

'You seem distracted,' Finn said when their portion of the set came to an end, his voice low, his presence potent beside her. She could smell the spicy, cinnamon scent of him, warm and welcoming, and yet the spice was a reminder of danger lurking beneath the surface for the unsuspecting.

'You've surprised me.' Catherine kept her eyes on the other dancers. He had surprised her. He was proving very good at flirtation with those dark eyes of his that knew just how to skim a woman's body with their gaze and his casual touches that conveyed confidence, offered provocative suggestion of other touches, more private touches that might be had under different circumstances. It was common wisdom in the Paris salons that a man who knew how to touch a woman in public would not disappoint in a more intimate setting. Catherine flushed; the thought of sharing such a setting with Finn heated her cheeks, the forbidden question rising to the fore: what would Finn be like as a lover?

It was a hypothetical question at best. She knew women in Paris who took lovers, but Paris was a far different society than

England. Here, she should not even think of such a deed and yet the very thought would not leave her. Throughout the second figure, through *La poule* and *La pastourelle* movements of the quadrille and into the finale, the thought persisted: the image of Finn naked in the candlelight, his body covering hers, his hands clasping hers as they reached over her head.

She had to stop. These wanderings of the mind were precisely the dangers her mother had warned her of. Finn bowed to her, the quadrille over and thankfully so. Lord Richard claimed her for the next set and Finn moved off, hopefully unaware of her imaginings. She wouldn't see Finn again until the third waltz, the dance that would close the evening hours away. She had her reprieve.

Chapter Eight

Before she knew it, Channing had claimed his waltz, the first one of the night while Lady Alina glowered a little further down the floor in the arms of the squire who looked positively thrilled at his good luck. To their left, Finn took up a position with Lady Eliza. On the sidelines, Catherine noted, his parents looked on with smiles.

'Your parents seem pleased to see Finn with Lady Eliza,' Catherine said as the dance began.

Channing gave a mock frown. 'I haven't seen you all evening and that's the first thing you can think of to say?'

She gave a playful smile. 'You could have seen me earlier.'

Channing swung them into a turn. 'I did, I simply couldn't get away. I was bowled over at the sight of you in that dress. I still am, so is everyone else. I'm dancing with the prettiest girl in the room and they know it.' Channing winked. 'Maybe my parents are smiling because I'm dancing with you. They might not be smiling at Finn at all.'

Catherine laughed. 'I don't think you've changed a bit.' The comment was just like Channing. He saw the world through his eyes and that world revolved around him. He was his very own Copernican theory, the planet around which all the minor suns orbited. It didn't make him selfish. Channing was a kind-hearted individual, she knew that. It simply made him Channing and it made him different from Finn. Conversation with Finn wasn't necessarily all about Finn.

'Cat, I want to talk to you,' Channing began. 'There's something I need to ask. Do you think we might slip off somewhere quiet?' She was aware of his hand at her waist, holding her closer than the rule. But this was Channing, handsome, charming Channing, and this was what she'd come home for.

Channing led them to a little sitting room down the hall. He checked to see that it was empty. 'You never know what some people get up to at a dance,' he said with a chuckle, ushering her inside. Catherine stood before the fire, her hands clutched, her insides churning with butterflies. She told herself it was because the fairy tale was about to come true.

Channing raised a hand to her hair, smoothing his hand over it, a smile on his face, his blue eyes intent. 'You're lovely, Cat. I meant it when I said I was bowled over by your beauty this evening. There isn't a woman in there who can match you.'

'Not even Lady Alina?' she had to ask. That relationship seemed murky at best.

Channing shook his head. 'She's business.' He cupped her jaw and ran his thumb along her cheek. The gesture was soft and gentle, but it raised no prickles of heat down her arms or sent any shivers of delight down her back. 'You, Cat, you are my pleasure. I have obligations in London I must see to, but when I come back?' He paused. 'What I'm trying to say is will you wait for me? When I return, we can announce our engagement if you'll have me.'

The proposal was so *Channing*. It had been all about him; his obligations, his return. 'Don't you think you should ask me first?' Catherine laughed.

He took her hand. 'Will you marry me?' There was a winsome boyish hope in his voice that excused the lack of pomp behind the question. 'We'd be the most dashing couple in London. We'd do all the parties, all the balls. Everyone would want to have us.'

He was sincere in his own way. She knew him well enough

to know that. But in those moments he was laid bare to her in a way he'd never been. As a friend, as a childhood playmate, his bonhomie, his love of a party, an outing, any social activity, had been enough. He had been the centre of attention and it had been fun to be in the centre with him. Catherine pulled her hand free. She didn't want to hurt him, but she knew what her answer had to be. It was an answer she'd never thought to make. 'Marriage has to be more than fun, Channing.'

He knitted his fair brows. 'I don't understand.'

Of course he wouldn't. Perhaps he couldn't. It might not be in his make up to understand that things had to be more than fun, more than dares and larks.

'Can't you see it?' he pressed softly. 'You and I just bashing around London?'

Catherine gave a sad smile. 'I *can* see it, that's why I must decline.' It would be fun for a while. Channing would lavish every extravagance on her, they would live in the Deverill town house, have every convenience. Most of all, she'd have the one thing Channing didn't even know he was offering. She'd have what she always wanted—a chance to be part of the Deverill family. She would have it all and it would have been relatively easy to achieve.

Too easy. She'd been taught easy answers were to be suspect. When something was too good to be true, it usually was. Life would be merry until…until parties were no longer enough, until she wanted to do something meaningful with her life, until Finn came to town, a reminder of what she could have aspired to.

'I thought you liked me.' Channing seemed genuinely wounded.

'I do like you, as a friend.' She reached for his hand. 'We'll always be friends, Channing. Some day you'll find the right girl and you'll thank me for turning you down.' It seemed surreal, standing in the sitting room where she and the girls had played with their dolls on rainy afternoons and turning

down Channing Deverill, turning down her chance to be part
of the family for good.

'I could make you happy, Cat.'

'For a while.' Catherine gave a wan smile. She didn't want
to see him beg. Channing Deverill was the sort of man who
should never beg.

'A while? What's that supposed to mean?'

She was getting a bit impatient now. Wasn't there a figura-
tive bone in his body? Did everything have to be so literal? 'It
means I *am* honoured, Channing. I just want something that
lasts a little longer.' She nodded towards the door. 'I need to
be getting back.' It was a vague excuse for a departure, but
they both needed this scene to end. She didn't want to second-
guess her decision, didn't want to start thinking of dangerous
practicalities; maybe marriage to Channing would be worth
it if it meant she could be a Deverill.

Out in the hallway, Catherine pressed her head to the cool
panelling. What had she done? She'd thrown away her chance.
She couldn't stay here in the corridor. If Channing saw her
regretting, he would push his offer. She needed to get back
to the ballroom and lose herself in the crowd. Lord Richard
would be looking for her. A country dance might be just what
she needed to lift her spirits.

So she danced, and she danced some more until she felt
the beginnings of a little hole in her pretty slippers and still
she danced. Catherine laughed and flirted politely with the
young men on her dance card. She was her dazzling best in
the hopes no one guessed there was a hole in her heart as well
as her shoe. If she couldn't have Finn, then she'd have no one.
She very much feared that wasn't simply hyperbole.

No one but Finn. 'What's the matter, Catherine? Your smile
has been pasted on so long it might never come off.' The inevitable had arrived: the last dance of the evening, the third
waltz. Finn steered them to an empty spot on the crowded
floor, everyone wanting to be part of the beautiful dance. The

candles in the chandelier had been dimmed and the ballroom had taken on the glow of a starry night.

'It's nothing,' she lied with yet another smile. None of the protocols she'd learned in Paris had prepared her for this. How did one tell another, 'I've refused your brother in hopes of something better and that something better is you?' Even if she'd been bold enough for such words, what was the etiquette? Did the one who'd done the refusing politely wait for the one who'd been refused to make the situation public? Should Finn hear about Channing's proposal from her or from his brother?

Finn fitted his hand to her waist as the music started. 'I'll wait and hope for better.' He smiled down at her. 'You always were a bad liar, Catherine.'

'Not now. Waltz with me, Finn.' She placed her hand at his shoulder and gave him a private smile as he adjusted his grip at her waist, pulling her closer. She didn't want to talk about Channing's proposal. She simply wanted to dance with Finn Deverill, for what might be the one and only time.

She gave herself over to the moment. Finn's dark eyes were hot, burning with unexpressed emotion, his hand strong at her back as he propelled them through the crowd. She was aware only of the unspoken message of Finn's body as it manoeuvred them through the turns and figures of the dance. For the first time, she understood the whispered rumours about the suggestive nature of the dance, the nuances nicely bred girls giggled over behind their fans when they thought no one was listening. She and Vivienne had done the same, but those nuances had no real meaning, no substance until now: the man in pursuit, the closed position of the bodies, the twining of legs and arms, the draw of his arm pulling her closer, the pressure of his hand, all determining her position, the brush of his thighs against the silk of her skirts.

Finn was a master of it all and she revelled in that mastery, matching him step for step, boldness for boldness until the crowd fell away leaving them space in the centre of the floor. They turned, they spun, her eyes riveted on the intensity of

Finn's gaze, not the usual traditional spot of nothingness over a gentleman's shoulder. But Catherine was aware of none of it until the dance was over and it was too late. Applause erupted from the sidelines. She glanced away from Finn's face, realising for the first time that they'd danced alone, their private waltz suddenly public. Everyone had seen them.

Not everyone approved. Her mother's mouth was set in a firm line. Tears threatened in Lady Eliza's eyes, her cheeks flushed an unbecoming shade of begonia. Channing looked like a wounded martyr. The countess was looking at Finn with an icy smile that matched her decorations, her manners too refined to show the slightest crack over this latest development.

'Chin up, my dear,' Finn said quietly beside her. 'On the bright side, the other one hundred and ninety-six people in the ballroom thoroughly enjoyed it.'

'Of course they did, the same way people enjoy a scandal not their own,' Catherine retorted under her breath.

Finn chuckled, escorting her back to the perimeter to her mother's side as if nothing were wrong. 'You're exaggerating,' he whispered. 'All those people don't see anything wrong. They only see something beautiful, a moment's magic on a winter's night in the middle of a magical season. Christmas brings out the best in people. Good evening, Mrs Emerson.' He bowed to her mother and relinquished her hand.

'Good evening, Lord Swale.' Her mother was frosty.

Finn turned in her direction. 'Goodnight, Catherine. I trust I will see you at the Yule log cutting tomorrow?'

'Yes,' Catherine said quickly, overriding any temptation her mother might have to refuse the invitation.

Her mother barely waited until they reached her room. Her entire life, Catherine had never heard her mother raise her voice when giving vent to her disapproval. But the lack of volume only made it worse.

'Catherine, what were you thinking?' her mother asked calmly. 'To dance like that with Lord Swale in front of anyone who matters? There will be a scandal. Did you see Lady Eliza's face? She felt positively betrayed after all the attention Swale has paid to her.' Well, that made two. She and Channing both.

Catherine sat on the bed, pleating her skirt between her fingers, unable to meet her mother's grey eyes. She had to tell her. She couldn't have her mother finding out from the countess. 'That's not the real scandal,' Catherine whispered. 'I've refused Channing.'

The change in her mother was instantaneous. Empathy filled her grey eyes as she sank down on the bed beside Catherine. 'Oh, my dear girl, what have you done?'

It all came out then, stolen kisses and all. When she was finished, her mother kissed the top of her head as if she were a little girl again, smoothing her hair. 'We can leave in the afternoon.'

Catherine shook her head. 'No, I don't want to go. It will only make things worse.' If Finn was right and no one else suspected anything, leaving would only call attention to the fact that something was wrong. Tomorrow was Christmas Eve. She had to go to the Yule log cutting and Christmas mass. She had to laugh and smile and pretend everything was fine.

'Don't worry, I'll talk to Millicent tomorrow and sort things out,' her mother said softly. But it didn't escape Catherine's notice that this was one of the few times her mother had called the countess by her first name. 'Mothers are good at this type of thing.'

'You were romancing Catherine right under Lady Eliza's nose,' Millicent Deverill all but shouted at Finn. Admittedly, his mother was not good at this type of encounter, Finn thought, watching his mother struggle to address the situation at hand with some sense of decorum. Conflict was not her strong suit. She was a staunch believer in the idea that if one had manners to begin with, conflict would never occur in the first place.

'It was just a dance,' Finn reminded her calmly, aware that everyone in the room was staring at him, all three of them. His mother had called the whole family together in her private office. Channing was glaring daggers at him from his chair and his father paced the far side of the room.

'You didn't dance with Lady Eliza like that,' his mother accused. 'I invited her here for the express purpose of—'

'Yes, *you* invited her,' Finn broke in.

'That does not give you leave to romance a neighbour's daughter. You are showing Lady Eliza a flagrant disregard.'

Finn sighed wearily. 'I am not. I've spent time with her, I've sat with her at dinners.' He couldn't recall either he or Channing being in this much trouble since Channing had locked the tutor in the wine cellar so he could go fishing.

'You've been kissing Catherine.' Channing broke his glowering silence. Dear Lord, were they boys all over again? He couldn't believe Channing had said that. Channing turned his gaze towards Finn. 'You knew I liked her and now you've stolen her.'

'Wait a minute…' He would not sit here and let Channing play the martyr, not when Channing had brought his London business home to the house party in the form of Lady Alina Marliss and asked him to keep the business portion a secret. 'I'm not the one who brought home a special friend. You walk around with Lady Alina on your arm while you make eyes at Catherine. If anyone in this room is playing someone false, it's you.'

Finn's anger began to simmer and then it began to boil. He would not concede the field. Inside, some integral part of him knew it would kill him to see Channing with Catherine—Channing, who couldn't even remember she hated nicknames, Channing who didn't know the first thing about history.

'Well, you don't have to worry about it any more.' Channing's fists curled into tight balls at his sides. 'I spoke with her tonight and she refused me.'

The room went silent for a brief moment and then it erupted, his mother and father talking at once. Now he knew what it was Catherine hadn't told him. Finn placed his head in his hands. It was going to be a long night.

Chapter Nine

'I think cutting the Yule log is just an opportunity for men to remove their jackets and show off their muscles.'

'I don't mind that tradition at all.' The girls standing near Catherine gave high-pitched laughs. The house party had tramped out to the woodland with saws and a long sled for the annual log cutting. The snow had stopped, but it was terribly cold. She doubted there'd be much jacket removing today, no matter how virile the man.

At the thought of virile, her eyes went straight to Finn. Unlike her, he'd not had the luxury of sleeping late and, as a result, looked tired, with a pale, haggard appearance to his face. There'd been no time to talk, no time to catch him alone. Which she supposed was fine. She hadn't any idea what she'd say to him and was regretting not telling him about the proposal. Finn would know by now. Channing had never been any good at keeping secrets. Nor was Channing a gracious loser. He'd stayed back at the house today, warm and toasty next to the fire with Lady Alina while Finn had to keep up appearances as host out in the cold.

'This one,' Finn called out after looking over several possible logs. The men with him dragged over their tools and they set to work, a man at each end of the saw. It was heavy work cutting through a thick log, but Finn made it look easy.

'Catherine, are you in?' Alyson nudged her. 'We're wagering pennies on who will be the first to take off his coat.'

'I think it will be Lord Swale,' Jenny Brightly put in slyly. 'I hadn't noticed how divine he was until last night. He's so tall and those shoulders just go on for ever.' She gave a dramatic shudder.

Meredith came to the rescue. 'I have to bet on Marcus.' But the diversion wasn't enough. Meredith shot Catherine an apologetic look. Every female there wanted to talk about Finn: his shoulders, his long legs, the dark brooding stare he was wont to wear. One girl went so far as to speculate she wouldn't mind if he spouted Latin phrases while he kissed her.

'He's so mysterious.'

'You know what they say about the quiet types.' The other girls laughed as if they knew the answer. They wouldn't be laughing if they did. They were wrong, of course. Finn was much more than the sum of his physical parts, much more than broad shoulders and brooding stares. If they knew Finn at all they'd know he was committed to family, that he loved animals, that he climbed apple trees to rescue a scared little girl who had disobeyed him when he himself had a dreadful fear of heights. And they would know he smiled. At least he did when he was with her.

'Catherine?' Meredith said softly at her side, jolting her out of her thoughts. 'Are you all right?' But Meredith answered her own question, her eyes travelling the path of Catherine's gaze to where Finn and Marcus worked the saw and back. 'Oh, my dear, you love him.'

'Yes, I'm afraid so.' Catherine was very much afraid of what loving Finn would mean. It would mean leaving. A rapid plan formed in her mind. She would go back to Paris as soon as Christmas had passed. She couldn't stay here and watch him court another, marry another. Catherine knew what it meant. It would mean spending the rest of her life alone or settling for a marriage that was less than what she wanted.

'It will be all right,' Meredith intoned the necessary words.

'I doubt anything will ever be all right again.'

Meredith squeezed her arm. 'It will, trust me. I felt the same way with Marcus. Things will come out right in the end.'

But Catherine didn't think so.

She still wasn't convinced as she dressed for the evening trip to the chapel in a warm walking costume of deep-blue merino wool. Finn had to marry someone better than she and he would do it because of the thing she admired so very much in him—family before self.

It was Christmas Eve, the most magical night of the year, the one night she looked forward to above all other nights. But tonight the magic was missing. Catherine wished she could feel it. She'd hoped coming downstairs to join the gathering in the drawing room would lift her spirits. There was no reason to be glum. The drawing room was a picture-perfect image of holiday cheer.

The Yule log was in the giant hearth, burning brightly and warmly. A huge buffet of cold meats and breads was laid out, mugs of mulled wine were in the hands of the gentlemen who had cut the log and everyone else's spirits were high. All about her was the merriment of the season. Meredith laughed up at Marcus, her face reflecting her joy. Alyson clung to Jameson Ellis's arm with shy pride. Lord Richard smiled a greeting at her and she almost recoiled.

Catherine could hear her mother's voice in her head: *the youngest son of a marquess is quite a match for a gently bred girl, much higher than we could have hoped for.* Beside Lord Richard, his sister positively beamed, looking well in a cranberry ensemble trimmed in white fur. Catherine's stomach pitched. Lady Eliza knew something, anticipated something. Catherine knew it instantly. Lady Eliza expected an offer. All at once, pieces fell into place. Lady Eliza hadn't come down to the village and neither had Finn. Finn had talked of desire and duty in the sleigh. It seemed the supreme confirmation that her mother had been right. She was the desire, Lady Eliza the duty, not the Caribbean and the earldom.

Catherine swallowed hard and tried to hide her growing disappointment. Soon, they'd bundle into coats and set off for the church. Maybe she could pray for a miracle. Guilt struck her for such a selfish thought on such a holy night, but the thought was there all the same.

Finn sat in the family pew, his mind swamped with guilt of all types: guilty pleasures, guilty thoughts. The guilty pleasure was his covert and somewhat dangerous effort to catch sight of Catherine across the aisle in the Emerson pew, an effort which required him to move his head without leaning forwards and setting his clothes on fire.

The latter was proving harder to do than one might expect given he had years of experience. Passing the light was a long-standing Christmas Eve ritual at the Deverill midnight service, the church taking on a peaceful cast as unlit candle after unlit candle was bent to the light of the lit candle next to it and so on until the place looked ethereal.

This year the peace of the candles did not have their usual effect on him. His thoughts were *not* centred on the vicar's Christmas reading of the story from Luke or on the familiar hymns. His thoughts were centred most firmly on Catherine, even if he couldn't quite see her in full, yet another source of guilt. His feelings had shamed her. He'd broken the most cardinal of rules instilled in him by his father when he'd come of age for women: treat women with respect. Never take from her what you cannot give back should the need arise to return it.

A more literal sort would think of this advice only as an approach to dealing with virgins and it was for the Channings of the world. But it was also more. Women had other items to guard beyond maidenheads. They had pride and they had reputations. He'd imperiled Catherine's reputation last night with that dance. He'd not liked his mother taking him to task over it, but she'd been right to do it. Although he had not needed the reminder. He'd known the moment the dance had ended what he'd done.

But how could he have done differently? Finn leaned forwards, catching a glimpse of Catherine's profile, of her auburn hair long and sleek in the candlelight, the light dancing across her fine features, the delicate curve of her jaw, and the perfect slope of her nose. He liked to think she felt his stare in that moment. She looked his way and smiled, then made a brief, panicked gesture at his coat. He pulled the candle away just in time to escape a singeing. He gave her a quick grin back and shrugged.

He was doing that a lot lately. Grinning. Smiling. Catherine brought it out in him, he supposed. His mistress had thought he never smiled. Perhaps he'd not had a reason to smile. But now that he had one, he had to figure out what to do about it. He knew what he wanted. It was just that it had happened so fast.

The vicar gave the signal for all to rise for the last hymn, 'Adeste Fideles', his favorite. Finn let the lines of the beloved song swell and echo around him. The congregation sang it in Latin, of course. There he went, smiling again.

The congregation began filing out during the last verse and Finn felt his father at his side, his voice low and supportive. 'Go to her, my son. If she's what you want, nothing on earth will be able to stop you.' Finn heard more than saw the smile in his father's voice. 'Don't worry about the haste of things. Who can explain love once it happens? Besides, she's practically been one of us since she was eight and could walk over. If you love her, she will be a credit to you and to all of us.'

Finn clasped his father's hand. 'Thank you.' It was a blessing, a confirmation. He'd spent the afternoon closeted with his father, talking it over, making his case more to himself than to his father. He wanted to be sure, for Catherine's sake. Over his father's shoulder his mother smiled softly, her eyes sparkling with gentle tears.

Finn let the others move ahead. He waited until Catherine

stepped into the aisle and approached the Emersons. 'Might I walk you back, Catherine?' he asked quietly.

The eyes that searched his face were worried. He wanted to erase that concern. What did she imagine he had to say? 'I'd like that.' Catherine stepped away from her parents before they could answer for her. She slipped an arm through his and let him lead her away, careful not to light any clothing on fire with their flames.

Outside, they blew out their candles. 'Make a wish, Catherine,' Finn whispered, closing his own eyes and blowing out the flame.

'That's only for birthday candles,' Catherine corrected.

'I think Christmas candles count too,' Finn argued softly. He drew her apart from the crowd gathering and dispersing in the churchyard. It was too cold for anyone to linger for long, but for now, the crisp air felt good after the heat of bodies in the church. Overhead the sky was midnight velvet pierced by the diamond sparkle of stars—a silent night, a holy night, a night of love and for love.

'I need to tell you why I didn't come on the Yule log cutting this afternoon.'

Catherine paled, her eyes going to the toes of her boots where they peeked from beneath her dress. 'I thought so. You seemed like you had something on your mind when you picked me up yesterday.' She looked up and bit her lip.

'I did. It's not something a man shares easily or without risk and I needed more time to work up my courage, I suppose.'

'I've never known you to need any more courage than what you already had.' Catherine gave him a half-smile, although he could see the effort cost her. Whatever she thought was coming, she was trying to make it easy for him. 'You were brave enough the day you climbed the apple tree. I might still be up there.'

Finn gave a short laugh. 'I was very scared that day. I don't like heights, you know.'

She smiled, a little wider this time, and nudged him in the ribs with her elbow. 'I know and you did it anyway.'

Over her shoulder he was aware of Lady Eliza staring, her cheeks flushed before his mother put an arm about her and led her away to a sleigh. Catherine turned and followed his gaze.

'Did you have something to tell me about Lady Eliza?' Catherine prompted. 'A happy announcement, perhaps?' Finn could hear the strangled pain and he understood. She'd thought he'd come to tell her he was marrying Lady Eliza. Some of the guilt he felt in the church came racing back. He'd not meant to hurt Catherine. Oh, how differently she must see events than he did! The realisation galvanized him into action.

'I'm not going to marry her,' Finn said, relishing the relief that flooded Catherine's face. 'I'm going to marry you. If you'll have me,' he added. He rushed on. 'I know it's only been a few days, but really we've known each other for a lifetime, if you think about it. It's not all that strange. We don't have to go on expeditions if you'd rather not. I don't know if I can stop spouting inconvenient Latin phrases, but I can try. We—'

Catherine put a hand to his lips. 'Wait, let me answer. You don't have to explain anything. Yes. Yes, I will marry you and, no, you don't have to stop the Latin phrases. They're a part of you. I don't care if we go or stay, I just want to be with you, wherever you are.' Then she was crying. 'I thought...'

'I know what you thought.' Finn gripped her gloved hands between his. 'I didn't mean for you to think that. Please, Catherine, don't cry any more.'

She looked up at him. 'I love you, Finn Deverill.'

'*Te amo,* Catherine. *I* love *you*,' Finn said, enunciating each word carefully because when a man tells a woman he loves her for the first time, he wants to remember it his whole life. When that man was Finn Deverill, he wanted to remember it in English and Latin.

They were alone in the churchyard. Far ahead of them, the sounds of carols drifted back from the sleighs. Assured of their solitude, Finn bent his mouth to hers and kissed her, once for love, twice for for ever under the Christmas sky. When he'd wondered what the holidays held in store for him, he'd never imagined this, but the things one *can't* imagine often make the best gifts of all for precisely that reason.

* * * * *

The Captain's Christmas Angel

—

Margaret McPhee

Dear Reader,

Christmas is a time for hope and trust. It is a time when the magical sparkle of miracles is in the air, and also a time when people travel far to celebrate with family and friends. These four separate strands weave together in *The Captain's Christmas Angel*.

I was inspired to write the story while I was watching seals play in the sea and spotted an open-water swimmer in the distance. I did a double take through my binoculars but I wasn't imagining it; some hardy soul had braved the chilly water of the Firth of Clyde for a swim. It set me thinking of a man alone and close to drowning in the middle of the ocean, and the woman who spots him from the deck of a passing sailing ship. The man became Daniel Alexander, the hero in *The Captain's Christmas Angel,* and the woman, Sarah Ellison, my heroine. And I got to write another story about the sea, which I love! I love its smell, the way its colors reflect the sky, and the speed and diversity of its changing moods.

I would like to thank Jim Allen for all his help and advice on nautical matters, and for answering my numerous questions with patience and good humor. Any mistakes are my own and I hope that Jim and all other mariners, past and present, will forgive me the liberties that I've taken for the sake of romance.

So here is Sarah and Daniel's story, of love and miracles and angels, at this special time of year. May your Christmas be happy, and may your own tall, dark and handsome First Footer bring you all the very best for the New Year! You can find out more about my writing at www.margaretmcphee.co.uk.

With warmest wishes for the season,

Margaret McPhee

DEDICATION

For Helen—hope you like the extra special hero!

Chapter One

November 1807

The sun was low in the clear winter sky as Sarah Ellison scanned the expanse of ocean before her. Water lapped against the bow of the boat, making a rhythmic slap against the planks of oak, and the rock of the vessel was slow and easy. Sarah's stomach began to settle. She breathed in the cool fresh sea air, tasting the tang of saltiness against her lips, and felt glad that she had abandoned the cramped, dim cabin below.

A chill wind was blowing, playing with the ribbons of her bonnet and nipping at her cheeks. In the distance the water was as pale and smooth as the blue silk that made up her favourite evening dress, but closer it dulled to grey and crowned small waves white. She contemplated the journey that lay ahead, crossing the Atlantic Ocean to take her back to England, and knew so late in the year a poor choice for a good crossing. But Sarah had every wish to be gone from New York before Christmas.

She looked again into the distance. The vastness of the ocean soothed her. The water was polished like a looking glass, its surface unbroken save for one small dark shape. Her eye focused on the shape. She peered harder, wondering what it was—a whale or dolphin, or, more likely, a seabird. But it was none of those things. The realisation kicked her heart to a gallop. With a gasp she turned, calling as she ran.

'Mr Seymour! There is a man in the water! Over there, in the distance!'

James Seymour, the sea-worn first mate, glanced where she pointed, removed his pipe from his mouth and regarded her with an expression of weary patience. 'The *Angel* has carried many passengers alongside her cargo in her crossings of the North Atlantic and you would be surprised at just how many of them fancy they see men, and more, within this here ocean. Rest assured, ma'am, there's nothin' out there save the fishes.'

Sarah's eyes swivelled to where the shape had bobbed. There was only the endless stretch of water.

'Just a trick of the light, ma'am.' Mr Seymour turned away.

Sarah's gaze returned again to the empty waves. She saw him then, quite clearly in the distance. There could be no mistake. 'No!' she cried. 'Look!'

Mr Seymour peered at where she pointed and, with an exclamation beneath his breath, was off and bellowing for the captain.

Sarah kept her gaze on the man. Each time he slipped beneath the surface the breath caught in her throat, only releasing when he bobbed up again.

His arm raised, reaching towards her.

Sarah responded, reaching to him, as if their two hands could meet, as if she alone could save him.

'Hold on,' she whispered, knowing that he would not hear even had she screamed it at the top of her voice. The distance was too great, the wind too strong.

In the background, voices shouted amidst the clatter of the crew's footsteps. Wood creaked, ropes slid, canvas billowed and cracked in the wind. The *Angel* was changing course, tacking into the wind so that she might reach the stranger.

'Hold on. Just a little longer,' she willed the man. 'We're coming.'

The schooner crept closer, defying the wind to reach him.

As the distance diminished she saw him more clearly. Dark hair, slick and sodden. A pale face. A white linen shirt that both clung and swirled in the water. He tried to swim, but his strength was spent and the current too strong.

'Please God…' Sarah prayed. 'Please.' It was all she could do other than stand helpless and watch his struggle while the jolly boat was lowered on to the waves.

Two men rowed out to fetch him, catching hold of him, pulling him and a gallon of seawater into the little boat, bringing him back to the *Angel* and safety.

The sailors quietened, the murmur of voices dropping away. She was right there when they laid him on the wooden deck.

Even laying his length she could tell he was a tall man, used to activity and well formed. His feet were bare, his dark breeches hugged tight around the muscled length of his legs. He wore neither coat nor waistcoat, only the white shirt transparent against the flesh of his chest and gaping wide at the nakedness of his throat.

Her eyes slid higher to his face. Her heart stumbled and missed a beat, then raced all the faster. His eyes, which were staring into hers, were the colour of the ocean from which they had fished him, pale and blue and piercing. Something arced between them. Something that Sarah had never felt before. Time stood still. Seconds became aeons. Until, eventually, his eyes flickered shut and he was gone. Even then she could not look away, but continued to stare at the pale skin that glistened with water and the dark hair slicked back smooth… and the bloody gash that stood jagged and stark at the edge of his forehead.

Her mouth was dry as a desert. 'Is he…?' The words faltered against lips that were almost as bloodless as his. Her fingers curled tight, the nails cutting into her palms.

The captain glanced up, noticing her for the first time. 'This isn't a sight for a lady's eyes, Mrs Ellison. We need to get him below and warmed up if he's to survive. You should return to your cabin, ma'am.'

But she could not move. Her eyes returned to the man who lay so limp and still upon the damp deck, seawater seeping from his clothing.

'Mrs Ellison…' Captain Davies urged.

It took real will-power to walk away. 'Of course, sir.' With a nod of her head she returned to her niece and maid in the cabin below, but in her mind remained the image of a man who had defied death in the Atlantic ocean on a cold November day.

The first thing that Daniel Alexander became aware of was the pounding in his head. In those initial few seconds he thought that he was still aboard the *Viper*, held captive by Higgs. But as the foggy confusion cleared he remembered the events of those last hours and exactly what Higgs had done.

Somehow, Higgs had failed. God only knew how.

Daniel kept his eyes shut and tried to gauge his surroundings. There were voices, two men talking quietly. He listened.

'There was naught on him to give a clue to his identity,' said the first voice.

'Well, he'll no doubt tell us who he is and what exactly he was doin' floatin' around out there all covered in bruises and cuts…if he ain't lost his memory, that is,' replied the second, with a West Country accent.

'As like he cracked his head when he was up the riggin' on watch. Probably went into the water while it was still dark. No one to see him, if the rest of the crew were asleep.'

The other—older, if the gravel of his voice was anything to go by—man snorted. 'If he'd been in the water that long he'd be dead. And he's no ordinary seaman. Look at his hands.'

Daniel knew they would be staring down at him.

'He's a gent, that one.'

'Then what the hell was he doin' swimmin' in the Atlantic?'

'Now that's the question, lad.'

Daniel had heard enough. Whoever the men were, they neither worked for Higgs nor knew who he was. Ignoring the ache in his head, he cracked his eyes open and looked up at the men. One was perhaps thirty years his senior, grey-haired, sinewy, a man who had spent his life at sea. The other was a youngster, perhaps eighteen years of age, fair-haired and fresh-faced.

'So you're awake at last.' It was the older man that spoke. The boy just stared with curiosity.

'Where am I?'

'Aboard the *Angel*,' said the same man.

'The *Angel*?' Daniel's accent was soft in comparison to theirs, his voice, weak. Indeed, he felt as if something had chewed him up and spat him out.

'A merchant schooner, under Captain John Davies, that transports cargo between America to England. I'm the first mate, James Seymour.'

Daniel gave a nod and then wished that he hadn't. The pain in his head intensified to make him feel nauseous.

'Head hurt?' Seymour asked.

'Like the de'il himself were pounding upon it.'

'And it'll get worse before it gets better.' The man gave a grunt. 'So, you're a Scotsman, are you?'

'The last time I looked.'

Seymour cracked a smile, then gestured to Daniel's head. 'Nasty bump that is. Hit it before you went into the water, did you?'

Trust no one. The words whispered again in Daniel's mind and he knew, after Higgs, that he would listen to them. There was no way of knowing which men or ships were involved.

Daniel shrugged. 'Came to in the water with no sign of the ship.'

'Best fetch the captain,' Seymour instructed.

The boy returned with a man who was squat and packed with power. His eyes were sharp as he offered Daniel his hand.

'Captain Davies of MS *Angel*. And you are?'

'Alexander, Daniel Alexander.' To his relief no one gave a flicker of recognition at the name.

Captain Davies wasted no time in pleasantries. 'Oakley here tells me you were knocked overboard in an accident.'

Daniel said nothing.

'From which ship?'

'*Miss Lively.*' It was the name of a merchant ship Daniel had had dealings with in the recent past. Lawful cargo and passengers were not the only things *Miss Lively* carried.

Davies didn't even pause to think about it. 'Never heard of her. Have you, Mr Seymour?'

Seymour shook his head.

'I thought they would realise I was missing and come back for me.' The naivety of his statement fitted the part that Daniel was trying to play.

Davies did not correct him.

'With my business in New York concluded I meant to travel to London and thus paid passage to Plymouth with Captain Murchie on *Miss Lively.*' Daniel could feel the fatigue tugging at him and kept the deception as simple as possible.

'Murchie?' Captain Davies's eyes narrowed as he tried to place the name.

Seymour slid a look at the captain. 'Friendly with Jim Walker was Mr Murchie.'

'I see.' Davies did not pursue the matter, just as Daniel had anticipated. Walker had gone to the gallows for smuggling.

'I owe you and your crew my thanks, Captain Davies.' Daniel fought the urge to close his eyes. 'Mr Seymour said you are for Plymouth. I will, of course, pay my passage in full, if you do not mind waiting until we reach England. At this minute I find myself without funds.'

'I'll wait, sir. But it is Mrs Ellison, not me, who deserves your gratitude for she spotted you in the water and raised the alarm.'

Mrs Ellison. The angel in a dying man's dream. Except he had not imagined her.

'Your wife, sir?'

'My passenger. A respectable widow of four years, travelling to Plymouth with her niece.'

'Then I will be sure to offer my thanks to the lady.' The words sounded slow and stilted. He wondered if his mouth and his brain were still connected.

The Captain nodded. 'If you will excuse me, Mr Alexander.' Davies left, taking Seymour and the boy with him.

Daniel could no longer defy the darkness that was creeping to claim him. But in the gloom he saw the face of the angel again and he smiled.

Three days passed before Sarah saw the man again.

She was taking the air with ten-year-old Imelda and their maid, Fanny. As the only passengers on the schooner Captain Davies allowed them to come up on deck as they pleased, weather permitting.

The sky was grey-white, the water, cold and choppy and dark. The wind was stiff and unremitting, blowing its damp chill through every nook and cranny of the boat. Yet still Sarah sought it out at every opportunity.

'I think I see something over there!' Since the rescue of the man they had learned was a businessman returning to London from New York, Imelda still had not given up hope of spotting something equally exciting in the water.

'It is just the wind on the waves, Imelda.' Sarah stared out at the place to which her niece pointed.

'I bet that's what Mr Seymour said to you when you saw Mr Alexander in the water.'

Sarah gave a wry smile and breathed in another lungful of air.

'Perhaps it is another of Mr Alexander's pirate crew.' Imelda had spent the past week reading *An Investigation into Monsters, Myths and Villains of the Oceans* and so was obsessed with the idea that the rescued man was a pirate. 'They have hatched a ploy to sneak on to the *Angel* one by one.' Imelda was warming to her theme. She had read the chapter on pirates twice already. 'They mean to rob us and make us walk the plank. And we will be eaten by sharks.'

Fanny's eyes slid to Sarah's and the women exchanged smiles before Fanny answered the little girl. 'Do you really think so, Miss Imelda?'

'Of course, why else would Mr Alexander be in the Atlantic ocean waiting to be rescued by the *Angel*? I tell you he is a pirate captain with a plan to steal our jewels.'

A deep masculine voice sounded. 'My, I cannot help but notice what a very pretty bracelet you are wearing, miss.'

The three figures spun round. Imelda gave a shriek of horror, Fanny's face flushed puce, and Sarah found herself looking into the eyes of the man she had last seen lying half-drowned upon the deck.

'Forgive me if I startled you,' he said, 'but as there is no one to introduce us I find I must introduce myself.'

Imelda and Fanny were staring at him, eyes like saucers. Sarah felt like doing the same.

He was a devastatingly handsome man. Now that it was dry, his hair was a light ashen brown, cut short and feathered in the wind. His nose was strong and straight, his mouth, both determined and sensual, with a hint of amusement about it. He was taller than she had anticipated, and the borrowed brown coat he was wearing was too tight across his broad shoulders. Fortunately the clean white shirt beneath it decently covered his chest this time and he was wearing a dark neckcloth. Sarah swallowed.

'I am Daniel Alexander.' His soft Scottish lilt stroked against her ear to the nape of her neck and all the way down her spine. He bowed. 'And I am very pleased to meet you, at last.'

Sarah ignored the increased patter of her heart and curtsied. 'I am glad to make your acquaintance, Mr Alexander.' She met his gaze with a cool calmness she did not feel. 'I am Mrs Ellison and this is my niece, Miss Bowden.'

Imelda appeared to have been struck dumb and motionless.

'Imelda,' prompted Sarah.

Imelda dropped a hurried curtsy.

'It seems that I owe you my life and my thanks, Mrs Ellison.' He extended his hand to shake hers.

Her eyes took in his lack of gloves, and the long bare fingers, making her heart speed all the more. She hesitated, but knew she could not refuse to shake his hand.

His clear blue eyes were calm and steady and smiling as she finally grasped just the tip of his fingers. Even through the kid leather of her gloves his touch was warm and disturbing, sending tingles of awareness all the way up her arm.

'I did no more than any person would have done.' She withdrew her hand too quickly, turning to the ocean view once more, both to hide her embarrassment and to terminate the conversation.

But Mr Daniel Alexander was not so easily dismissed. 'Not according to Captain Davies.'

'Captain Davies is too kind.' She allowed just enough of an edge to her voice—of reserve and distance. She kept her gaze fixed on the grey-blue waves with their white-flecked heads.

From the corner of her eye she saw him smile. 'Then I must be thankful that your eyesight is so keen and your powers of persuasion so determined.'

She said nothing, just stared out to the sea, waiting for him to leave, but much to her consternation Mr Alexander showed no sign of leaving. The silence stretched until Sarah was embarrassed by her rudeness to the man who had come so close to death.

Unable to bear it any longer, she glanced round at him, her eyes moving over the bandage fixed upon his forehead and the fading bruising on his cheekbone and jawline. 'Are you recovered from your accident, sir?'

'Very well recovered, thank you.' His voice was easy. He smiled again. A self-assured smile. A smile that made her stomach flutter with nerves and other things. *Oh Lord!* She was *not* attracted to him.

She gave a curt nod and turned back to the safety of the ocean. The civilities had been exchanged. He should walk away now.

There was another silence in which only the wind blew and the water slapped against the boat.

'Are you travelling on from Plymouth, Mrs Ellison?'

'I am, sir.' She glanced across, meeting his eyes, and holding them with the clear message, *Go away, sir. I have no wish to converse with you, or tell you anything of myself.*

But Mr Daniel Alexander's gaze was unfazed. Indeed, she could see in it something that looked like amusement.

'We are for Bowden, near Totnes in Devon. My Aunt Sarah is returning me to my family for Christmas. I stayed on a little longer after their recent visit to my aunt's home in New York.'

Sarah suppressed the sigh.

'I'm sure you must be looking forward to the reunion, Miss Bowden.' His eyes were laughing, even though his mouth was all politeness.

Imelda's face was a picture of honesty. 'Immensely so.' She grinned, before hastily adding, 'Not that I would not have enjoyed Christmas in New York. I loved staying with my aunt.'

'Naturally.' Then, with a look at Sarah that said he knew he was baiting her, asked, 'So, how long have you lived in New York, Mrs Ellison?'

'Some years.'

He smiled. 'And yet your accent…'

'Is as unAmerican as yours,' she finished.

Their eyes duelled across the small distance, his with provoking merriment, hers, with a coolness she was finding increasingly difficult to maintain.

'Your voice does sound funny.' Imelda peered up at him. 'Where are you from, Mr Alexander?'

'Young ladies do not ask such questions,' Sarah warned.

'Do not scold the lass. She has a natural curiosity, and my accent *is* different from most she will hear in Devon or

New York.' He looked at Imelda. 'I'm from the Highlands of Scotland.'

'A Scottish pirate!' Imelda breathed with something akin to reverence.

Sarah felt the blush warm her cheeks. 'Imelda!'

'Indeed, but let that be our secret, Miss Bowden.' He lowered his voice, 'You'll help me keep a look out for any of those Royal Navy ships that come to catch me?'

'Or your own pirate ship come to fetch you?' Imelda nodded. 'I will start straight away.'

'I am in your debt, Miss Bowden.' He bowed a deep formal bow.

Imelda dipped a low, wobbly curtsy.

Only then did he meet Sarah's gaze again, with the hint of a smile playing about his lips. 'I will leave you to enjoy the peace, Mrs Ellison.' With a bow he walked away.

Sarah turned her back and faced out to the ocean once more, but her sense of peace had gone, shattered by the tall handsome Highlander. She was too aware that there were two more weeks to go before they reached Plymouth and, short of staying in her cabin, it was going to be very difficult to avoid meeting him again.

Daniel's thoughts were on Mrs Ellison as he made his way to the small cabin that had been assigned to him. She was different from other women, most of whom were only too willing to talk, to flirt…and more. That slight standoffishness and prickly demeanour determinedly sent the message that she was not available, not interested. He smiled at that, remembering the transparency of her feelings before she had reluctantly agreed to shake his hand.

She was a very attractive woman. Too young to be a widow. Tall with silky dark hair and velvet brown eyes that hinted at passion and secrets hidden beneath that aloof respectability. And beautiful—perhaps not in the conventional sense of the word, but there was something about her that rendered her unforgettable. As if he ever could. Her image had been impressed upon his mind since he had seen her across the waves, standing on the *Angel*'s deck. Though Daniel had much more important things to be thinking about than a woman. Things that meant the difference between life and death. Things like Higgs.

The cabin door closed behind him. Sitting himself down at the little table, he put Mrs Ellison from his mind, dipped the pen in the inkwell and wrote the letter.

It was a letter he hoped would never be needed, but one that was a necessary insurance were the worst to happen. And as for Higgs... Daniel's eyes narrowed with deadly intent. Until he reached England there was not a lot he could do about Higgs. The ship's progress to the English coast was out of his hands; he could not will the wind to blow her there faster, no matter how much he wished it. For now, he was stuck here on the *Angel*, with the beautiful Mrs Ellison.

Had he not been up to his neck in this mess... Had she not been the woman who saved his life... Had it been any other time of year... Daniel Alexander shook his head and smiled at the irony of it. Fate could be both merciful and cruel in the games that she played upon a man.

Chapter Two

The moon was a silver crescent high in the sky when Sarah wiped the cold sweat from her face and sat the chamber pot aside, resting a little as the latest bout of retching subsided. The remnants of the evening's paltry meal had long since been emptied from her stomach. At this rate she wondered if she would survive another fortnight and could only be thankful that Imelda and Fanny, sound asleep in the next cabin, were not here to witness the worst of it. The *Angel* heaved upon the waves and Sarah's stomach followed suit. A quiet moan escaped her lips and, unable to bear it a moment longer, she rose from the bed, grabbed her cloak and lantern and quietly slipped from the tiny cabin.

Up on deck the wind was howling, catching beneath the long dark lengths of her cloak to billow it like wings on her back, and snatching the ribbon that secured her hair from the nape of her neck to set it free. The cold air nipped at her face, chasing away the nausea that roiled in her stomach. She breathed in great gulps of it, relishing the freshness, and with her lantern swaying in the wind, made her way to the bulwarks.

Gone was the smooth pale stretch of water. In its place was something dark and fierce and alive. The sea spray stung against her cheeks, the wind's chill was like a knife through her dress and cloak, but she welcomed it. The cold heat in her head receded. The constant background roar of the ocean was louder up here than in the tiny cabin below, competing with the wind to fill her ears and yet still she heard the tiny noise and glanced in its direction. The dark figure was leaning against the bulwark only a few feet away.

She jumped and sucked in a small shriek.

'Forgive me if I startled you, Mrs Ellison.'

'Mr Alexander,' she breathed. In the lantern light his face was all harsh planes and angles, dangerously handsome.

'I did not expect company,' he said.

'Nor I.' His presence made her glance behind to the hatch that would take her back down to the safety of her cabin below, the cabin in which the buck of the ship seemed so much worse. Her nausea rose just at the thought. She swallowed hard and dismissed any idea of leaving.

She gripped a hand to the top of the bulwark to steady herself, staring out at the blackness beyond, breathing deep to halt the sickness, swallowing again and again, determined not to reveal such weakness in front of him.

A large wave rolled beneath. The *Angel* dipped and kicked.

Sarah's stomach reacted. The lantern slipped from her fingers to crash upon the deck as she leaned over the side and retched for all she was worth.

A strong arm fixed itself around her waist. A hand captured her wild flail of hair into a tail and held it secure. Daniel Alexander stood behind her.

'What…?' She tried to speak, tried to pull away, but the sickness was too pressing and the man too strong. 'Oh, dear God…' Her stomach heaved again.

'Easy, lass,' he soothed by her ear. 'Any ocean can have a slyness to it. The waves are not always what you think and I've no mind to lose you over the side. One of us having a winter dip is enough to be getting on with.' His grip was gentle but unyielding.

She stopped fighting both him and the sickness.

'Breathe,' that Highland lilt instructed. And again, so soft and soothing, 'Breathe.'

And she obeyed. One breath of the bracing air, and then another, until eventually the nausea passed, leaving her spent and embarrassed.

'You can release me,' she murmured. 'I'm all right now.'

He loosed his arm slowly as if he did not trust her words, moved to stand by her side, but stayed close. The wind caught at her freed hair, streaming it to dance long and wild. All her efforts to catch it back met only with minimal success.

'Is it just at night that you suffer the seasickness?'

She shook her head and some more hair escaped. She gave up and let it billow free in the night. 'I have felt sick since the moment we sailed out of New York. But it is worse at night.'

'Sometimes it is the way of it.'

She closed her eyes and took a deep breath as another wave of nausea clenched tight at her stomach. 'Being up on deck helps. The fresh air, the openness…'

'But this will help more.' Through the darkness his hand took hers to press a small pouch into it. 'Crystallised ginger.'

'Just the thought of eating…' She swallowed down the retch that threatened.

'One piece, three times a day.'

A large wave reached up the bulwark to spray them both.

Sarah gave a sharp intake of air and backed away. 'I will leave you to your contemplations.'

'Shall we, Mrs Ellison?' She sensed his movement to escort her.

'I am quite capable of making my own way, sir.'

'I am quite sure that you are.' Again that smile in his voice. The high lantern on the mast caught the glint of the glass as he passed her her own expired lantern.

She looked to where the hatch should be and saw only shadowed shapes.

'But I am finished my contemplations for the night.'

There was a tiny silence before she tucked her fingers

within his arm, yielding to what she told herself was only common sense, and let him guide her through the darkness all the way to her cabin door.

'Goodnight, Mrs Ellison.'

He turned and, heading for his own cabin, disappeared into the blackness.

She stood there until she heard the quiet open and closing again of his door before she slipped within her own.

Sarah was standing at her favourite spot out on deck. The waves were not too high nor the wind too strong. A fine smirr of rain was slowly wetting the wool of her cloak, but she did not mind. It was not the nausea she was escaping this morning. She touched a hand to her pocket and Daniel Alexander's pouch of crystalline ginger—it had worked a magic just as he had said. Down below Fanny was dressing Imelda's hair while Imelda imagined stories of Mr Alexander's pirate past. Sarah had no wish to hear of any more of the tall handsome Scotsman—even aside from last night and the memory of what he had witnessed.

He disturbed her in a way she had sworn never to let any man disturb her again. Not after Robert, and not after Brandon Taverner, who had brought back all those awful feelings she had thought finally laid to rest. She swallowed and it seemed she could still taste something of the bitterness, of the hurt and the shame. The memories from across those years, stirred up afresh, haunted her even now, standing here, looking out at the expanse before her, of sky and ocean merged in shades of sombre grey. They made her strong. They made her determined. They made her turn away from men like Daniel Alexander.

One breath and then another, focusing on the here and now, on the damp-chilled air with its tang of salt and seaweed. Closing her eyes, she let the wind blow the memories away so that she did not think, but only felt this moment. And there was peace in that.

Footsteps sounded behind her. The nape of her neck tingled and a shiver rippled down the length of her spine, banishing the peace. She did not have to open her eyes to know the man's identity.

He was standing at the bulwark some distance away, looking out at her view of the ocean.

'Mr Alexander.'

'Mrs Ellison'—that soft lilt of the Highlands that made her name sound like a lover's upon his lips. She blushed at the thought.

'Do you mind if I join you in your view?'

Yes, she minded! Because she had no interest in encouraging any gentleman. Especially not gentlemen like him, men who made her feel… Made her feel nothing, she finished harshly. 'The view is all yours. I was just leaving.' Her voice was sharper because of the heat in her cheeks.

'And you have no mind to talk to me this morning.' He turned his face to look at her then, his eyes meeting hers.

She stopped, ashamed of her rudeness. He unnerved her. He made her behave in a way that would have had her mother turning in her grave. She took herself in hand. He was just a man like any other, and she would be polite. To be anything other would be an admission that he affected her. And he did not affect her. No man affected her any more. 'Forgive me, I did not mean to be so ill mannered.'

'Perfectly understandable. You are enjoying the peace and I am disturbing you.' He smiled as if he understood exactly how he disturbed her.

She returned to her original stance at the bulwark, keeping her eyes out on the gentle movement of the waves rather than on the man by her side. A small silence opened between them. 'Thank you for helping me last night when I was…unwell.' Her cheeks burned all the hotter.

'I was glad to have been of assistance.'

'The ginger is most effective.'

'So I see.'

She swallowed, but did not look round. 'Do you suffer with seasickness yourself?'

'Never. But I know many that do.'

She gave a little nod.

'You take a great risk in coming up here alone at night. One larger-than-expected wave and you could be swept overboard without a soul to know your fate.'

'Should I take the advice of a gentleman with a penchant for taking the midnight air and who ended up alone in the ocean?'

The flicker of a smile pulled at his lips. 'If you've a mind to take the midnight air any night, knock upon my cabin door and I will accompany you.'

She laughed at his sheer audacity. 'Just like that?'

'Just like that, Mrs Ellison.'

'Mr Alexander, I am not the sort of woman who goes knocking on a strange gentleman's cabin door in the middle of the night.'

His eyes met hers as if to say that was a shame. 'In that case, I'll wait for you on deck. Try not to drop the lantern this time.' He smiled.

She shook her head and tried to stifle her own answering smile. He was unbelievable.

'Enjoy the view, Mrs Ellison—undisturbed.' He smiled again and was gone.

But Sarah did not return her gaze to the view. Rather she watched the retreating back of Daniel Alexander and wondered at the ease with which he had just disarmed her and turned what should have been an awkward encounter into something else. It was only when he had gone and she looked once more at the ocean that she thought to question what a man who did not suffer from seasickness had been doing alone up on the deck in the middle of the night.

Daniel found Mrs Ellison at the larboard stern the next day, diametrically opposite her usual spot and hidden from casual view by the aft mast and wheel. He knew he should not have sought her out, but it seemed natural and harmless, and besides, he wanted to know why a woman like her had built her defences so strong and high.

'Are you hiding from someone, Mrs Ellison?'

'Not at all. Whatever gave you that impression?' The cool confident look had not been fixed in place quite quickly enough to mask her reaction to his approach.

So much for a man's ego. He smiled.

'It is beginning to rain, sir.' She made to leave.

'Are you about to tell me that you must rush away to the confinement of your cabin to which the rain...' he glanced across to the horizon where the sky was dark and heavy and blowing towards the *Angel* '...that will soon come in earnest will banish you for the rest of the day?'

She checked her movement. 'Your words persuade me otherwise.'

'Not the prospect of my company?'

A reluctant smile curved her lips and he felt something of her rigidity relax.

'You wound me, madam.'

'And yet I think you must feel the confinement worse than I.' Her eyes flickered over him. 'The top of *my* head brushes the ceiling.'

'One grows used to it over time, with the aid of a few bruises.'

Her focus shifted to the exposed, newly healing scar on his forehead.

'Although that is one more than I anticipated,' he murmured, then sought to steer the conversation away from that subject. 'No taking of the midnight air last night?' He teased, knowing he had ensured she would not risk that again.

She smiled, easier this time, and returned her gaze to the stretch of ocean once more. She was a woman who had been made to smile, yet he had the feeling that whatever life had dealt her, happiness was not foremost on the list.

They stood in silence watching the weather roll towards them.

'When do you return to America, Mrs Ellison?'

A shadow flitted across her face. 'I am not sure I will.' She glanced away, but not quickly enough to hide the unease in her eyes. 'It has been on my mind that I might move back to England for good.'

'You are not happy in New York?'

'Perfectly happy.' But she was lying—he could see it in the way she did not meet his gaze.

'Do you sail often for business, Mr Alexander?'

'Very often, indeed.'

'Even over Christmas?'

'Especially over Christmas.'

She met his gaze directly and this time there was nothing of the cold mask there. This time, it was as if she were allowing herself to look at him properly. She smiled again, a slightly shy smile, a warm smile. Whatever unhappiness she had left behind in New York was forgotten and he had no wish to remind her of it.

'How terrible.' She said it teasingly.

'Not so terrible, at all.' He leaned slightly closer. 'I confess to preferring it that way.'

'You do not like Christmas?'

'Not in the slightest.' He admitted it freely enough, as if it meant nothing.

'You are a cynic, sir.'

'Undoubtedly.'

She smiled and so, despite the topic, did he.

'Whereas Christmas is your favourite time of year, Mrs Ellison.'

'You are a mind reader, sir.'

They chuckled.

'We Scots prefer New Year.'

'New Year celebrations are paltry in comparison to Christmas.'

'Paltry? With the ceilidh dancing on Hogmanay? The first footing after the bells? And a fine feast on Ne'erday?'

'First footing? I have not heard of it.'

'After the stroke of midnight the first foot to cross your threshold sets your fortune for the year to come. A tall, dark-haired, handsome man brings the best luck. He carries with him a lump of coal that your hearth shall not grow cold, a black bun that your belly will not be empty and a dram of whisky to toast the New Year.'

'It does sound rather good.' She smiled and a little thinking line crinkled between her brows. 'But I still do not understand what there is to dislike of Christmas.'

'What is there to like?' he countered. 'You will not persuade me as to the merits of Christmas, Mrs Ellison.' So easily said and with a good nature that hid the darkness of that truth.

'Really?' There was a hint of mischief in her eyes, a glimpse of the woman she must have been before... Before what? 'Have you considered the snow?' She looked at ease. She looked happy and Sarah Ellison happy was a sight to warm any man's heart.

Daniel encouraged her all the more. 'Snow is an impediment to travel and transport. It argues against Christmas rather than in its favour.'

'Bah, humbug!'

'The point still lies with me,' he insisted.

'What of the song of red-breasted robins?'

'Annoying wee beasties.'

'Deep-green polished holly and evergreens and kissing boughs of mistletoe?'

'I concede I could perhaps be persuaded by the latter.'

'Roasted chestnuts and mince pies?'

'I'm warming further to the idea.'

'Christmas hymns sung loud with cheer?'

'You would change your mind were I to sing, Mrs Ellison.' Her smile widened. 'Gifts exchanged on Boxing Day?'

'Of what kind of gifts are we talking?'

She laughed, a woman's laughter, soft and pure after the harshness and stench of the days with Higgs. Like soothing fingers against a brow tense with knowledge he would rather not possess but could not forget. But when he was with Sarah Ellison he was not thinking of Higgs.

'Not to mention the mulled wine made by my own hands to my great-grandmother Bowden's recipe. I've a portmanteau full of the stuff. It is a most potent brew.'

'Now you're bringing out the big guns. Mulled wine, indeed.'

She smiled. 'Have I won the challenge and convinced you?'

'No, lass,' he said quietly and shadows from the past stirred when he would have left them undisturbed. And even though he wanted to keep her smiling, and even though he was already lying to her, that was one lie he could not bring himself to tell. 'That's a challenge you'll never win.'

The blue of her bonnet had grown damp from the drizzle and the ribbons that tied it no longer fluttered, but stuck to her neck. The fading of her smile was soft and gradual, but the unhappiness did not return, nor were the barricades re-erected. Instead, her eyes studied his in the silence, as if she could see something of those things he kept hidden deep and dark within. Daniel turned his gaze away and felt a relief that the rainclouds opening in full meant the end of the conversation.

She was a widow of nine and twenty.

He was a man she scarcely knew. The wrong sort of man. She only ever attracted the wrong sort of man—scoundrels, men who lied and cheated, men who were never what they said they were. And yet that look in his eyes when they had spoken of Christmas… She shook her head, knowing the rawness she had seen there was something she had never seen in any man's eyes before. It touched her to the core. A man with such depths in his eyes couldn't be like Robert. Could he? She frowned at the direction her thoughts were taking.

She was here to take Imelda home and escape another wrong sort of man, not enter into some flirtation. And yet... She bit her lip, not wanting to admit the truth even to herself.

Daniel Alexander wanted her. She could see it in his eyes, and in a way the knowledge repaired something of the tattered shreds of her self-confidence. All those years of humiliation, all those times she had held her head high in the best of New York's drawing rooms and ballrooms, pretending she did not see the knowing looks or hear the whispers. Robert had not even had the decency to be discreet. All the doubts came crowding back, all the fears.

In the small peering glass fixed on the cabin wall, Sarah checked her hair for the tenth time and then chided herself for doing so. She should be steering well clear of him, not going up there to meet him—again. But she would go today, just as she had gone all the others, because when she was with him he made her forget all of those shadows and insecurities. Because he made her feel as if the darkness of the past had never been. And what was wrong with a few days of that? Whatever she thought of men in general, of relationships and sex and marriage, this was nothing of any of those. This was nothing but a journey home, a journey conducted in front of a captain and his crew, a journey in which nothing could happen.

'You like him, don't you?' Imelda grinned.

'If you are referring to Mr Alexander, I barely know the man enough to say whether my sentiments towards him are those of like and dislike. But we must, as ladies, contrive to behave in a civil manner to all persons at all times.' Lord, that sounded pompous!

Imelda was not dissuaded. 'He likes you, too.'

'I am quite sure that Mr Alexander is not concerned in the slightest with me.' But he was. She knew he was, and the knowledge relieved and excited and worried her in equal measure.

'Fanny and I think him very handsome...for a pirate. Isn't that right, Fanny?'

'Hush now, Miss Imelda,' Fanny warned.

'If you and he were to marry, would that make him my uncle?'

'What nonsense you talk, Imelda. One husband is quite enough in any woman's lifetime.' A husband ground a woman's pride in the dirt before the eyes of an entire city. And had Robert not been proof enough, there was Brandon… She shook the bitter thoughts away and did not allow her mind to travel down that dark route.

'But I would like to have a pirate for an uncle.'

Sarah raised an eyebrow, determined to nip such talk in the bud. 'Have you started your French study for today?'

'Oh, Aunt Sarah!' protested Imelda. 'I couldn't possibly concentrate on French. Besides, this is our time for taking the air.' She smiled sweetly. 'And Mr Alexander will be waiting.' Grabbing her cloak but without a heed for her bonnet, Imelda ran out of the cabin.

'Sorry, ma'am. Shall I fetch her back?' Fanny asked.

She shook her head. 'We probably *should* take a little air.'

But Sarah knew, even as she and Fanny slipped on their cloaks and bonnets, that she was not going up there to take the air.

She stood there by the bulwark, looking out to sea, and Daniel knew by the way she did not turn her face to his that she was very aware of the growing desire between them.

All these days of talking and he did not yet know her story. Most women wanted to spill that within hours of meeting. Yet Sarah Ellison parried his every attempt to tread close, especially when it came to her late husband, although Daniel took some solace in her subtle enquiry as to whether he was married. Heaven only knew why! He didn't even know why he had pushed them to this routine of daily meetings. Why he was pursuing her when he could not, in all honour, have her.

He raked a hand through his hair. The way things were he needed neither games nor complications. Part of him craved

to bed her and be done with it. By God, she would be a salve
to the underlying ache that always came at this time of year.
And part knew he should walk away from her and focus only
on Higgs, on what the hell he had stumbled into. But Daniel
could do neither, and not just because they were stuck together
within the confines of a ship. He closed his eyes, knowing he
had a complication whether he wanted it or not.

And in nine more days they would be in Plymouth.

Her voice when she finally spoke was soft, her words echoing his thoughts. 'In nine days we shall be in Plymouth.' She
still had not looked at him, just kept her gaze fixed on the
expanse of ocean.

'There is much that can happen in nine days.' He did not
know why he was saying it, only that he could not help himself.

He could see the slight tensing of her body in response to
his words.

'You are mistaken.'

'Am I?'

'I am not the sort of woman who indulges in dalliances.'

'I am not the sort of man who dallies with the woman who
saved his life.'

She swallowed. 'Nor am I seeking another husband.' She
gestured down at her dark skirt. 'I am still mourning the first
and always will be.'

'I am not seeking a wife.'

'Then we understand one another.'

He did not challenge her assertion. They understood each
other too well, yet it served not to alleviate the underlying
sensual tension between them, but only to tighten it.

She took a breath. 'And I hardly saved your life.' She
glanced round at him.

'What did you do that day?'

She averted her gaze again.

'Shall I remind you?' He did not wait for her reply. 'You
were standing on this same deck, wearing the same cloak

and bonnet, as dark a blue as to appear black. I thought I was dreaming, for what man cast into the North Atlantic midwinter is rescued?

'I watched you run to Seymour. I watched you persuade him. I tried to swim to you, but the current was too strong and my strength was spent. You reached for me, as if you would pluck me from the water yourself. "Hold on," you said. "Just a little longer. We're coming."'

She moved so that they stood facing one another squarely, one hand still anchoring her to the bulwark. 'How could you possibly have heard my words?' Her eyes were wide with shock, her voice, barely above a whisper.

'I saw them shape upon your lips. I heard their whisper in my ear.'

Her eyes never shifted from his. Brown velvet, ringed in charcoal grey. Beguiling as the woman herself. Daniel forgot everything else. Forgot Higgs. Forgot the lies he was weaving. Even forgot Netta. All he was aware of was Sarah Ellison.

He stepped closer, never breaking his gaze. 'Mrs Ellison, Sarah…' And despite all that he did not intend, he lowered his face towards hers. And despite all that she had said, she moved her mouth to meet his.

'Mr Alexander!' Imelda's voice shouted from the other side of the deck.

Sarah started.

'Come and look! I see your pirate ship in the distance!'

The moment was broken, allowing him to regain his senses. He stepped back from the brink, from where Sarah stood blinking at him in shock before her composure slotted back into place.

'If you will excuse me, sir.' He could hear the breathlessness in her voice, and see the embarrassment that coloured her cheeks. 'I must attend to my niece.'

'Allow me to accompany you, Mrs Ellison.'

'I think it better if you do not, Mr Alexander.'

They looked at each other, the desire that pulled between them strong as the wind blowing across the ocean, finally unmasked for what it was. But Daniel's control was back in full, and so too were all of Sarah Ellison's barricades. But whatever he would have said to repair the damage was forgotten in the next moment.

'Ship ahoy,' came the call from the seaman who had climbed up into the crow's nest.

Sarah watched Daniel change as the man's words reached them. His expression hardened. His jaw tensed. His eyes narrowed with focus, and through his body rippled a wariness, an alertness, an edge of steel.

Regardless of what she had said, he followed her over to where Imelda and Fanny stood peering into the distance.

'I *told* you so. Can you see it?' Imelda pointed.

There, just visible on the horizon, was the tiny shape of a ship.

Sarah's heart was still racing from what had just almost happened between them, her blood still rushing, her cheeks still scalding. She glanced at Daniel Alexander, but his gaze was focused firmly on the distant ship. Nothing could disguise the presence that emanated from him—strength and power and determination. His hair ruffled in the wind. The angles and planes of his face sharpened, honing his handsomeness. His eyes darkened and all around him she felt the aura of danger. Sarah shivered just to see it.

'Aunt Sarah?'

'I see it, Imelda.' But she was not looking at the ship.

'Is it a pirate ship?' whispered Imelda.

'There are no pirates in these waters,' replied Sarah. 'Only merchant ships such as the *Angel* and ships of the King's navy.' There were other navies too, not all of whom would be friendly towards a British merchant vessel, but Sarah did not want to frighten her niece by saying so.

'But what about…?' Imelda gestured her eyes towards Daniel Alexander.

Sarah pretended not to notice.

'Aunt Sarah?'

'I think it is time we retired to our cabins.'

'But the ship…' protested Imelda.

'Is sailing away from us,' said Daniel Alexander in a low serious voice.

Imelda cast big wide eyes at him.

He became aware of the way they were looking at him and the harsh focus dropped from his face. He smiled and was transformed to the man that they had come to know. 'You need not worry, Miss Bowden, if they are pirates they have changed their mind about coming back for me.'

'And if they are the King's navy looking to catch you?'

A shadow moved in his eyes—there, then gone in a second. 'Then I have had a lucky escape.' Daniel Alexander gave a cheeky tug at one of Imelda's pigtails and grinned.

Imelda giggled.

It was as if the moment had never happened…almost. For Sarah could feel the tension about Daniel Alexander and see the way his focus returned to linger long and cool on the distant ship.

She followed Fanny guiding Imelda back down to the cabins, leaving him to watch the last trace of the ship disappear. But what she had seen reminded her that Daniel Alexander was a man she did not know, for all it felt otherwise. And what had almost happened between them, in broad daylight, before Imelda and the *Angel*'s crew… She closed her eyes at how close she had come, despite all that she had resolved about men. But Daniel Alexander was different from other men. The time had come to stop lying to herself and admit the truth—that she was attracted to him, more than attracted to him. She wanted him in all the ways that a woman could want a man. And that was too risky a place for Sarah. Especially when the man involved was a tall handsome Highlander who was dangerous possibly to more than just a woman's heart.

She knew now, that when it came to Daniel Alexander she could trust neither herself nor him. Nine days to Plymouth and she was going to have to avoid him for every one of them.

Chapter Three

Sarah Ellison's niece and maid were alone when they appeared on deck the next day.

'Oh, there you are, Mr Alexander.' The wee lassie had already knocked her bonnet askew and was fidgeting at the ribbons. 'Any sight of the pirate ship today?'

'Not one, Miss Bowden,' he said. *Thank God!*

'Maybe tomorrow.' She seemed cheerily hopeful.

'Maybe.'

'They are sure to come and fetch you.'

Daniel hoped not. 'Your aunt does not accompany you today?'

'She says she is busy with her needlework.' Busy avoiding him, more like, after his carelessness the previous day. Imelda came to stand by his side. 'You like Aunt Sarah, don't you?'

'I like Mrs Ellison very much.'

'I thought so,' said Imelda. 'She likes you too.'

'I am glad to hear it.'

'Although she will not admit it.'

Daniel gave an encouraging nod. 'Because she misses Mr Ellison?' He knew it was unfair of him to ask the bairn, but he wanted very much to know what it was that Sarah Ellison was hiding.

Imelda snorted. 'I do not think that likely!'

'Why not, Miss Bowden?'

Imelda poked at a mark on the deck with the toe of her shoe. 'She did not like him very much.'

'Miss Imelda…' warned the maid.

Imelda sent her an insolent look in return.

'Mrs Ellison told you this?'

'Of course, not. Aunt Sarah would never say such things to me. I am only ten years old!' She looked at him as if he were a simpleton, then glanced away with a guilty expression. 'I once overheard my mama and papa talking about it. They said he was a scoundrel.'

'But your aunt still wears her widow's weeds four years after his death.'

'Only to dissuade gentlemen. Aunt Sarah is very pretty,' said Imelda and drew him a knowing look. 'And very rich. Lots of gentlemen want to marry her.' Imelda smiled.

'That is understandable,' said Daniel.

'But Aunt Sarah doesn't want to marry again, so she pretends she is still in mourning so that she doesn't have to go to balls and routs, and be thought on the marriage mart, but the gentlemen called just the same. Mr Mallory, Mr Watkins, Mr Taverner—' Imelda's list was interrupted by the maid.

'That is quite enough, Miss Imelda. Your aunt would be very angry if she knew what you were saying.'

'Do you really want her to marry Mr Taverner?' Imelda demanded.

'Of course not, miss, but—'

'Is your aunt then interested in marrying this Mr Taverner?' Despite his apparent relaxed stance, Daniel's senses sharpened as he waited for the answer.

Imelda gave a visible shudder at the thought and checked around before leaning forwards in a conspiratorial fashion. 'It is true that they *were* courting…'

'For the past few months,' added the maid. 'First man since Mr Ellison passed away. A real charmer is Mr Taverner, when he wants to be, and right handsome too.'

'Anyway,' Imelda resumed the story again, 'Mr Taverner came to visit two weeks ago, late at night. Fanny and I sneaked downstairs and spied on them.'

Daniel raised an eyebrow at the maid, whose entire face flushed scarlet.

'I was worried for Mrs Ellison, sir.'

'We both were. I know it is not a nice thing to do, but Uncle Robert wouldn't have fitted that spy hole through from his library to the drawing room if spying were really so terrible, would he?' The wee lassie looked up at Daniel in total innocence.

'I suppose not,' he said, wondering what manner of man Sarah Ellison had been married to.

'So that was how we came to see Mr Taverner pushing Aunt Sarah against the wall and hear him shouting that the gossip was a lie—that he hadn't kissed another lady—' she added as an aside.

'Oh, the louse more than kissed her, sir,' said the maid, puffing up her chest in righteous indignation.

'He said that if Aunt Sarah did not marry him he would tell everyone…' Imelda screwed up her face in confusion. 'I didn't really understand what it was he was going to tell everyone, only that it would ruin Aunt Sarah's reputation.'

Daniel looked at Fanny for further explanation.

The maid's lips tightened. She cast a sideways glance at her charge before bringing her eyes back to his and saying diplomatically, 'Mrs Ellison is the height of respectability, but he was going to tell them otherwise, that she had succumbed to his…' she raised her eyebrows '…charm.'

So the bastard was blackmailing her.

'He said that Aunt Sarah had until Christmas to give him her answer. The next day my aunt decided we should go home to England for the holidays.' Imelda narrowed her eyes. 'So you see now why it would be a good thing if someone else was to marry Aunt Sarah before she goes back to New York. Someone who could run Mr Taverner through with his cutlass.'

'I see perfectly.' Little wonder that Sarah Ellison was thinking of moving to England for good.

'You do have a cutlass, don't you?'

'I have a sword that is much better than a cutlass for running villains through, Miss Bowden.'

'Good.' Imelda gave a sigh of relief. 'You will not speak of what I have told you to anyone else will you, especially not Aunt Sarah.'

'My lips are sealed, lass.'

'Shake hands on it.' Imelda looked very serious.

She had forgotten to put on her gloves and her small hand was both cold and sticky beneath his, but the bairn loved her aunt and she had told him something of what he wanted to know, and he was grateful for both.

'I knew I could trust you, Mr Alexander.'

There was a curious dearth of wind. Through the porthole in the cabin that Imelda shared with Fanny, Sarah watched the sky change. It was the third day she had kept to her cabin and even now, even watching what she was, and even knowing what she did, there was a part of her that wanted to be up there on deck, to see the sky overhead, and feel the wind on her cheeks…and be with him. She pressed her lips firm and concentrated on the view.

Great clouds, dark and thick, belched across the sky, drawing with them a deep dull grey curtain tinged faint with yellow hue. She watched it close until only a peek of brightness remained in one small corner. And then that, too, was gone. The wind picked up, cracking the canvas stretched tight against the strain. From up on deck came shouts as the *Angel's* sailors raced to lower the sails.

A knock sounded at the cabin door and Fanny answered it.

'I wish to speak to Mrs Ellison.'

Sarah's heart stumbled at the deep Scottish voice that sent delicious shivers chasing across her skin, and then kicked to a gallop. She stood where she was and did not look round.

'Mr Alexander is here to see you, ma'am. Are you in to visitors?' Fanny stood by her side, saying the ridiculous words. The door gaped wide. He stood so close he could have reached across and touched her shoulder.

She wanted so much to turn and look into those steady blue eyes.

'No visitors today, Fanny,' she said and knew that, however wrong it felt, she was doing the right thing.

'Yes, ma'am.' Fanny dipped a curtsy.

Sarah kept her gaze fixed on the darkening sky and held her breath. The click of the closing door never came.

'Mrs Ellison, you may be avoiding me, but…'

She turned and saw Daniel Alexander with his hand splayed firm against the door.

'How dare you, sir?'

'There is a storm coming,' he said calmly, ignoring both her protestation and her wishes, which fuelled her outrage all the more.

'You overestimate your importance, sir! I have *not* been avoiding you.'

He crooked an eyebrow. 'Three days without a foot on deck. Taking the ginger, are you?'

Her cheeks burned. 'If you would be so kind as to leave now.'

He made no move. 'As I said, ma'am, there is a storm brewing.'

'I can see the sky, Mr Alexander. I am quite well aware there is a storm brewing.'

'Good. You'll be ready to be secured to the mast then.'

'What on earth are you talking about?'

He produced a coiled length of rope.

She looked at the rope and then at him. 'Is this your idea of a joke?'

'It is no joke, Mrs Ellison.' But it was the look in his eyes, more than the grave sincerity of his words, that made her realise he was in earnest.

'We are not dogs to be tethered, sir!'

'It is clear, madam, that you underestimate the ferocity of a storm at sea.' His voice was soft but determined.

'Sir, I will have you know that we suffered a storm two days after leaving New York.'

'That was not a storm.'

'How do you know?' she demanded. 'You were not here to see it.'

'I know because you are arguing with me rather than begging to be tied to the mast.' He gestured towards the great thick wooden mast passed through the deck, but his eyes held hers with a strength that made it impossible to look away.

'But I do not want to be tied up!' Imelda protested.

'And neither you will be,' said Sarah.

'Mrs Ellison, perhaps I am not making myself clear—'

But she cut him off with a fury. 'We will be fine in our cabins, Mr Alexander. As we were before. I bid you good day, sir!' She moved to close the door.

But Daniel took a step forwards to meet her. He stood there, so tall and imposing that she had never been more aware of his strength or masculinity.

'I must insist, Mr Alexander.' They were standing so close that she had to tip her head back to see his face.

'So must I, Mrs Ellison.'

'You cannot seriously mean to tie us to the mast?' Her eyes flicked to the rope coiled in his hand.

'You'll thank me afterwards.'

There was a heartbeat of horrified silence as she raised her gaze to his once more.

'No!' Imelda dodged round him and ran.

'Imelda! Stop!' But Sarah's shouts went unheeded.

At the far end of the deck the *Angel*'s crew were busy securing the cargo.

Imelda did not stop. She ran straight for the hatch ladder that would give her escape to the upper deck.

Sarah chased after her niece, but Daniel was faster, reaching the bottom of the ladder and climbing just as Imelda stepped off the top.

'Stay below, Mrs Ellison. I'll fetch her.'

But Sarah knew, with Imelda so frightened, that if anyone had a hope of fetching her it was Sarah herself. She took the rungs two at a time, desperate to reach her niece, but what she saw when she emerged on deck was a place she did not recognise.

Sarah stood there and stared around her in horror. It was like a scene from hell except there was no fire, no colour, only wildness and darkness and rain that was not rain. It was a deluge, heavy, icy, stinging as a vertical sheet of hail, deafening as Thor's fingers, drumming against the wooden deck. Furious. Ruthless. Relentless. It felt like it was flaying the skin from her bones. And through the horror there was no sign of either Imelda or Daniel Alexander.

'Imelda!' she screamed. 'Imelda!' So loud as to scrape her throat raw, but it was as nothing against the onslaught.

Shadow figures rippled through the dark curtain of water and Sarah stumbled towards them, shouting Imelda's name for all she was worth. Her heavy, cold skirts wrapped themselves around her legs, impeding her all the more. Her hair was plastered against her face. Blinded by the rain, she felt her way.

And then running out of the hell scene came Daniel with Imelda in his arms.

He grabbed Sarah's hand and dragged her with him as they sprinted towards the open hatch.

He took no notice of the ladder, just swung Sarah round and lowered her into the hole. She jumped the rest of the small distance to the deck below, turning just in time to see Daniel slide with his feet alone down the edges of the ladder, as if he had done such a thing a thousand times before.

From up above the wind screamed a war cry against the ocean's roar and the *Angel* began to reel.

'To the foremast. Now!' he commanded.

And this time, not one of them disobeyed.

The rope was where he had dropped it halfway along the deck. He caught it up as they ran. And when they reached the foremast he stood Sarah, Imelda and Fanny around it and bound them in place.

'Where are you going?' Sarah asked.

'The main mast.' He gestured to the aft of the ship. 'Just there. No further.'

She nodded, took a breath and felt the rain run from her sodden hair to drip down her face.

'Are you all right, Imelda?' She glanced down at her niece.

'I'm frightened, Aunt Sarah.'

'Everything is going to be fine. It is just a storm and storms pass.' She squeezed Imelda's little hand within her own and forced a smile. 'Is that not so, Mr Alexander?' She met his gaze, afraid that it was not going to be fine at all.

'It is, Mrs Ellison.' His voice was calm and reassuring, his eyes steady upon hers.

I'm sorry, she wanted to say. *What is coming?* she wanted to ask. But she knew she could utter not one word of it before Imelda.

'Let go of the fear, lass.' He touched his fingers lightly to her cheek, in what was almost a caress, and she had the feeling that it was not only fear of the coming storm he was talking about. The moment stretched as they stared into one another's eyes. Then it was gone and he was bending down to Imelda and chucking her under the chin. 'Your aunt is right. All storms eventually pass. Everything is going to be fine.'

'Do you promise?' The tremble in Imelda's voice touched Sarah's heart.

'I promise, Miss Bowden.'

Fanny's gaze met Sarah's across the small distance. Sarah gave a nod and a smile of reassurance she did not feel.

'But it will get worse before it gets better again. And as a pirate's friend you will have to be brave. Can you be brave for me?'

'Have you been through many storms, Mr Alexander?'

'Very many.'

'And it has always worked out fine?'

'Always.'

'Are you the captain of your pirate ship or just an ordinary pirate?'

'I am the captain.'

'Then I will be brave, *Captain* Alexander.'

'Good lass.' He smiled at her.

The wind had returned with a vengeance and the *Angel* was already rocking and swaying in the swell of the sea as Daniel secured himself to *Angel*'s aft mast.

The howl of the wind grew louder, the heave beneath their feet stronger. The nausea was in Sarah's stomach again, worse than it had ever been, but this time she did not know if it was seasickness or fear, or a combination of the two. The ship pitched so steeply that it seemed that it would tumble right over. Almost everything had been tied down or chained into place. The few small items that had not were launched like rag dolls into the air. Fanny and Imelda screamed. Sarah held her breath, and then, at the very last minute when it seemed that the ship were about to capsize, the *Angel* was buoyed back up from the depths again. The items in the air smashed against the deck. From the cargo hold came the dreadful sound of splintering wood, and from the cabins a violent crash and clatter. Sarah listened in horror, knowing that she would have kept Imelda and Fanny in there with her had not Daniel Alexander insisted otherwise.

Imelda and Fanny's screams ebbed to cries and sobs. Sarah could do nothing more than hold both their hands and whisper words of reassurance they would not hear.

Please God, help us!

But the tiny lull was over and the *Angel* bucked again and dived down as the waves swept to cover her and there was terror and screaming and the enormous crushing power of the wind and the waves, and the gaping mouth of the ocean sucking them down, swallowing them whole, then spitting them out again. It was violence like nothing Sarah had ever known. They were helpless before its furore, could do nothing other than hold on, endure, wait.

All storms pass eventually. His words whispered again in her ear. He had to be right. He had been right about the rest of it.

But the storm was not done with them yet. A flicker of light forked in the sky, illuminating the whole of the lower deck, the whiteness of the crew's faces that she only now saw were lashed around it and the water that poured through the closed hatch. A rumble of thunder crashed in the distance.

Time ceased. The terror stretched to an eternity of icy darkness and roaring while the *Angel* was thrown and dropped and shaken like a hare in the jaws of a great hound. The lightning flashed again and again, and up above the skies were being ripped apart and down below the ocean was trying his best to pull the ship apart.

All storms pass eventually.

But still the rain lashed and still the waves crashed high and all the ocean was deep and wild and snarling, until, at last, it began to soften and the rain became once again just rain and the wind eased, so that the waves only battered, but did not tear at the *Angel*. Until, at last, the thunder passed into the distance and there was only the thrum of the rain and the rhythmic splash of waves thudding against the ship. Until, eventually, there was only the beat of her heart and the grip of Imelda's and Fanny's fingers against hers.

None of them moved. None of them spoke. They stood stunned.

'It is over,' she heard her own voice say. 'We are safe now.'

And then Daniel was there, unfastening the rope, catching Fanny up before the maid hit the ground. Imelda was sobbing as she threw herself into his one available arm and wrapped her arms around his waist.

'Well done, brave lass,' he said.

And then Imelda was in her arms. 'Oh, Aunt Sarah!' Imelda sobbed.

Sarah held her niece and stroked her hair and made shushing sounds. 'The storm has passed.' She gently wiped away the tears from Imelda's face and hugged her tighter. 'And we are fine', the words were no more than a whisper, barely believable to herself.

Daniel's arm encircled her and she let herself lean against the strength and warmth of his body. The relief made her legs weak, made her head spin, made her cling to him.

'Brave lass,' his lips murmured against her ear.

Chapter Four

The sun shone from a beautiful blue sky the next morning. The ocean stretched endlessly smooth and calm. As if the storm had never been—save for the *Angel*.

Daniel stood on deck and surveyed her damage.

The rigging had been devastated. The bowsprit and jibs were gone. The fore topgallant had snapped off, taking out a great section of the bulwarks and ripping a hole in the deck, before being claimed by the waves. The flags were missing. Ropes dangled limp and useless. Canvas shreds fluttered, the only remnants of great sails that had been taken, lowered or not. The rudder had been torn off and the hull was leaking. The *Angel* was the ghost of the ship she had been. But that was not why the pit of Daniel's stomach felt cold and tight.

Sarah Ellison's niece had woken up with a fever.

Imelda's cheeks were flushed bright, her head burning and sweaty, yet the child shivered and moaned beneath the covers of the cot.

'I'm so cold, Aunt Sarah.'

Sarah soothed Imelda's sweat-dampened hair from her forehead. 'Take another little sip of ale.' The fresh-water supplies had been lost in the storm.

Imelda did as she was bid. 'I don't feel well.'

'I know, little honeybun. You have caught a chill from being soaked in the rain yesterday.'

'I'm sorry that I ran away, but I did not want to be tied to the mast.'

'None of us wanted to be tied to the mast.'

'But I'm glad we were. Captain Alexander was right, wasn't he?'

'He was.' Sarah did not want to think what would have happened had he not been there.

Imelda's eyes fluttered shut. She fought to open them. 'You do like him, don't you? Even though you were angry with him.'

'Yes, I like him,' said Sarah quietly, admitting it openly for the first time.

Imelda's eyelids were already closed, but she smiled at the answer.

'Now rest.' Sarah dropped a kiss to Imelda's forehead. 'Rest and you will be better by the end of the day,' she hoped, not letting her mind follow down other dark paths.

But Imelda was not better by the end of the day. With every hour that passed the fever grew worse until, by nightfall, it racked her, tormenting her rest, making her thrash and moan, burning her hot in the chill of the cabin. And nothing that Sarah did, not compresses or cool icy air, not cold weak beer dripped into her niece's mouth or stripping the covers from the bed, made any difference. And the relief that she had felt from surviving the storm was a distant memory and in its place was a fear that squeezed the breath from her lungs.

When Daniel entered the tiny cabin, the wee lassie was dressed in her nightdress and lying uncovered in her cot. Even in the dim flickering light of the lantern he could see the scarlet flush of her cheeks and the glisten of sweat upon her skin. Sarah sat by the bed on a small wooden chair, watching over the bairn.

'I brought you some stew and wine.' He sat the tray down on the tiny table.

'Thank you, but I am not hungry.' Sarah's face was pinched pale with exhaustion and worry.

'She has not eaten a thing all day, sir.' Fanny's forehead was creased with concern.

'Please do not start again, Fanny!'

Fanny's mouth tightened. 'But, ma'am—'

'Go and rest in Mrs Ellison's cabin, Fanny,' Daniel interrupted. 'There is not room in here for us all. I will stay with Mrs Ellison.'

The door closed with a quiet click behind the maid.

Sarah bit her lip.

Daniel moved to the bed where the bairn stirred and moaned in her sleep. 'Is she any better since this afternoon?'

'She grows worse. I gave her a little laudanum to aid her rest, but the fever will not let her go.' Sarah's voice was quiet and strained.

He touched a hand to Imelda's forehead and felt the scald.

'I have tried everything I can think of and nothing makes any difference.'

'There is time enough yet.' He rested his hand against Sarah's shoulder.

She ignored him. 'She was soaked through to the skin from the rain. And then all those hours tied to the mast in the cold…' Sarah closed her eyes. 'You should have explained better to me about the storm. You should have…' She shook her head. 'She ran away because she was frightened.'

He said nothing, knowing the real reason she was blaming him.

'She's ten years old. Ten!' The anger flashed in her eyes as she stared up at him. She got to her feet, angrily shrugging his hand from her shoulder and facing him. 'She thinks you are a pirate captain!'

Still he said nothing, just absorbing her need to vent her frustration and fear.

'If you had not come with the rope in your hand… If you had not…' Her voice broke. She closed her eyes and began to weep. 'It was my fault! I argued against you when you wanted to anchor us to the mast to keep us safe. Had I not…'

'It would have made no difference.'

'You cannot know. I was angry with you and angry with myself, over what had almost happened between us up on deck. And because of that…' She sobbed. 'I am supposed to look after her. I am supposed to keep her safe.'

'Sarah,' he said softly and pulled her against him.

'It is my fault.' She wept in earnest and he held her, just held her, giving her what little comfort he could, knowing he would have taken her pain a hundred times over rather than have her suffer like this.

'There is nothing of fault. A storm is a force of nature, nothing more.'

She wept, this woman who through their journey had struggled so hard against revealing weakness. She wept until the tears were spent, until the sobs died away and she was just standing there with her face pressed against his chest.

'I am sorry.' She tilted her face up to look at him.

Her cheeks were wet and blotched from the weeping. He wiped away her tears. 'You have nothing to be sorry for.'

'If she dies…'

He knew he should tell her that everything was going to be fine, just as he had done in the storm, but this was different, far different, and he could not. False hope was worse in the long run. 'She's a plucky wee thing. She'll fight the fever every inch of the way. All we can do is wait this night out.' Strands of hair stuck to the dampness of her cheeks. He stroked them away.

Her eyes clung to his. All of her defences were gone, broken down and washed away by the prospect of losing the bairn. Without them he could see all of her fear, all of her vulnerability, all of her courage, and the sight of it reached into his chest and squeezed a fist tight and hard around his heart.

'You are right. All we can do is wait.' She sat down to re-sume her vigil.

Daniel lifted the second chair from the other side of the cabin and sat down beside her.

'Daniel…'

He slid his hand to cover hers. 'I'm not going anywhere, lass.'

Her fingers closed around his.

He passed her the dinner tray. She accepted it without pro-test, eating and drinking a little before setting it back down on the table.

They sat in silence for a while, their fingers entwined, watching the child's fitful rest.

'I lied to you,' she said at last, breaking the silence. 'When I told you that I was still mourning my husband.'

He said nothing, just let her speak.

'His name was Robert and I hated him. He was an En-glishman emigrating to a new life in America when we met. I did not realise that he only needed a wife to help further his career. He was so handsome and charming…at first.'

Handsome and charming, the same words the maid had used to describe Taverner.

'But he was a scoundrel and a liar, with eyes that turned too readily to any pretty woman.' She gave a soft laugh that was not of happiness. 'He bedded half the women in New York before we were wed a year.'

'The man must have been a fool.' He understood now why Sarah Ellison had built her defences so high. Betrayed by every man she had trusted—first the husband and then the suitor.

'He contracted a fever on a business trip to the South. A fever like Imelda's. I nursed him in the weeks before he died.'

'I am sorry, Sarah.' He gave her hand a gentle squeeze, knowing how much it must be costing her to open up to him.

'Mourning weeds are like armour against men.' She met

his eyes. 'But I want you to know the truth. I am sorry that I lied to you.'

'Sometimes lies are told for the best of reasons. For defence. To protect.'

'Yes.' She shivered in the chill of the cabin.

'Thank you for telling me.' His thumb stroked against the back of her hand.

Sometimes Imelda's eyes fluttered open, sometimes she cried out in her fevered sleep. Every time the wee lassie stirred, Sarah rose to check on her, wiping the sweat from the bairn's brow and dribbling weak beer through the dry lips. The hours of the night crept slowly by.

'Why do you dislike Christmas so much, Daniel?' It came out of the silence, the question he least expected.

He did not want to answer. But she looked at him with her soul stripped bare and he knew he would tell her, even though he had never told another, never even spoken the words.

He looked into her eyes. 'Because I lost my wife and babe at Christmas.'

'Oh, Daniel…' her words were soft as breath '…I am so sorry.'

'Childbirth is a treacherous thing.'

He felt her fingers tighten around his. She raised his hand to her lips and pressed a kiss to his knuckles. 'So I have heard.'

He pulled her closer, wrapping his arm around her as she laid her head against his shoulder.

'I am glad you are here, Daniel.'

'So I am, lass. So am I.' And despite everything, it was the truth.

Sarah woke with the gentle light of a winter morning. For the first time in such a long time she felt safe. She breathed in the scent of fresh wood and tar, of sea and the underlying pleasant scent of Daniel Alexander. The muscle of his chest was hard and warm beneath her cheek, and the steady reassuring beat of his heart loud in her ear. Curved protectively around her spine she could feel the weight of his arm. She shifted her legs beneath the blanket that covered them both and opened her eyes.

Daniel's blue eyes looked into hers and he smiled the most handsome smile in the world. 'Good morning, Mrs Sleepyhead,' he said softly. 'There is a young lady only just woken up before you.' He shifted his gaze to the cot and winked.

Sarah followed his focus to find Imelda looking at her.

'Imelda!' The whisper conveyed all of her relief and joy and thankfulness. All sleepiness vanished. She hurried to the cot. 'Oh, Imelda.'

'Aunt Sarah.' Imelda's voice was rusty with lack of use.

'Thank God!' Sarah stroked her niece's face.

'Captain Alexander saved us.' Imelda smiled.

Sarah heard the quiet click of the door and knew he had gone.

It was the middle of the afternoon before Sarah had a chance to seek out Daniel Alexander. She found him up on the main deck.

The men were all busy repairing the damage the storm had wrought. And for all their sawing and hammering the destruction was great indeed. Shirt sleeves rolled up to reveal a pair of strong arms, and hatless so that his hair was dishevelled in the sea breeze, Daniel was lifting what looked like a tree trunk. His face was rugged, his jaw stubble-shadowed where he had not shaved. She knew now why the scent of fresh wood and tar had been in his clothes last night. He had been working all the time, making the *Angel* safe, and yet still found time to help her.

Daniel's eyes met hers across the deck and she felt her heart grow warm. He hefted the spar into position, then made his way over to her.

'Mr Alexander.'

'Mrs Ellison.' He smiled. 'How is Miss Bowden?'

'She grows stronger with every hour and wished to ac-

company me up here to find you. It was all I could do to keep
her in bed.'

His smile deepened. 'I am relieved to hear it.'

One of the seamen passed between them. Daniel guided
her over to a quieter spot by the bulwark. She gripped a hand
against the wooden wall, but neither of them looked out at
the ocean.

She lowered her voice so that only he would hear. 'Last
night, had you not been there…' She could not bring herself
to admit the rest of it aloud. 'Thank you,' she finished instead.

'No thanks are required between friends.' His bare fingers
surreptitiously touched against hers in a small reassuring gesture. *Let go of the fear, lass.*

And when she looked into his eyes, this man who was like
no other she had ever known, she knew she had done just that.
A happiness welled up within her and she could not help herself from smiling.

It was like the brilliance of sunshine on a dreich day seeing her smile. And inside his chest were feelings that Daniel
had not felt in such a long time, not since Netta, feelings of
tenderness that he had thought never to feel again. There un-
bidden, unwanted, and yet, at that moment, with Sarah Ellison standing before him he could not resent them.

Sarah glanced away, to further along the deck, to the place
where they had stood so often to take the air and view the
ocean. Rope now cordoned off a section of missing bulwark.

'It can be repaired,' he said, following her gaze.

'Are you trying to make me feel better, Mr Alexander?'

'Am I succeeding, Mrs Ellison?'

'You always do,' she confessed.

The admission warmed his heart. 'I am glad of that.'

There was a small comfortable silence.

'How bad is the damage, Daniel?'

'She is still afloat.' Just.

'Are we going to make it?'

'We can secure her so that she is watertight. But the *Angel* is too small a ship to carry much material for repairs. Captain Davies has not the spares needed to repair the mast and rigging. We can stay afloat, but—'

'We cannot sail,' she finished.

He nodded. Neither of them spoke of the peril of that position. It would not take another storm to finish the *Angel*.

'What are we to do?'

'Wait until another ship arrives to tow us to port.'

'In all of the past week we have seen only one other ship and that was far in the distance.'

'We are without sail and any other vessel that sees will come to our aid. The storm has not blown us far off course. We are north of the Azores.' He saw she did not realise the significance of the location. 'There are many naval ships in these waters. We should not have to wait long.' He turned his mind away from what that might mean for him and focused, instead, on the relief on her face.

Rain began to patter softly around them.

Seymour's head appeared at the hatch, shouting over at the captain, 'We need more men down below, Captain.' And then Captain Davies was bellowing for Oakley and Struthers to go with Mr Seymour.

Daniel smiled. 'I should get back to work.'

'I should get back to Imelda.'

'We will talk later, Sarah.' But he was not sure he wanted to talk. Not with the knowledge that in all probability a naval ship would soon come to their aid and their journey would be over. And most of all, not feeling the way he did. Daniel was not sure that he wanted to care so much about a woman again.

He walked Sarah to the hatch for the deck below.

But there was no opportunity for either of them to talk over the next days.

The weather grew worse and the repairs more urgent. Daniel worked with Davies and Seymour and the rest of the crew from first light in the morning, all the day through and into the night, straining to see by the light of their lanterns. The hull had been patched and would hold if the seas did not grow too violent. They repaired the hole in the main deck as best they could, and the bulwark where Sarah and Daniel had stood. But there was little they could do for the rudder or the mast. The *Angel* stood stripped and bare. Everyone knew they were at the mercy of the ocean and everyone prayed for the sight of another ship before the next storm found them.

It grew so cold that they could see their breath clouding before them even when below deck. A fire burned constantly in the galley, but it made no difference to the men up on the deck. They wrapped themselves in layers of clothes, but the wind whistled through them as if they were naked. Sarah and Fanny stayed within the galley to keep Imelda warm, both helping the cook as best they could. The only time Sarah saw Daniel was when he came in with the others to eat, and the sight of him tired, soaked through and half-frozen tore at her heart.

Sarah tucked Imelda up safe with Fanny and retired to her own cabin, but, exhausted though she was, she could not sleep. There were too many thoughts in her head, all of them centred around one man. A book lay limp within Sarah's hands. She gave up the pretence of reading, closed its pages and watched the lantern light flicker against the cabin walls.

She had suffered a storm and the near loss of a child she loved. She was adrift in a wrecked ship in the North Atlantic in the midst of winter, at risk of sinking, of being attacked by pirates, or drifting undiscovered until they died of dehydration and hunger. She had worked like the lowliest maid. She had learned to peel potatoes, wash dishes and clean lantern glass. She had scraped wax from tables and dug out ashes from a fire, and drunk beer. Her fine dresses were marked with soot and grease and gravy. Her hair was a mess. She had never experienced so much fear, never felt so cold or tired… or so happy.

Imelda was alive and well. And for the first time in all her life, Sarah felt alive too. Perhaps it was because of how close she had come to losing everything. But she knew it was not.

She had never met a man like Daniel Alexander. She knew virtually nothing of him. Nothing save that he had lost a wife and babe. Nothing but that he had saved their lives during a storm. Nothing except he had been there to help her when she needed him during those long dark hours when the fear of losing Imelda had almost broken her apart. And to hold a woman's hair while she retched her stomach overboard on a winter night. She knew, too, the smoulder in his eyes when he looked at her and the way her heart thrilled when he was near.

Robert had never looked at her like that. Robert had never been kind or protected her. After two years of marriage Robert had remained a stranger to her. After little more than two weeks with a man who really was a stranger it felt as if she had known him a lifetime. It felt as if she had loved him a lifetime.

Men's voices murmured as they passed by her cabin, making their way to their own cabins. The sounds trailed off into the distance. Across the deck she heard a door open and close, and did not have to look out to know that it was Daniel's.

All would change when they were saved. *If* they were saved. She would go back to her own life, turning away from men lest she make the same mistakes she had made with Robert and with Brandon Taverner. But here and now in this little window of time, Sarah had been granted something magical, a chance to know real happiness, the chance to love, for however short a time. It did not matter if it was weeks or days or only hours. She set the book down on the lipped shelf and, pulling her shawls tight around her, slipped from the cabin.

Her lantern swayed softly in the draught, illuminating the darkness. There was only the creaking of timber and the sound of wind and waves. Her heart began to thud as she made her way across the deck.

Chapter Five

Daniel had taken off his coat and was sitting on his cot, unwinding his neckcloth when he heard the quiet knock at his door. He gathered up his coat and with a weary sigh got up to open the door to Davies, but it was not Davies that stood there.

'Sarah.' The sight of her chased away all exhaustion, only to be replaced with a sudden worry. 'Has something happened? Imelda…?'

'Is well.' She glanced away, and when she looked at him again he could see the nervousness about her and he knew why she had come, knew what had always been inevitable between them from the very start, but still he gave her one last chance to turn away from it.

'Do you wish to take the midnight air?' He smiled.

'No. Not that.' Her voice sounded breathless. Her eyes, so dark and soulful, met his. There was a smudge of soot on her cheek, her hair was escaping its pins, she was bundled beneath two shawls, and she was the most beautiful woman Daniel had ever seen. He knew the level of trust she was putting in him by coming here, and his heart was tender with the knowledge.

'Come in, lass.'

Her teeth nipped at her lip. She hesitated, her eyes meeting his again.

Further along the deck there was the creaking sound of

the deck hatch being opened and the thud of footsteps coming down the ladder.

He reached for her hand and pulled her inside.

The door was hard against Sarah's spine, Daniel, close before her, his hand still warm around hers so that she could feel the little rough scar on his thumb. She opened her mouth to speak, but he touched a finger to her lips to hush the words.

Two sets of footsteps passed by outside his cabin. A voice recognisable as young Oakley complained that he was starving.

Sarah stood frozen where she was, her lips burning beneath his touch.

It seemed they stood that way for ever, so close that she could smell the intoxicating scent of him, so close that she could see each lash that lined his eyes and feel the brush of her breasts against his chest with every breath. At last the footsteps and voices disappeared into the distance. A door slammed.

His finger dropped away.

Neither of them moved, just stood as they were, looking into each other's eyes. The lantern trembled where it hung in her free hand, casting shadows to flicker and dance upon the chiselled planes of his face.

He took the lantern from her and set it upon the shelf.

Nerves wriggled and danced in her stomach. The enormity of what she was doing and all that it meant hit her. 'Oh, Lord! I've never done this before. I should go.'

But he caught her hand in his. 'Stay. Please.' The Highland lilt was so soft and beneath it she heard a depth of emotion and need that matched her own. He stroked a hand against her cheek and she could smell the scent of cold air and tar and soap from his skin.

'It turns out I *am* the sort of woman who knocks on a strange gentleman's cabin door in the night.'

He smiled, and so did she.

'Sarah.' He took her face gently between both his hands and kissed her. His lips were everything that she had imagined—warm and tender and giving, nothing like Robert's, nothing like Brandon Taverner's. He kissed her and her heart overflowed with love for him.

Beneath the flat press of her palms against the linen of his shirt she could feel the beat of his heart, strong and steady as the man himself.

He kissed her and it felt like all the broken parts fixed back together, that all her insecurities, all her fears and worries paled to nothing. He made her feel as if she were the only woman in the world and he, the only man. All the shadows and darkness of the past faded and there was only light. Their lips met again and again, sharing, giving and taking in equal measure. It was as if she had waited all of her life for this moment, for this man, as if this had always been destined to happen between them. There was no one beside him. He was the one, she thought. The only one.

Her hair tumbled loose around her shoulders and she was not aware that he had unpinned it. He slid his fingers through its lengths, bunching them against her scalp, angling her face to his, kissing her all the more.

She skimmed her hands over his shirt, gliding them around to reach his back, feeling the ripple of the muscles beneath. He was lean and hard and strong. She clutched him closer to her, feeling the echo of his heart against her own.

Their tongues danced together, their mouths inviting deeper intimacies.

Her shawls were gone. His hands stroked over her shoulders, over her back, against the curve of her hips, over her buttocks. Low in her belly the heat flared hotter. She melted against him, pressing herself to him and all of his masculinity, acknowledging that she had wanted him from that first day on deck. She wanted him as a man, as a lover. She more than wanted him, she needed him, in a way she had never needed before.

She pulled his shirt free from his breeches and slid her fingers beneath the linen, sighing with the relief of touching his naked skin at last. He was so big, so strong, so warm. She traced her fingers over the hardness of his chest, down over his stomach and abdomen, feeling the ribs of muscle contract beneath her touch. All that power and yet there was nothing of brutality in him, nothing of greed or the rush to satisfy only himself. He wooed her with such gentle enticing persuasion.

It was only when he unfastened the buttons of her dress, sliding it down to land, with a soft rumple of wool, upon the deck that she began to tremble. What if he, too, did not want her when he saw her? But she forced the thought away and turned her back for him to unlace her stays, catching them before they fell away and hanging them over the chair back. Standing there before him clad only in the thin shift that revealed too much, the trembling had advanced to a blatant shivering and there was nothing she could do to stop it. She wrapped her arms around herself, knowing hers was a body that had made a husband seek other beds.

'You are cold.'

'A little.' But it was not the cold that was making her shake.

'Then let me warm you.'

He came to her and wrapped his arms around her and kissed her again with such passion, such desire, caressing her breasts, stroking her hips, revering her as if she were the most beautiful woman in the world. He chased the chill from the night air, made her forget her embarrassment. She was aware only of him and her need for him. He made her burn. He made her ache and throb for his long hard length that pressed against her belly. She wanted him in her, filling her.

'Daniel,' she pleaded.

He stripped off his clothes and, scooping her up into his arms as if she were small and light as a child, carried her to his cot to place her beneath the blankets.

She loosed the tie of her shift, pulled the thin linen over her head and dropped it to the deck.

He climbed in beside her, the lantern light revealing her nakedness as he did so. He stilled, his gaze sweeping with appreciation over her breasts, over her stomach.

'God, lass, you're beautiful!' His fingers traced the path his eyes had led before his body moved to cover hers. His eyes smouldered dark with desire and his smile was both teasing and sensual. 'But I'm supposed to be warming you.'

He took her mouth again, harder this time, with a hunger that matched her own. He kissed her chin, trailed kisses all the way down her neck to her breasts, taking her fully in his mouth, to work a magic with his tongue, while his hands caressed her waist, her belly, her hips, working ever closer to the place between her thighs. Until he reached his destination.

She gasped aloud, threading her fingers through his hair, arching into him all the more.

Daniel did things to her that no man ever had. He made her feel things she had never felt. He made her gasp and moan and beg. Pushed her body and mind to a place high in another world where she shattered in an explosion of blinding unbelievable pleasure, before he entered her, as he made her truly his own, and again.

He loved her with everything he was. And she loved him.

And afterwards he held her in his arms and stroked her cheek and dropped a tender kiss to her forehead. And she took his hand and kissed the crescent scar that marked the pad of his thumb.

They both knew that what had just happened between them was more than a bedding, so much more than coupling.

It was a sharing of souls, a union that could never be undone.

It was love.

Daniel found Sarah in the galley the next morning, with her niece and maid. It looked like Fanny was teaching them how to make bread. All three were wearing long white aprons over their dresses and stood busy kneading dough.

It was the first time he had seen her since returning her to her own cabin in the wee small hours of the morning. Last night had been nothing of dishonour. He could no more have turned her away than stopped breathing. And what they had shared... God help him! Why the hell did it have to happen now? Of all the worst bloody timings in the world!

'Mr Alexander,' she said and he saw the flush of pleasure that touched to her cheeks, the way her beautiful dark eyes sparkled, and the smile that curved her mouth, shy from the intimacies that had passed between them. And there was both an agony in his heart and a dread of what was coming.

'Mrs Ellison, Miss Bowden.' He could not take his eyes from Sarah's, could not smile in return. 'A ship has been sighted.'

Imelda clapped her hands and yelped with excitement.

But Sarah knew. The smile faltered upon her lips, even as she wiped her floury hands on her apron and forced it back into place. 'That is good news.'

'Can we go up and see? Please, Aunt Sarah, please!'

'Fetch your cloak first.'

'Ohh, Aunt Sarah!' the bairn grumbled.

'Do as your aunt says, then go on up on deck with Fanny. We will follow on shortly.'

'Yes, Captain Alexander!' Imelda gave a whoop of delight and ran off across the galley, leaving the maid to hurry after her.

The galley door banged shut. The patter of small footsteps faded to the distance.

He took Sarah's hands in his own.

'The ship is good news, is it not, Daniel?'

'Of course it is.' For the *Angel* and her crew. For Sarah, Imelda and Fanny. But not for him.

'Then what is wrong?'

'Probably nothing,' he lied. Given the *Angel*'s location the probability was stacked against him. He knew too well the frigates that patrolled this area, and one more so than the others. There was no time. The minutes were counting down and even were they not, he could not tell her.

'There is a favour I must ask of you, Sarah.'

'Anything.' The level of her trust flayed him. After all she had been through. She trusted him, just as he trusted her—with his life and more.

He would have given much not to have to do this, to wipe the worry from her face and have her smile at him again as she had done only moments ago. But too much was at stake. He had to ask her.

'Sarah… If something happens to me and we cannot finish this journey together…' He produced the letter from the pocket of his coat. 'Take it. Keep it hidden. Tell no one. As soon as you reach England send it on to whom it is addressed.'

'What do you mean "if something happens to you"?' She stared up into his face, her eyes wide with concern.

'There is no time to explain. Please, Sarah, will you do this?'

'Of course.' She accepted the letter and hid it within her own pocket.

'Swear it. For the sake of all that is between us.'

'Daniel…?'

'Swear it, Sarah.'

'I swear.' Her eyes held his. 'This is to do with the ship that comes to our rescue, isn't it?'

He nodded, knowing what the waves were bringing closer even while he stood here in these last few precious moments with Sarah. There was so little time. He knew what Higgs had told them all. He knew, too, the procedure that would ensue, and that there was nothing he could do to deny it until they got him back to England. And he knew what that was going to do to Sarah. And that knowledge hurt more than everything else that was coming.

'Daniel, why—?'

But he did not let her finish. Instead, he cupped her face in his hands. 'Whatever happens, know that what is between us is no lie. In this, at least, I have been honest, I swear with all my heart. I hope you can forgive the rest.' Forgive him his lies. Forgive the dishonourable scoundrel they would reveal. Forgive him what he was going to have to do if the worst of the possibilities over the ship sailing towards them proved true. He prayed to God it would not come to that, for, even without it, he was asking a lot of a woman who had been betrayed by lies and dishonourable scoundrels in the past. And then his mouth took hers, and he kissed her, knowing that this might be for the very last time. He eased back and studied her face, memorising her every detail. 'Thank you, Sarah.'

She took off her apron and rolled down her sleeves.

Hand in hand, they walked towards the galley door.

Chapter Six

The light was bright, causing her to screw her eyes up after the dimness of the lower deck. A weak sun struggled in the winter sky. Men were lining the bulwark on the larboard side of the vessel. Captain Davies and Mr Seymour stood together at the stern.

Sarah was conscious of Daniel walking behind her, of the letter in her pocket, and, more than anything, of a terrible sense of foreboding.

'There you are, Aunt Sarah, do come and look!' Imelda shouted and ran towards the stern.

Sarah and Daniel followed.

Captain Davies removed the spyglass from his eye to glance round at them. 'Mrs Ellison, Mr Alexander.'

Daniel gave a nod in return. The anguish she had seen on his face in the galley was masked, as if it had never been, but she knew it was still there beneath the surface.

'The ship has seen us?' she asked.

'I believe so,' said the Captain.

'She is heading directly for us,' said Daniel quietly.

Sarah peered at the blur of the vessel on the horizon.

'Is she a pirate ship?' asked Imelda.

'We shall have to wait and see.' Daniel smiled, but Sarah could feel the tension that rippled through him just as if it were her own. And that shared feeling was not one of relief or excitement at the prospect of rescue, but dread.

Imelda beckoned him down to her level so that she might whisper in his ear.

'Imelda, Mr Alexander is busy.'

'Never too busy to speak to Miss Bowden.' He lowered his head to hear what Imelda wanted to say.

'If they are pirates, you will protect Aunt Sarah, Fanny and me, won't you?'

'You've no need to worry, lass. I'd lay down my life to protect you ladies.' His eyes moved briefly to Sarah's and there was so much intensity and emotion in them that it took her breath away and made her all the more frightened of what the closing ship might be bringing other than rescue.

Imelda nodded her approval and came to stand at Sarah's side.

'Praise be to God!' exclaimed Captain Davies. 'She's a frigate of the line, flying the ensign.' He collapsed the spyglass. 'It seems that this is indeed the time of miracles. First we find Mr Alexander out swimming in the North Atlantic, and now one of His Majesty's frigates has found us!'

Daniel showed nothing of relief at the news. 'May I?' His voice was relaxed as he held out his hand for the spyglass, but Sarah was not fooled for a minute. His face was a stony mask. He was alert, honed, ready, as if waiting to face an enemy.

One of His Majesty's frigates. Captain Davies's words echoed in her mind. Surely the fact that it was a Royal Navy ship should allay his concerns, shouldn't it?

Daniel held the spyglass to his eye and studied the distant frigate. She saw his jaw tighten, saw the flair of his nostrils, saw the way his eyes closed. It was the thing he had feared. Her stomach clenched with the certainty of it even before his eyes sought hers across the small distance.

'Ladies,' exclaimed Captain Davies, 'and gentlemen, we are saved!'

All across the deck the men broke into spontaneous applause and cheered at the captain's words.

Daniel did not cheer. He stood stock-still, grim-faced, his eyes on hers as he spoke the quiet words, 'Remember the letter, Sarah, and all we have sworn. I love you, lass, for all that it will appear otherwise.' And then he turned away, leaving Sarah standing there reeling.

Thirty minutes later HMS *Viper* drew alongside the tiny *Angel*'s larboard. She was indeed a British frigate, thirty-eight guns, built of solid English oak and painted in the familiar yellow and black of Nelson's chequerboard.

Her jolly boat was lowered and a small party of uniformed men rowed across to the *Angel*. Daniel did not need to see the men's faces to know who they were and what was coming. The worst of his nightmares. The worst of Sarah's too, although she did not yet know it.

He watched the boat rowing closer, watched the men clamber up the boarding ladders and on to the *Angel*'s deck. And all he could think of was Sarah.

Davies hurried to greet the boarding party and *Viper*'s captain that led them. Higgs shook Davies's hand, one captain to another, his eyes surveying what remained of the *Angel* as they spoke.

Daniel stood where he was at the stern, everything in his body language distancing himself from the woman he had spent the night loving. Higgs's gaze dropped from the damaged mast, passed briefly over Daniel, and moved on. Then what Higgs had just seen hit him. He froze, jerked his eyes back to Daniel, and then made his way slowly over.

'Captain Higgs, this is Mr Alexander, *Angel*'s passenger.' It was Davies who made the unnecessary introduction. 'Although it is the most unlikely of stories how he came to be so.'

'I am sure that it is.' Higgs smiled, but his eyes were sly with menace.

'We found him in the ocean, nigh on dead. Indeed, he

would have been were it not for the fortuitous arrival of the *Angel* and Mrs Ellison, here's, keen eyes.'

'Fortuitous, indeed.' Higgs glanced at Sarah, noticing her for the first time. 'Mrs Ellison.' He bowed.

'Captain Higgs.' She curtsied.

'You have done your country a great service, ma'am.'

'How so, sir?' She shot a confused glance at Daniel.

'You see, Captain Daniel Alexander and I are already acquainted.'

There was silence across the deck.

'*Captain* Alexander?' he heard Sarah echo faintly, but he ignored her as if she were nothing more than a stranger. That tiny moment seemed to stretch and in it he heard the gentle *hush* of the ocean and the beat of his own heart.

'Oh, indeed, Captain Alexander and the whole of the Royal Navy are very well acquainted. He is a frigate captain of wide renown since his shore leave in New York a month ago when he decided he no longer wished to serve good King George and deserted.'

Daniel gave a low laugh at the words he had known were coming and shook his head.

'There is no point denying it. Everyone knows. There is a warrant out for your arrest.'

Higgs was nothing but thorough.

'Good God!' he heard Davies exclaim.

'Daniel?' Sarah's voice was barely more than a whisper. She came to stand close, staring up into his face with disbelief, waiting for him to deny it.

Oh, lass... His stomach sank and he closed his eyes, knowing what she had just revealed to Higgs and the only way that he could counteract it. He had been prepared to put a distance between them, a coolness, been prepared to be held up as a traitor. But not this. Not with such deliberate bare-faced cruelty. To look into her eyes while he slid a blade into her heart and his own. He thought of Netta and the babe. And he thought of Sarah Ellison's fragile trust. And it seemed to Daniel that sometimes life asked too much of one man.

Higgs's gaze moved to Sarah before coming back to rest on him again with a knowing expression. The bastard smiled.

'I see he has tricked his way into your friendship, Mrs Ellison.'

'I have no friends, Captain Higgs, but you were aware of that long before me,' Daniel said. 'And as for Mrs Ellison…' He shot a dissolute glance in Sarah's direction. 'Look at her. Can you honestly blame me for trying?'

Higgs gave a laugh. 'I am afraid, Mrs Ellison, that Captain Alexander has something of a reputation when it comes to beautiful women.'

'You lied to me,' she said, the accusation in those soft words more cutting than if she had screamed or shouted or raged. 'You lied to us all.' He could feel her stare even though he did not let himself look at her, could feel the weight of it crushing his heart.

Imelda came towards him, 'I don't understand, Captain Alexander. What are they saying?' But Sarah caught a firm hold of the wee lassie's hand and hauled her back.

'Stay away from him, Imelda.'

'Why?'

'Because…' Higgs bent down to look into Imelda's face. 'He is a very dangerous gentleman, young miss.'

'He is a pirate, sir.'

'I am afraid he is a deal worse than that, my dear.' Higgs gestured to the two marines who accompanied him. 'He is a traitor.'

Daniel watched Higgs standing there with Sarah on one side and Imelda on the other and knew he could risk nothing.

He let the marines tie his hands behind his back, let them take him away, to *Viper*, and all that awaited him there. And all the while he kept his gaze fixed steadfastly ahead.

And as he left he heard Higgs command his lieutenant, 'Transfer all bodies to *Viper* and make ready to tow the *Angel*.

Time is of the essence. We must reach Plymouth with this villain as soon as possible.'

'Aye, sir,' said the lieutenant.

Daniel knew he would not make Plymouth alive, Higgs would ensure that. He could only trust that, despite everything Sarah believed him to be, she would keep the oath she had sworn.

Two young lieutenants had given up their cabins for HMS *Viper*'s new female passengers. The frigate might have dwarfed the *Angel* but the cabins which housed the women were still cramped.

Imelda, sitting on her cot, looked as dazed as Sarah felt.

Sarah kept her face to the porthole, looking out of the passing ocean. She had wept in the night, but not now. And she would not let herself weep again, not over him.

All those little details made sense in the light of the truth. No wonder he had been through many storms and knew to tie people to the mast. No wonder he sailed so often and knew his way about a ship so well. And knew that crystalline ginger eased seasickness. How he must have laughed at her naivety!

She had trusted him. And he had lied. As they all did. How many men would it take before she learned? It felt like her heart had been ripped out and ground beneath the heel of his boot. Her whole body ached from the betrayal. And she knew why it hurt so much more this time. Even if he was a stranger. Even if she had known him only a matter of weeks. Because Daniel Alexander was the only man to have reached in and touched her soul. Because he was the only man she had ever truly loved. She closed her eyes against the realisation.

God in heaven, one man in the whole of the Atlantic Ocean and he had to be a deserter, a liar, a cheat. He had known exactly how to make her dance to his tune. When she thought of how she had gone to him, given herself to him... The humiliation was scorching, rendering that to which Robert had subjected her, before all of New York's high society, trivial in comparison. Had not Imelda been here to care for, Sarah dreaded to think what she might do. She was so angry, so hurt. But Imelda *was* here and so Sarah had no choice but to be calm and unemotional—and keep, as her brother Thomas said, a stiff upper lip.

She would not make the same mistake again. Ever.

Sarah sealed off her emotions and got on with the task in hand.

'Please come in and sit down, Mrs Ellison.' Captain Higgs stood while she took her seat in the leather chair set before his desk.

His cabin was vast in comparison with any other she had seen and furnished better than many a *ton* drawing room. The rectangular windows of the ship's stern ran the length of the back wall. The desk was in one corner of the room, with a small sofa and bookcase nearby. In the centre was a long mahogany dining table, its surface polished until its gleam rivalled that of a looking glass, its edge lipped. Two weighted flat-bottomed crystal decanters sat in the middle of the table—one filled with liquid that sparkled ruby red in the winter sunshine flooding though the huge windows, the other, tawny. Overhead hung an ornate gold-and-crystal chandelier.

'I am sorry that you have to be involved in any of this, Mrs Ellison. It is a nasty business.' He resumed his seat only once she was sitting down.

'It is.'

'And one into which I must conduct a full investigation. Which is why I am forced to ask you a few questions regarding Captain Alexander. I hope you do not mind.'

'Not at all, sir.' She showed not one sign of how just the mention of his name made her feel.

'I have already spoken to Captain Davies and his crew.'

'So I understand. Where is Captain Alexander now?'

'You need not worry, Mrs Ellison, he is safely imprisoned down on the orlop deck.'

'I am glad to hear it.' She truly was. He deserved every punishment they heaped upon his villainous head.

'We all are,' said Captain Higgs. 'He is not only dishonourable, but dishonest too. I need to know what lies he told you.'

I love you, lass—the cruellest lie of all.

'The same as he told everyone aboard the *Angel*. That he was a businessman returning to London from New York. That he fell overboard in an accident from a merchant ship named *Miss Lively*.'

'I do not know quite how to phrase this delicately, Mrs Ellison.' Captain Higgs paused. 'But as a lady, and a very attractive one at that, it is possible that Daniel Alexander may have sought to impress you with stories of his own importance, of treachery and imagined derring-do.'

'He made no such claims.'

'Not even to win your…affection?'

She faced him levelly, refusing to be cowed with embarrassment. 'What are you implying, Captain Higgs?'

'You called him by his given name aboard the *Angel*.'

She closed her eyes, knowing just how much that one small slip had revealed. 'He saved us in the storm. My niece developed a fondness for him.'

Not just her niece. The words whispered unspoken in the cabin between them.

'What did he tell you of himself?'

That he had lost a wife and a babe. That she was beautiful. That he loved her. Was anything of it true?

'He told me nothing of himself.'

She saw the scepticism in his eyes. 'Come now, Mrs Ellison, do you expect me to believe that you were on Christian-name terms with a man, a stranger plucked from the sea, of whom you knew nothing?'

'I am afraid I have a history of poor judgement in men, sir.' She glanced past him to the large stern windows and the rose-tinged sky.

'He did not tell you, for example, that he is the second

son of the Earl of Glen Affric? And the younger brother of Viscount Cannich?'

'He is an earl's son?' He was a stranger indeed. A man she did not know at all. She felt the wound she was struggling so hard to hide begin to gape.

Something of the truth must have shown in her face because Captain Higgs said softly, 'He really did not tell you.'

She stared down at her hands, determined not to weep.

'And he gave nothing into your keeping, no letter, no document?'

Swear it, Sarah. For the sake of all that is between us. The words of a deserter, a liar and a scoundrel.

I swear. Her own oath taken in such foolhardy ignorance.

'Mrs Ellison,' Captain Higgs pressed.

'Nothing.' The lie slipped from her lips.

'Then I will take up no more of your time, ma'am. I am sorry to have troubled you. Please allow me to show you out.'

The captain's cabin doors opened out on to the main deck, revealing the sun setting in the west—a glorious blaze in the white-grey winter sky, so vivid and beautiful amidst all the misery dragging at Sarah's heart. She stopped where she was and stared at it, remembering all the times she had stood watching the sun set by Daniel Alexander's side.

'May I ask you a question, Captain Higgs?' She did not look round at him.

'Of course.'

'Why did Captain Alexander desert?'

'He found himself a woman in New York that he was reticent to leave.'

She closed her eyes to control the pain.

'It bodes well for fine weather tomorrow.' Higgs glanced at the sunset. 'We shall make good speed for Plymouth.'

'I hope so,' she said and meant it.

'Thank you again for your help, Mrs Ellison.'

'You are welcome, sir.' She turned to leave, but what she saw coming down the deck stopped her dead. Daniel, flanked by two armed red-jacketed marines, his hands bound behind his back, his ankles shackled together with irons, was being manhandled towards her. A third marine walked behind, the muzzle of his musket pressed against Daniel's back.

Daniel's face was scraped and bleeding. One eye was dark bruised and there was a cut on his lower lip. The borrowed brown coat was gone and the white of his shirt was crimson-speckled with blood. As she stared in shock and horror his eyes met hers and she saw the man she had known aboard the *Angel*, the man who had saved her, the man who had loved her. She saw trust and love and a plea for understanding. There for a flash, then gone, as quickly as it had appeared. His eyes were cold and hard as he turned them to Captain Higgs.

Sarah could not move, could not tear her stare from Daniel.

'You are early,' snapped Captain Higgs at his men, before barking at the blue-uniformed officer who accompanied the marines and Daniel. 'Get Mrs Ellison out of here, Lieutenant Peyton. She should not have to witness this.'

'At once, sir.' The lieutenant took her arm and began to guide her away.

She glanced back and saw them take Daniel into Captain Higgs's cabin.

The door slammed shut.

Sarah sat that night alone at the tiny desk in her cabin. All was quiet save for the roar of the wind and ocean that was always there in the background. She barely noticed it any more. From up on deck she heard the faint chime of six bells. An hour before midnight and still she had not slept a wink, nor even pretended it could be so.

Her mind could not forget that image of Daniel Alexander. It had haunted her for every minute of every hour since. That they had beaten him made her heart bleed. But it was that look in his eyes that she kept coming back to again and again.

Inside her pocket the letter lay snug. She was so conscious of its presence she could feel it burning through the layers of clothing like a touch from Daniel's fingers. She fished it out, laid it on the table before her.

It was addressed to Lord Mulgrave of Admiralty House in Westminster, London, written in a hand that was surprisingly artistic for so physical a man. But then he was an earl's son, and a Royal Navy captain!

He found himself a woman in New York that he was reticent to leave.

She rubbed a hand against her forehead, feeling bitter at how much of a fool she had been, and was still being. She should have given the letter to Higgs and been done with it; should have chalked Daniel down to just one more mistake and moved on with her life.

She closed her eyes and saw again Daniel with his eye blackened and his lip cut and that look in his eyes, and knew she could do none of those things. And if Daniel had deserted for a woman in New York, what was he doing sailing back to England aboard a ship on which no one noticed him missing?

With great care she turned the letter over. The red wax seal bore the indent of no signet or seal, only the mark of a man's thumbprint with a distinctive scar in the shape of a crescent moon. She swallowed and touched her fingers against it, resting her thumb where his had been.

I love you, lass.

It was what men like him said. He had lied. Just like Robert and Brandon Taverner. And yet, sitting here, she knew he was nothing like either of those twin imposters. She thought of that night on *Angel*'s deck when he had held her as she was sick. She thought of the storm and how he had saved them. She thought of how he had stayed with her at her lowest ebb through Imelda's fever. And of the tenderness of his lovemaking.

I love you, lass—for all that it will appear otherwise.

She looked again at the red wax seal.

What is between us is no lie. In that at least I have been honest, I swear.

There was one way to know for sure.

Sarah hesitated no longer, but broke the wax seal.

And the words that Daniel had penned on that sheet of paper made her heart turn over. For a few moments she just sat there letting the truth sink in before resealing the letter and replacing it in her pocket. She understood now why Daniel had lied and why he had behaved so abominably towards her before Higgs. Protection. She closed her eyes. Amidst all the lies he was the only man who had shown her the truth of himself.

Sarah prepared very carefully. And when she was finally done she fastened her cloak around her shoulders, fitted her bonnet to her head. Lifting up her basket and her lantern, she went to find the orlop deck.

Chapter Seven

From the gloom and silence of his dank prison down in the bowels of the ship Daniel heard the light tread of a woman's footsteps and looked up to see Sarah—the angel who appeared when darkness threatened and all hope seemed lost.

He uttered not one word, made no move other than to fix his eyes upon her, unsure of what she could be doing here.

Sarah did not so much as look at him. She smiled at the two marines who stood, muskets in hand, guarding the locked bars of his cell.

'Forgive my intrusion, gentlemen. Captain Higgs told me that rogue who has so dishonoured the King's uniform was imprisoned down here.' She flicked a glance of utter contempt at Daniel.

'As you see, ma'am.' The tallest marine gave her a small bow.

'You are sure he cannot escape?' There was an edge to her voice that sounded like fear.

The marine smirked. 'We are very sure.'

'Do not laugh at me, sir. I have seen that of which he is capable. He is dangerous in the extreme.'

'Begging your pardon, ma'am.' The marine looked contrite. 'But he is shackled and locked behind iron bars.'

'And the keys are safe from his reach?'

The marine glanced at the second bunch of keys that hung on the wall opposite Daniel's cell. 'Rest assured they are, ma'am.'

'You will be here to guard him in person? All night?'

'Indeed. Corporal Clarke and I have that honour. Captain Alexander is locked up safe. He won't be leaving his cell before we anchor in Plymouth.'

Her relief was visible even from where he sat so still within the gloom. 'Thank you for your reassurance, Lieutenant.' He saw her smile.

The marine smiled, too, and glanced away, pleased but embarrassed. 'It's just plain Corporal Brown, ma'am.'

'Well, Corporal Brown, I will sleep easier tonight for having spoken to you.'

Brown gave a nod.

'I will leave you to your guarding, sir.' She turned to leave, then stopped as if a sudden thought had occurred. 'I have spent the night delivering some small gifts to the officers of HMS *Viper* who so valiantly rescued my niece and myself.' She pulled back the cover of the basket hooked over her arm. Daniel could not see what was within, only the way the lantern light glinted on something dark.

'I made a whole batch before leaving New York, to give as Christmas gifts when I reached England. But it is almost Christmas, and if any two gentlemen deserve something warming on this cold December night it is most certainly Corporals Brown and Clarke.' She handed Brown a bottle of mulled wine. 'Goodnight, gentlemen.'

Not a look. Not a glance. Only hostility that bristled.

But with the scent of cloves and cinnamon and rich red wine strong as Brown and Clarke shared the wine Sarah had left, Daniel smiled and felt his heart blossom.

Almost an hour had passed when Sarah returned.

Brown and Clarke were sprawled face down on the guard's

table. He watched her fetch the keys from their hook on the wall and unlock the door of his cell.

'You should have told me,' she said as she fitted the smaller keys into the locks of his shackles.

'That I was a deserter?'

'I know you are not a deserter, Daniel.'

The shackles loosed and fell away.

'You read the letter,' he said.

'Of course I read the letter!' She glanced up at him and everything that was between them welled up and overflowed.

'Sarah, lass… God help me!' It would have taken so many words to tell her and Daniel knew he was not an eloquent man. Instead, he pulled her into his arms and with his kiss showed her the truth of what was in his heart.

The time was not enough, but he made the best use of it. And when he eased back to look into her eyes he smiled before flicking his eyes to the basket that sat by her feet.

'You were not lying when you said Great-Grandmother Bowden's mulled wine was a potent brew.'

'I added a little extra special ingredient to help it along—laudanum.'

He laughed. 'Shame you haven't enough to drug the whole ship.'

'I managed most of the officers.' She lifted the basket and opened its cover to reveal two duelling pistols, complete with bullets and rods. 'They were Robert's. After a little incident between myself and a gentleman in New York I thought it wise to bring them with me. A lady cannot be too sure of what manner of scoundrel she might come across on the high seas these days.'

'Sarah Ellison, what would I do without you?' What would he do without her in truth? She was the most amazing woman.

'Not mutiny a frigate of His Majesty's navy, that is for sure.'

He slid his hand over her hip, pulled her close and kissed her lips quick and hard. 'You know I love you, don't you?' He loved her, and everything else that he was about to do was easy because of that.

'I know,' she said softly, then stronger, 'You best get to it, Captain Alexander. I have a niece to keep safe.'

The night had almost passed when Sarah finally made her way up to the main deck of HMS *Viper*.

The first thing she noticed was the chill. The second was the beauty of the clear night sky. The moon hung fatter than the sickle on Daniel's thumb and, all above, covering the lush velvet darkness was the twinkling of stars. She breathed in the cool night air and moved her gaze lower.

He was standing up on the quarterdeck, his lone figure silhouetted against the moonlight. The tension that had been tight in Sarah all night eased.

'Sarah?' He turned at her approach and against his hip was fastened a naval captain's sheathed sword with the two pistols tucked within its belt.

'Where is Higgs?'

'Shackled on the orlop deck with the few that were party to his treachery. With a little bit of persuasion Higgs squealed like a pig, confessing his all before his crew and Davies's too.' She saw the way his fingers touched to the hilt of the sword at those words, saw the bruises and scrapes against his knuckles and did not ask the manner of persuading. Daniel was a formidable warrior. 'They are decent men. *Viper* is under my control. I did not want to wake you.'

'As if I could sleep.'

He gave a chuckle and held out his hand to her.

She took it and moved to stand by his side at the bulwark, just as she had done so many times before.

They stood in silence, looking out over the beauty of the night seascape, with the wind on their cheeks, and the damp salty scent of the ocean in their noses. The luminous moon bathed them in its ethereal light and turned the sea to rippling molten silver. All was silent save for the creak of timber and the rhythmic wash of the waves. The men on the morning watch high above on their lofty perch made no sound.

'I need to tell you the truth, Sarah.' He had wanted to for so long.

'You do not need to tell me anything. Words can lie. Actions show the truth of a man's heart and I already know the truth of yours, Daniel Alexander.'

He smiled. 'I want to tell you, Sarah. Nothing of lies.'

She gave a nod.

He looked directly into her eyes, and began to talk. Of his father, who was the Earl of Glen Affric, his mother and his brother, Viscount Cannich. About his career at sea. And then he told her of his fellow frigate captain Albert Higgs and how Daniel had found that he was taking payments to give clear passage to ships transporting slaves from Africa to the West Indies. And not only that, but that Higgs had protected the slavers from other frigates. Admiralty had suspected corruption and had tasked Daniel to discover who was involved. He had been sworn to absolute secrecy even from his crew.

'It is the worst of trades and Higgs has been bought off with vast sums of money. Little wonder how far he went to prevent discovery.'

'It was Higgs that left you to drown.'

'We have a contact in New York who had in his possession a letter naming the English officer we were after. I was in New York for the letter, but when I got to the meeting place, Jeffries was dead and a gang of ruffians waiting for me.'

Sarah's fingers tightened around his.

'I did not know that it was Higgs, not until they removed the hood from my head.' He remembered that moment. 'He was my friend.' And Higgs had betrayed a lifetime of trust.

'Is that why he did not bind you when he threw you into the water—for the sake of your friendship?'

Daniel gave a cynical laugh. 'He did not wish there to be any evidence of foul play in the remote chance my body was discovered. The corpse would have been an unknown man dead through an accident.'

'And that is why he removed your uniform—so that you would not be identified.'

'He wanted my disappearance to be taken for desertion. Before he dumped me overboard he delighted in telling me the seeds he had sown for that ultimate dishonour.'

'But I still do not understand why you did not reveal your true identity to those on the *Angel*. They were not of the Royal Navy.'

'The slave trade is like a club with members through all manner of shipping, legitimate merchant vessels included. I could trust no one.'

She nodded her understanding.

'I am sorry for the façade I had to play before Higgs. Had he realised what was between us, that I might have confided in you…' He shook his head. 'Higgs would have stopped at nothing, Sarah, not women, not even bairns. I couldn't risk that.'

'I worked it out…eventually.'

'And I'm sorry, too, that I lied to you, Sarah. I know how you feel about men that lie.'

She took his face between her hands, looking deep into his eyes. 'You did what you had to do, Daniel. As you said aboard the *Angel*, sometimes lies are told for the best of reasons. Who, more than I, knows that? All those years pretending I did not know of Robert's infidelities before his death and pretending that I had loved him afterwards. And never more so than here aboard the *Angel*. Lying with my mourning weeds, lying with my mouth, because I was so afraid of what I felt for you.'

'There is nothing more of lies between us, lass, nor will there ever be.'

The winter dawn was breaking as HMS *Viper* approached Plymouth.

The sky glowed a glorious pink as the rising sun emerged from its slumber. Only the deep-blue west remained of the fleeing night even though, still high in the sky, hung the same clear crescent moon, defying the dawn.

Sarah ignored the chill that goose-fleshed her skin, and watched the west cling to the vestige of the night, as she clung to the last of this incredible journey. It had been nothing that she had imagined, but so much more in every way. Christmas really was a time of miracles.

Plucking Daniel from the waters of the North Atlantic had been the first.

The *Angel* surviving the storm, the second.

The third was Imelda's recovery.

The fourth miracle was the miracle of love for a woman who had spent a lifetime without it.

She had found a man who was true, a man whose heart was merged with her own.

Daniel moved to stand behind her, wrapping his arm around her waist, snuggling her close before lowering his mouth to her ear. 'You know I must take Higgs before the Admiralty in London and clear my name before anything else, Sarah?'

'I know,' she said and let herself relax against the warm strength of his body.

He kissed the top of her head and rested his chin there, and together they watched Plymouth come ever closer in the magnificence of the winter sunrise.

'*The Times* makes mention of the naval frigate you travelled upon,' Sarah's brother, Thomas, commented as they sat before the fire in the drawing room of Bowden House. 'Apparently its captain, one Albert Higgs, has been arrested and charged with accepting bribes, dereliction of duty and the attempted murder of a fellow officer. My word, quite the villain!'

'Indeed.' Sarah sipped at her glass of warmed mulled wine.

'I always knew Captain Alexander was not the one who was the villain.' Imelda climbed upon her papa's knee.

'And how did you know that?' Thomas enquired.

'Because he saved us.' Imelda gave a grin. 'And he liked Aunt Sarah very much.'

'Did he now?' Thomas shot Sarah a glance. 'Your Aunt Sarah made no mention of that bit of the story.'

Sarah felt a traitorous heat blossom in her cheeks. 'Imelda exaggerates.'

'No, I don't. He told me it was so. And then there was the time in my cabin, when I was unwell and he cuddled you.'

'You had a fever, Imelda, and were imagining things.'

'It seemed real.'

'It always does.'

Her brother said nothing, but there was a speculative look in his eye when his gaze met Sarah's.

'Come now, it is time we readied ourselves for the midnight service, or have you forgotten it is Christmas Eve?' She smiled to lighten the slight tension that had erupted and wished that Daniel would come soon.

And, as if to save her, Imelda's two little sisters came running into the room, all excited at staying up late for the special Christmas church service.

Sarah celebrated Christmas with her brother, his wife and their three children. There was no letter from Daniel, and no mention of Captain Alexander in any of the Admiralty columns of the newspapers even though Sarah scoured each one.

The days passed and Sarah looked for him on each one with mounting anxiety. How long did it take to deliver Higgs to London and report the truth of what had happened? Surely not this long, even allowing for the weather? At first she worried that something had gone wrong before Admiralty but she knew that, were that the case, it would have been reported in one of the newspapers. And then the doubts began to whisper, like devils, in her ear.

There had been no mention of marriage. He had never

actually said he would come and find her. Those had been assumptions.

I love you, lass.

He had meant it, *then*, she was sure. But *now*, when they were apart, and back in the real world with all its pressures and truths? Maybe there was another woman waiting for him at home in Scotland. Maybe his father did not approve of his son marrying a widow or thought she was not good enough for an earl's son, even though hers was one of the oldest and richest families in England. Maybe... There were so many possibilities. And the truth was she knew so little of his life, just as he knew so little of hers. Foolish as a green girl, she had thought love would be enough.

She tried to put him from her mind, but everywhere she looked were reminders. It snowed and she thought of their Christmas challenge aboard the *Angel*. On Boxing Day the family exchanged gifts and, amidst all the squeals and excitement of her nieces, Daniel was in her thoughts. He was there in the red-breasted robin darting through the hedges as she accompanied her brother and his family on a visit to old friends. And every time they sang the Christmas hymns in the church. And there was a bigger reminder than all of those. One of which she was not entirely sure yet, but just the prospect of which made her pray all the more that he would come for her. Because she knew what she was going to have to do if he did not...and it did not involve scouring the country for a man who did not want her.

But as the days passed and still she heard nothing from Daniel, the old insecurities came back to haunt her.

Sarah stopped looking for his letter. She ceased listening for the thud of his horse's hooves, or the creak of his carriage wheels through the snow. Daniel might love her, but what was love to men? He might love her, but he wasn't coming for her. What had been between them had ended with their journey. If she found him, if she told him, he would marry her. Out of duty. Out of necessity. Not because he wanted to. And, because she loved him, that knowledge would kill her. Better a man she hated than that.

He was a naval sea captain who had chosen a life without her.

And because of her recent discovery, she was a woman who was going to have to return to New York and marry a man she did not want to marry.

It was the last day of the year when her brother took her out riding alone.

The sky was a cloudless blue and bright with pale sunshine that glittered on the snow that still dusted the fields all around. The air was fresh and smelled of earth and winter. Blackbirds scurried beneath bushes. She turned her eyes away from the robin that sat in the bare brown boughs serenading their progress along the country lane.

'What happened between you and Captain Alexander, Sarah?'

'Nothing happened.' She kept her eyes straight ahead to hide the lie.

The horses ambled on at their slow steady pace, but she could feel by the way her brother was looking at her that he was not fooled.

'Perhaps I should find Captain Alexander and ask him the same question.'

'Don't you dare!' Her eyes shot to his.

His expression remained impassive. 'You are no longer wearing your mourning weeds or wedding band.'

'It means nothing.'

'I am not a fool, Sarah. I see how unhappy you are beneath the smile.'

'Don't.' She squeezed her eyes shut to prevent the tears that prickled there. 'Please, Thomas.'

'Did he seduce you?'

She let the question hang in the air before looking squarely at her brother. 'I seduced him.'

She saw the shock that flared there. 'Good God, Sarah!'

'You have a scandalous sister.' Possibly more scandalous than he realised. And in her heart she prayed that it was so.

'I could contact him. I have friends in London who could—'

'No.' She swallowed back the emotion that threatened too near the surface. 'I will be leaving for New York at the end of next week.'

'I thought you said you did not wish to return to America.'

'Change of plan.'

'If you think it is for the best.'

'Most definitely.' She forced a smile and cracked a joke to hide the truth. 'Do not worry, I will not seduce anyone on the return journey.' The smile faded. She glanced down at the leather reins held loosely between her gloved fingers. 'There is a gentleman in New York who has proposed marriage.'

'You could stay here, with us.'

'No, Thomas.' She met his eyes. 'For the sake of all our reputations, I do not think that I can.'

They looked at one another for a moment.

'Oh, Sarah,' he said softly.

The horses walked on in silence.

The children were long in bed. Sarah, Thomas, and his wife Anne, sat in the drawing room of Bowden House, each with a glass of warm mulled wine, watching the hands of the clock on the mantel approach midnight. Soon the old year would pass and a new one begin—one that would take Sarah back to New York and a lie. But it was as Daniel Alexander had said, sometimes lies had to be told for the best of reasons. To protect and defend—those that you loved…and those that were innocent.

The clock struck twelve and from down in the village the

church bells pealed, ringing out the old year and welcoming in the new.

Sarah took a breath and did the same. Turned her back on a past she would never forget or regret and faced her future.

'Happy New Year, Sis.' Thomas made the toast and Sarah responded.

'Happy New Year, Thomas…Anne.' She chinked their glasses with her own. 'May it be a good one for us all.' But she saw the glance that Anne shot Thomas and knew that her brother had told his wife.

The last chime was still echoing in the air when the knocker sounded against the front door.

'Who on earth comes visiting in the first minute of the New Year?' Thomas frowned.

Sarah felt the blood rush from her head. Her fingers gripped so tight to the stem of the wine glass that her knuckles shone white.

Mr Thomas Bowden's expression was glacial when the maid announced the name of his first caller of the New Year and Daniel stepped into the drawing room.

Sarah's eyes met Daniel's and he saw the shock in them before she lowered them to hide it. She looked so pale that he thought she might swoon.

He bowed to Bowden. 'I am ridden from Scotland to first foot your sister.' He saw Bowden's hostile gaze drop to take in his mud-splattered boots and breeches and rise again to the faint beard that stubbled his jaw, before meeting his eyes. 'If I might be permitted to address her?'

'About damn time, Captain Alexander.'

'Thomas!' Sarah jumped to her feet, knocking over her glass in the process. The deep red of the wine soaked to merge with the red wool of the Turkey rug and the glass rolled away unnoticed.

'If you would be so kind as to grant Mrs Ellison and me a

few minutes alone.' Daniel was polite enough, but his expression brooked no refusal.

Bowden glared at him as if he wanted to run him through.

'Thomas, please!'

Bowden's eyes flicked to his sister, then with a curt nod he and his wife left the room.

The closing of the door echoed in the silence.

Sarah did not move, just stood where she was, with her head held high. 'Daniel.'

'Sarah,' he said softly.

For all her face was a mask of composure he could sense her tension. From his pocket he produced a lump of coal and offered it to her.

She made no move to accept it, so he sat it down on the nearby table.

'A lump of coal that your hearth shall ne'er be cold.'

From his other pocket he took a small oil-skin package, and unwrapped it before placing it beside the coal.

'A black bun that your belly shall ne'er go hungry.'

And then the bottle of whisky that glowed amber in the firelight.

'And a dram to toast the New Year…and more.'

Her eyes dropped to move over the items he had brought. 'Daniel…' He could hear the emotion she was trying to hide.

'I'm tall and I'm handsome, and in the right light my hair might be construed as dark…' he raised his eyebrows '…and I will bring you good fortune if you will have me as your husband, Sarah Ellison.'

He heard the breath that escaped her, saw the way her eyes clung to his. 'I thought you were not coming.' The tears spilled from her eyes.

'Oh, lass!' He crossed the room to take her in his arms and capture each precious tear. 'I am sorry for the delay, but there was something in Glen Affric I had to fetch.'

He kissed her, with tenderness and passion and then looked

into her eyes. 'I brought a few other things with me, from Doctors' Commons in London…' He handed her the paper from his pocket.

Sarah opened the special marriage licence.

'And from Glen Affric.' He produced the small brown velvet box and opened it to reveal the ring inside. 'It was my grandmother's. The gold is from the Lowther Hills in south-west Scotland, the sapphire, from the Isle of Lewis in the Outer Hebrides.' He looked into her eyes. 'So, Sarah Ellison, will you have me?'

She nodded. 'I'll have you, Daniel Alexander.'

He slid the ring on to the third finger of her left hand and when she had kissed and hugged him she looked into his eyes. 'I am glad that you came, for more reasons than my love for you.'

'Oh?' He looked at her teasingly.

'There is something I have to tell you. The night I came to your cabin…' She blushed and hesitated. 'My monthly course is late. And it is *never* late…' She bit her lip and looked at him with worried eyes.

'I thought that your heart was the best gift a man might receive. Now you give me something to rival it.'

'I thought that after…I thought you might not…' She took his hands in her own and looked into his eyes. 'You do not like Christmas,' she said by way of quiet explanation.

'An angel came and healed my heart. You won the challenge, after all, Sarah.' The tears sprung fresh in her eyes, as he gathered her to him and kissed her. 'I love you, lass.'

And up in the heavens of the clear winter night, the stars twinkled all the brighter.

In the quiet of the Bowden Parish Church, on the morning of the second day of 1808, Sarah married her handsome Scottish captain. Eight months later their son, Wee Alex, was born. Christmas and the New Year had brought her true love, a husband and the child she had always dreamt of.

Sometimes the magic of Christmas really did make miracles happen and a heart's desire come true.

* * * * *

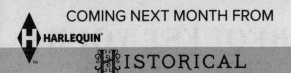
Available November 19, 2013

THE TEXAS RANGER'S HEIRESS WIFE
by Kate Welsh
(Western)

Helena Conwell has built a successful ranch, but now raiders are hungry for her land. Only one man can protect her—Brendan Kane, the wild Texas Ranger she married at gunpoint.

NOT JUST A WALLFLOWER
A Season of Secrets • by Carole Mortimer
(Regency)

Ellie Rosewood is the talk of the *ton*. Her guardian, Justin, Duke of Royston, has one job—to find her a husband. But confirmed rake Justin wants Ellie all for himself!

RUNNING FROM SCANDAL
Bancrofts of Barton Park • by Amanda McCabe
(Regency)

David Marton lives a quiet life, until Emma Bancroft comes sweeping back into his world. She will never be the right woman for him, but sometimes temptation is too hard to resist....

FALLING FOR THE HIGHLAND ROGUE
The Gilvrys of Dunross
by Ann Lethbridge
(Regency)

Disgraced lady Charity West lives in the city's seedy underbelly. She's used and abused, yearning for freedom, and her distrust of men runs deep...until she meets Highland rogue Logan Gilvry.

**YOU CAN FIND MORE INFORMATION
ON UPCOMING HARLEQUIN® TITLES,
FREE EXCERPTS AND MORE AT
WWW.HARLEQUIN.COM.**

REQUEST YOUR FREE BOOKS!

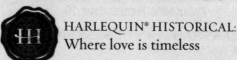

HARLEQUIN® HISTORICAL:
Where love is timeless

2 FREE NOVELS PLUS 2 FREE GIFTS!

YES! Please send me 2 FREE Harlequin® Historical novels and my 2 FREE gifts (gifts are worth about $10). After receiving them, if I don't wish to receive any more books, I can return the shipping statement marked "cancel." If I don't cancel, I will receive 6 brand-new novels every month and be billed just $5.44 per book in the U.S. or $5.74 per book in Canada. That's a savings of at least 16% off the cover price! It's quite a bargain! Shipping and handling is just 50¢ per book in the U.S. and 75¢ per book in Canada.* I understand that accepting the 2 free books and gifts places me under no obligation to buy anything. I can always return a shipment and cancel at any time. Even if I never buy another book, the two free books and gifts are mine to keep forever.

246/349 HDN F4ZY

Name	
	(PLEASE PRINT)

Address	Apt. #

City	State/Prov.	Zip/Postal Code

Signature (if under 18, a parent or guardian must sign)

Mail to the Harlequin® Reader Service:
IN U.S.A.: P.O. Box 1867, Buffalo, NY 14240-1867
IN CANADA: P.O. Box 609, Fort Erie, Ontario L2A 5X3

Want to try two free books from another line?
Call 1-800-873-8635 or visit www.ReaderService.com.

* Terms and prices subject to change without notice. Prices do not include applicable taxes. Sales tax applicable in N.Y. Canadian residents will be charged applicable taxes. Offer not valid in Quebec. This offer is limited to one order per household. Not valid for current subscribers to Harlequin Historical books. All orders subject to credit approval. Credit or debit balances in a customer's account(s) may be offset by any other outstanding balance owed by or to the customer. Please allow 4 to 6 weeks for delivery. Offer available while quantities last.

Your Privacy—The Harlequin® Reader Service is committed to protecting your privacy. Our Privacy Policy is available online at www.ReaderService.com or upon request from the Harlequin Reader Service.

We make a portion of our mailing list available to reputable third parties that offer products we believe may interest you. If you prefer that we not exchange your name with third parties, or if you wish to clarify or modify your communication preferences, please visit us at www.ReaderService.com/consumerchoice or write to us at Harlequin Reader Service Preference Service, P.O. Box 9062, Buffalo, NY 14269. Include your complete name and address.

HHI3R

"She held still, as if she had not noticed the growing warmth in the room. The heat between them. And then he lifted her hand in his, carefully, as if it could be broken by his greater strength. Eyes fixed on her face, he turned it over and, bending his head, touched his lips to her palm. A warm velvety brush of his mouth against sensitive skin. A whisper of hot breath. Sensual. Melting.

Her insides clenched. Her heart stopped, then picked up with a jolt and an uneven rhythm. She felt like a girl again, all hot and bothered and unsure. And full of such longings. Such desires.

But the woman inside her knew better. She craved all that kiss offered. The heat. The bliss. Carnal things that shamed her. Things she had resolved never to want again. They left her vulnerable. A challenge she could not let go unanswered. To do so would be to admit he had touched her somehow.

"Charity," he said softly, as he lifted his head to look at her, still cradling her hand in his large warm one, his thumb gently stroking. "Never in my life have I met a woman like you."

The words rang with truth. And they pleased her. She leaned closer and touched her lips to his, let them linger, cling softly, urging him to respond. And he did. Gently at first, with care, as if he thought she might take offence or be frightened. Then more forcefully, his mouth moving against hers as he angled his head, his free hand coming up to cradle her nape while the other retained its hold. The feel of his lips sent little thrills spiraling outward from low in her belly. On a gasp she opened her mouth and, with little licks and tastes and deep rumbling groans in his chest, he explored her. The gentleness of it was her undoing.

The way he delved and plundered her mouth as if making the discovery for the very first time was incredibly alluring. If she didn't know better, she might have thought this was his first time. Passion hummed in her veins. Dizzied her mind. Sent her tumbling into a blaze of desire.

He drew back, his chest rising and falling as if he, too, could not breathe, his gaze searching her face. And she melted in the heat in his eyes.

Has this bad boy Highlander finally met his match with English bad girl Charity? This time around, two wrongs could just make a right....

Don't miss
FALLING FOR THE HIGHLAND ROGUE
by Ann Lethbridge, out December 2013,
only in Harlequin® Historical!

ℋISTORICAL

Where love is timeless

THE PAST IS ALWAYS
HOT ON YOUR HEELS...

Emma Bancroft used to pride herself on her sensible nature,
but good sense flew out the window during her first Season in
London! Her reputation and her belief in true love in tatters,
she reluctantly returns home to Barton Park.

David Marton is trying to live a quiet life—until Emma
comes sweeping back. With whispers of scandal all about
her, he knows she will never be the right woman for him, but
sometimes temptation is just too hard to resist....

Bancrofts of Barton Park
Two sisters, two scandals, two sizzling love affairs
Look for

Running From Scandal

by Amanda McCabe

Coming December 2013

Available wherever books and ebooks are sold.